REA

P9-EEI-806

3 1833 05056 9703

"Something's going on," Ian said. "Something...unnatural. I feel it."

Icy tendrils wrapped slowly around Honor's spine. She felt it, too. "Someone's watching."

"I thought we'd get away from it by coming out here." He scanned the beaches and the dunes, seeking the watcher. "Let's get out of here."

Even as she went with him, she questioned his motives. For all that he seemed concerned for her safety, he spent an awful lot of time scaring her even more. What if he was trying to scare her out of her wits? To drive her away? Or drive her over the edge?

The man is an abomination. A witch's spawn. The words whispered through her mind again, cold and deadly. Once again she tried to ignore them. They were *not* real. They came from some buried corridor of the subconscious, and they were meaningless.

Or were they?

OCT 3 1 2006   SUPER ROMANCE

RACHEL LEE

USA TODAY bestselling author Rachel Lee
is the pseudonym of sisters Sue Civil-Brown
and Cristian Brown. They have written over
40 bestsellers, and have been published in
16 languages around the world. They split
their time between Florida, Germany and the
Caribbean.

RACHEL LEE

IMMINENT
THUNDER

Silhouette® Books

Published by Silhouette Books

America's Publisher of Contemporary Romance

If you purchased this book without a cover you should be aware that this book is stolen property. It was reported as "unsold and destroyed" to the publisher, and neither the author nor the publisher has received any payment for this "stripped book."

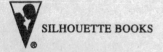 **SILHOUETTE BOOKS**

ISBN-13: 978-0-373-47081-5
ISBN-10:   0-373-47081-9

IMMINENT THUNDER

Copyright © 1993 by Susan Civil

All rights reserved. Except for use in any review, the reproduction or utilization of this work in whole or in part in any form by any electronic, mechanical or other means, now known or hereafter invented, including xerography, photocopying and recording, or in any information storage or retrieval system, is forbidden without the written permission of the editorial office, Silhouette Books, 233 Broadway, New York, NY 10279 U.S.A.

All characters in this book have no existence outside the imagination of the author and have no relation whatsoever to anyone bearing the same name or names. They are not even distantly inspired by any individual known or unknown to the author, and all incidents are pure invention.

This edition published by arrangement with Harlequin Books S.A.

® and TM are trademarks of Harlequin Books S.A., used under license. Trademarks indicated with ® are registered in the United States Patent and Trademark Office, the Canadian Trade Marks Office and in other countries.

Visit Silhouette Books at www.eHarlequin.com

Printed in U.S.A.

CHAPTER ONE

The midnight breeze had turned soft with the hint of thunderstorms and the scent of the nearby bay. It filled the night with the restless rustle of leaves in the old live oaks. Spanish moss swayed eerily before it, creating dark, rippling curtains of shadow. Mixed with the swish of the leaves and the sigh of the breeze was a distant, low rumble.

From the west came the approaching thunder of a storm and the flicker of sheet lightning, an ominous promise. From the north, too, there came a louder rumble, a more distinct thunder and a sharper flash of light, as bombers practiced on the military reservation. Both storms had their own kind of eeriness, the one wholly natural, the other wholly unnatural.

Just as Honor Nightingale pulled into her driveway, beneath the sagging shoulders of a row of old oaks, a thick cloud scudded across the moon, swallowing the last bit of illumination. The night abruptly devoured everything beyond the yellow beams of her headlights. It was a wild, beautiful night, she thought. The kind of night that always made her want to kick off her shoes and run barefoot through the grass like a frisky colt.

She pulled up to the detached garage that sat behind her ramshackle house and shoved the car door open, pausing to draw a deep breath of the northwest Florida air. Nowhere else on earth had nights like these. Nowhere else could you smell the sea and the thunder on a breeze as soft as silk and satin.

Climbing out of the car, she smiled to herself and threw back her head to soak it all in. The wind caught at her blue hospital scrubs, snatching the fabric and molding it to her trim body. Laughing softly, she turned her head a little and let the breeze tug her hair free of its pins and whip the long, dark strands around her. It was a beautiful, beautiful night, she thought, and for just this little while she felt free of all the sorrows that had haunted her for so long.

The wind suddenly whipped around her, feeling cold and damp, and snatched the car door from Honor's hand, slamming it shut. Damn—her keys were locked inside. She absolutely didn't want to cope with that right now. She had just come off a grueling shift as triage nurse in the emergency room, it was well past midnight, and not a light had been visible in any house along the dirt road leading to the highway.

And then she recalled the damaged screen on the kitchen window beside the back door, the window with the loose latch she had discovered only yesterday. With a little patience she could probably jiggle the darn thing open. If worse came to worst, she could break the glass. So what was she standing here dithering for? Giving a last toss of her head in the breeze, she stepped toward the back porch.

And froze.

She wasn't alone. How she knew that, she couldn't have said. But suddenly her heart was in her throat and she was paralyzed by the absolute conviction that someone was watching her from the house. Her house. The house with the torn screen and the loose latch on the back window.

Holding her breath, she sorted through the possibilities with lightning speed, the same speed that often meant the difference between life and death in the emergency room. The house up the road to her right was closer, but it was deserted. The house to her left was occupied by some kind of recluse. She'd lived next door to him for a month and hadn't seen him once, but Millie Jackson, who lived up near the highway, said he was some kind of military man who just wasn't sociable.

So okay, he probably wasn't a serial killer. He was probably some soured old warrior who would—

A thump. Distinctly, despite the rustling of leaves and the distant rumble of bombs and thunder, she heard a soft thump, as if something had been bumped. From the house. From her house.

That did it. Without another second's hesitation, she whirled and took off for the recluse's house. Whatever kind of crazy he was, he couldn't be as bad as someone who would be waiting inside a house for a woman alone after dark. No way. She'd seen too many women in the emergency room who'd come home to find a creep waiting for them. She didn't need to imagine a thing. She *knew*.

A holly hedge separated the two properties. The recluse might have preferred to let it grow into a forest, but someone had kept it neatly trimmed, so she was able to leap it with the grace that had made her a champion hurdler in high school. She covered the expanse of his yard like the wind and flew onto the porch without her feet touching a single step.

If the door had been unlocked, she probably would have barged right in, but the door was locked, which was probaby the only thing that saved her from getting a knife under the ribs. Or maybe not. Later she was never really sure that her neighbor would have done such a thing without checking out the situation first, though he definitely wanted her to think so.

She definitely thought so when, after thirty seconds of her hammering, a mountain of masculinity opened the door and greeted her with the ugliest-looking hunting knife she had ever seen. It was, in fact, exactly like the one her father had had. Recognizing it, she relaxed just a hair.

"In my house!" she gasped. "There's someone! Someone broke in...."

Recluse or not, the man was quick. He threw open the screen door and dragged her inside. "Where is he?"

"He was—he was watching me from the back window when I got home. The screen is torn and the latch is loose.... I heard a sound...."

She was talking to the air. Beyond the screen door, the night whispered of coming storms, the cicadas screeched as if the world were normal, and the air smelled like the sea.

He had gone over there. Numbly she stared out at the night and wondered why. Why hadn't he called the police? Any sensible person would have called the police...

And that was precisely what she was going to do right now. She saw the wall phone over by the kitchen table. Her hand barely touched it before she realized that he neighbor could get hurt if she called the police while he was over there. The cops wouldn't care who he was or why he was carrying that Ranger knife. They would be too hyped to care, too scared to take a chance.

Unable to do anything, she paced rapidly from one end of the large kitchen to the other, back and forth, until her nerves were stretched to breaking and she figured a primal scream wouldn't even begin to touch the tension.

God, what if he got hurt and she was responsible be-

3 1833 05056 9703

cause she had asked him for help? But he shouldn't have gone over there alone. He should have called the police. That was all she'd wanted. That was all he'd needed to do.

Maybe she should call the cops now anyway. He'd been gone too long. Maybe he was hurt and needed help. Maybe—

"He got away."

The abrupt words, spoken in a voice as deep as the night and as richly textured as black velvet, brought her spinning around with a gasp. Her neighbor stood just beyond the screen door, a dark shadow in the darker night, standing back from his own kitchen as if he feared his very presence would terrify her.

Her hand flew to her throat, and she clutched at her scrubs. "There was someone there? I didn't just imagine it?"

"I didn't see anyone, but that doesn't mean anything."

Evidently he thought she was calm enough to handle him, because he pulled open the screen door and stepped into the kitchen. She hadn't been mistaken, she realized. He *was* a mountainous man, surely one of the biggest, tallest men she had ever met, and every ounce of him was well-defined, well-developed musculature. He wore nothing but a pair of snug jeans, hastily donned when she'd knocked, to judge by the way they were unsnapped. Zipped but unsnapped, and that unfastened snap seemed to catch her gaze the same way the breeze had snagged her hair.

"I'm calling the cops, Miss, uh, Miss—?"

"Honor Nightingale." Dragging in a deep breath, she managed to tear her gaze from the arrow of dark hair that seemed determined to point out his maleness to her. Darn it, Honor, you're a nurse. There's nothing there you haven't seen a million times.... "Please, just call me Honor. You shouldn't have gone over there. You might have been hurt...."

The word trailed off as he flipped on the overhead light. Now nothing was left to her imagination. Hurt? He might have been hurt the way the Incredible Hulk could be hurt, or Dirty Harry, or... Heck, any rapist in his right mind would flee like the wind at the sight of this man.

If faces could be likened to landscapes, then his was the north face of Everest, all angles, planes, sharp corners. A glacial, unforgiving face. It was a face that would never be comfortable with a smile, yet just now it smiled. Sort of. Just a quirk of one corner of his mouth, as if he found the thought of being hurt by anyone amusing. Almost as if he wished there were someone in the world who was capable of posing a threat to him.

"Nurse Nightingale, huh?" He turned toward the phone. "Or is it Doctor?"

"Nurse. Just nurse. And I've heard all the jokes."

"I just bet you have." He punched in the police emergency number and began to speak to the dispatcher. "My name's Ian McLaren. I live at 4130 South Davis, and my neighbor's house, 4132 South Davis, has just been broken into. No, the intruder is gone now. Yes. No. The back window is open, and the screen is torn. Yes, of course." He glanced at Honor over his shoulder and suddenly frowned. "You'd better sit down, lady. You're as white as a sheet."

That was when Honor realized she had completely run out of steam. The kitchen was tilting crazily, and her ears were buzzing as if she had stepped into a hornet's nest. And her field of vision was narrowing....

Some last vestige of sense caused her to slump onto a

kitchen chair and drop her head between her knees. "I never faint," she muttered to her feet.

"Thank God for small favors," he replied, in a voice that sounded dryly amused. "Just keep your head down until I can hang up the phone. Then we'll find out if you've got any blood pressure left."

He might be gruff, he might be tough, his face might look as ravaged as a war zone, but he was essentially a nice man, she decided as she studied her white oxfords and noticed blood in the creases. There had been a lot of blood in the emergency room tonight. A three-car pileup, a woman who had been shot by her husband during a quarrel, a man who had removed half his hand with a table saw. No, she never fainted. She lifted her head.

The next thing she knew she was lying on her back on the floor, staring straight up at the overhead light.

"I told you not to raise your head," said a deep, dark voice. She knew that voice, didn't she? Oh, yes. Her neighbor.

"I don't faint."

"Nope, you sure don't. Just stay put, will you?"

That sounded like a good idea, she thought as her stomach did a curious flip-flop and beads of perspiration broke out on her forehead. Nausea caused sweating, and she was undoubtedly nauseated as a reaction to adrenaline. Pleased with her clinical observation of her own state, she closed her eyes and decided that she might faint, but she absolutely was *not* going to vomit. No way.

"Here," said that same deep voice a few moments later. Strong hands gripped her shoulders and eased her slowly into a sitting position. "Okay?"

"Yes." She gave an unsteady laugh, refusing to open her eyes, because she was afraid she would find herself face-to-face with that impressive expanse of hard, mus-

cled chest. As a nurse, she must have seen a hundred
thousand chests, but she'd never seen one under these
circumstances. This was…different. ''I think my blood
pressure is back to normal.''

He gave a grunt of some kind—maybe of agreement,
maybe of approval—and then scooped her up with astonishing suddenness to set her once again on the chair. He
had, she realized with shock, lifted her as if she weighed
nothing at all. She wasn't sure she liked the feeling. It
made her too aware of her defenselessness against such
great strength.

Outside, the wind gusted, rattling the screen door in its
frame and sending a wave of cooler air into the kitchen.
Honor shivered.

''I'll make coffee,'' said her neighbor gruffly. ''Or
would you rather have tea?''

''Coffee would be great. Thanks.'' Arms wrapped
around herself, she tried not to shiver again. ''I really
appreciate you helping me out.'' Her eyes followed him
helplessly. Nurse or not, she finally had to admit she
really hadn't seen a million chests like this one. Nor a
million backs that rippled under sleek muscle. Nor shoulders so broad or hips so narrow or legs so powerful…
Sternly she shook herself back to reality.

He scooped coffee into the basket of the coffeemaker
on the counter and started it brewing. ''Women are at
risk in this country,'' he said after a moment. ''The sta-
tistics are shocking.''

''I know.'' She did. Too well.

''Men aren't doing their jobs.''

''What?'' The word was startled out of her, coming
out as almost a shocked laugh.

He faced her, looking at her with cat-green eyes.
''We're the warriors,'' he replied offhandedly. ''Seems

like we're doing a lousy job of making the world safe for our women and children.''

"Oh." A philosophical perspective, not a practical one. At the moment, it was one she could live with. He had, after all, rescued her without question. "Well, I'm sure glad you feel that way. I don't know what I would have done otherwise. Just before I realized someone was in the house, the wind blew my car door shut. It's locked, and my keys are inside, so I couldn't even drive away." And then, helplessly, she shivered again. It really wasn't cold, but as the adrenaline subsided she was beginning to feel the fear, the reaction.

Without a word, on feet as silent as a cat's, Ian McLaren left the kitchen. Less than a minute later he was back, draping a soft blue thermal blanket around her shoulders.

"Thank you," she said.

He acknowledged her thanks with a nod, then placed the length of the kitchen between them again. He did so, she realized suddenly, so as not to frighten her. The funny thing was, she wasn't frightened of him. Not at all. Not even the merest quiver. Which, she thought as she looked up into his bleak, unforgiving face, might really be stupid. He didn't look like a safe man. He looked like danger on the hoof.

He swiveled his head suddenly toward the kitchen window. "The cops are here. That was fast."

She thought so, too. When there was no immediate danger, cops generally took their own good time about showing up. Now, through the screen door, she could see the swirling lights of a patrol car. They would, she figured, check out her place first, and then come over here to ask questions she didn't have any answers for.

Her freshly brewed cup of coffee had cooled just about

enough to drink when Ian McLaren ushered the two young police officers into the kitchen. He dwarfed them, she saw, and she didn't think either of the policemen liked the feeling. Their movements around him were defensive and uneasy. Poor guy, she found herself thinking. It must be awful to have people react to you as if you were a threat just because you're so big. In fact, thinking about it, she would almost bet that when he got in an elevator, women stepped off.

The first questions were the usual, boring ones. "My name is Honor Nightingale. I'm a registered nurse, and I work in the emergency room at Community Hospital. I was on the 3:30-to-11:30 shift this evening."

"Then you were probably on when Bill Cates brought in the little girl who was in the auto accident."

Honor nodded. There had been only one little girl involved, a four-year-old, mercifully unconscious.

"Bill was wondering if she was going to make it."

It wasn't exactly a question, Honor realized, but she answered it anyway. "It'll be touch and go for a while, I'm afraid. It all depends on whether they can keep down the swelling in her brain."

The young officer, Lambert, let it go. "So you got home a little after twelve?"

"A little. Maybe 12:20."

"When did you know someone was in the house?"

She explained about the wind slamming her car door closed with her keys and purse inside, and how she'd been thinking about the loose window latch and torn screen when she had the sudden feeling that someone was watching her from that very window. And then how she had heard the thump, as if something had fallen.

"Since I couldn't drive away, I came running over here to ask Mr. McLaren for help."

Lambert turned his attention to Ian, who stood leaning against the counter, one powerful arm crossed over his waist while he sipped coffee.

"You're Ian McLaren, the man who called us, right?"

"Right."

"Occupation?"

"U.S. Army, retired. I sometimes work on the air base as a consultant."

"What kind of consultant?"

Ian set his cup down and folded his arms. "I advise the Rangers and other special-operations groups on operational tactics and survival skills." The air base included a huge reservation of federal land set aside for training purposes. Not only did bombers practice actual bombing, but all the services practiced jungle-style combat tactics and survival skills back in there, as well. Among them were the army Rangers and the Special Forces, as well as certain elite marine units.

"So Ms. Nightingale came over here for help, and you called us?"

Ian shook his head, never taking his catlike eyes from the cop. "I went over there first. I found the window by the back door open and the screen torn. The back door was wide open, flapping in the wind. I imagine the intruder fled as soon as he realized Ms. Nightingale had become aware of him."

The young policeman nodded, satisfied. "You'll have to come back over there with us now, Ms. Nightingale. We need you to tell us if anything is missing, and what damage was done, if any."

That was when Honor got the strangest feeling. She wasn't a fanciful person by nature, not at all given to odd feelings and psychic impressions. She was a woman of cheerful, optimistic outlook and a very simple faith in

God that made her feel safe in the darkest of nights. But suddenly, unexpectedly, she shivered. Almost helplessly, she raised her eyes to Ian McLaren's.

"I'll go with you," he said abruptly. "I want to take a look at that window and see if I can't make the house safer for you."

She could have kissed him for that. Had he somehow understood her sudden uneasiness? Had it been that plain on her face?

She started to leave the blanket on the chair, but he picked it back up and wrapped it around her shoulders again. "You've had a shock," he said. "Better stay warm."

"Thank you."

First, much to her relief, one of the policemen retrieved a tool from his cruiser and unlocked her car for her so that she could recover her keys and purse. Then they climbed the creaky steps to the open back door.

"This house really needs a lot of work," Honor heard herself say. She wondered if anyone else could hear the nervous note in her voice. "I've been meaning to call all kinds of repairmen ever since I moved in, but I've been so busy…"

Ian gripped her elbow reassuringly, and she fell silent. There was, she reminded herself, no reason to be nervous. Not now. Not with two policemen and a former army Ranger beside her.

The policemen warned her not to touch anything and even went so far as to turn on the kitchen light with the tip of a key so that no fingerprints would be disturbed. A crime-scene unit would come out, one of them said, to see if they could find any fingerprints around the window or the door. She absolutely mustn't touch anything until the team had come through.

"How long might that be?" she asked politely, wondering wildly if she was expected to leave her house untouched for the next week or so.

"Oh, I'm sure they'll be here soon, ma'am," said the shorter of the two officers.

So she wasn't going to get any sleep, either. "Wonderful. I'd be willing to bet the man who broke in here is already tucked into his soft little bed for the night. How many hours or days does it take for this team to complete their work?"

"That'll depend on whether you find anything else missing or disturbed."

That could almost be taken as a threat, Honor thought tiredly. By chance her gaze met Ian's, and she saw a surprising amount of understanding in those cat-green eyes of his. She had the eerie feeling that he was reading her mind. Disturbed by the sensation, she turned quickly away.

Room by room she walked through the house, with the two officers hard on her heels. The survey tour served one purpose, she thought as she led the way upstairs. By the time she and the police had poked their noses into every closet, she could be sure there was no one else in the house. The intruder, whoever he had been, was definitely gone. Only as they returned to the kitchen did Honor realize how relieved she felt to know that for certain.

Ian McLaren, she noticed, had not intruded on her privacy. He had waited in the kitchen and was talking with the freshly arrived crime-scene team as they dusted for prints around the door and window.

"Nothing else has been disturbed," said one of the policemen to the new arrivals. He glanced at Honor. "That means they'll be out of here as soon as they finish what they're doing now, Ms. Nightingale. But if you happen to notice anything after we leave, don't touch it. Leave it alone and give us a call. Someone will come right out.''

A short while later, having received some needless advice about better locks, Honor found herself alone with Ian. He had snapped his jeans, she noticed irrelevantly. Or maybe not so irrelevantly. The wind gusted sharply, making the whole house creak before its force, and thunder marched closer, a hollow drumbeat. The fresh smell of ozone spiced the air.

''Well,'' she said briskly, trying to sound like her usual fearless, capable self, all the while knowing that it was going to be some time before she felt fearless again. ''I certainly can't thank you enough for all your help, Mr. McLaren.'' As she looked up at him, she wondered if she had ever before met anyone so expressionless. His face betrayed nothing, absolutely nothing. His walls, she realized, were all invisible, and utterly inviolable.

The man, she thought, was totally unique. Totally self-contained. Totally impervious to whatever the rest of humanity might think. He was a law unto himself, and he didn't care one whit whether she was grateful or not. He had done only what he believed to be right and necessary, and her feelings in the matter didn't come into consideration. He had acted purely out of principle.

He would be aware of her feelings, of anyone's feelings, she thought, but they wouldn't affect him. Not at all. Whatever decisions he made, he made to satisfy himself, and he judged them according to his own internal measuring stick.

Suddenly she sank onto one of her kitchen chairs and wondered if she was losing her mind. She couldn't possibly know these things about this man from a few words, a few actions, the lack of expression on his face. She couldn't know these things from a few glances of his cat-green eyes. No, she was overtired, overwrought and inexcusably fanciful.

"I'm sorry," she said, not knowing why she was apologizing. Maybe it was for dragging him out of his isolation and into her problems. "I need to sleep," she added suddenly. "And I don't think I'm going to be able to." Now why had she told him that? Why? "I'm sorry," she said again, pressing her palms to her eyes. She was losing it, she realized vaguely. She was going to sit here in front of this man with the expressionless eyes and the frozen feelings and go blubberingly, embarrassingly hysterical.

A heavy hand settled on her shoulder, and she jumped, startled. Looking up, she found him watching her.

"You go up to bed," he said quietly. "I'll be down here. Nobody's going to bother you tonight."

"But—"

"Look," he said, interrupting her, "there's no way you're going to feel safe tonight, and that's normal. And I don't see anyone else around here to watch out for you. Is there somebody you can call?"

Reluctantly she shook her head, unable to tear her gaze from his. "I just moved here."

"Exactly. And I'm not going to sleep over there, wondering if that creep might come back. So do me a favor and let me hang around over here so I don't have to worry."

At that precise moment something thudded in the living room. Honor gasped and froze, but by the time the sound had died away, Ian was already moving toward the living room. Somehow the knife had once again materialized in his hand, even though Honor would have sworn he hadn't brought it with him.

She wasn't built to handle this, she thought wildly as she waited. Her heart was hammering as if she had just run a marathon, and she was breathing in huge gulps that never quite dragged in enough air. She couldn't handle this. She couldn't stand this. Her knuckles had turned white from the strength of her grip on the blanket, and she wished she could hide, just hide. Like a child, she felt that if only she pulled the blanket over her head and closed her eyes tightly enough, if only she didn't move and didn't breathe and didn't make a sound, whatever it was would go away.

In the emergency room, she knew what to do. Instinct and knowledge guided her surely in the worst situations. Her choices might not always work, but she wasn't helpless. And there was nothing quite like feeling helpless, she thought now. Nothing quite as undermining or terrifying. She had been fearless all along only because she hadn't come up against something she couldn't deal with. She couldn't even begin to imagine how she was supposed to deal with this. *What if that man came back?*

Ian returned to the kitchen a few minutes later, knife once again hidden wherever he hid it. "The wind must have blown something against the house," he said. "Everything's okay. There's no one here."

"Oh." Even that sound was a triumph of self-control. She was shaking now, shaking steadily, uncontrollably. "I think…I think I want to go to a motel," she said between chattering teeth.

"What good will that do?" he asked flatly. "Will you feel safe here tomorrow night?"

That was the crux of the matter, Honor realized. She

wasn't going to feel safe again for a long time. Slowly she lifted her frightened, moist eyes and looked at him.

She was unaware of all that was written on her soft, young face and revealed by her damp blue eyes. The man who wore a mask of iron *was* aware, however. He read it all in a glance, and something in him shifted infinitesimally, like heavy stone dragging over stone.

Thunder boomed hollowly, and lightning flickered brightly enough to be noticeable. The wind whipped around a corner of the house and moaned gently. The live oaks whispered restlessly, and the cicadas were suddenly silent.

"You can stay at my place tonight," Ian said, his voice sounding as rusty as an unoiled hinge. "I've got a guest room that's all made up, and you're welcome."

He had a guest room? This isolated man had a guest room? "I couldn't impose—"

He shook his head. "Look, neither one of us is going to sleep tonight at this rate. Just come over to my place and try out the sheets on the guest bed. In the morning we'll see about making this place trespasserproof, okay?"

He somehow managed to make her feel as if she would be obliging him by accepting his offer, that she would be inconveniencing him if she didn't. "Thank you, Mr. McLaren."

Something in him shifted just a little more. "Call me Ian. Let's go up and get whatever you need for the night."

He stood in the hallway just outside her bedroom as she hastily stuffed the necessary items into an overnight bag. Her hands still trembled, but her terror was subsiding as she realized that tonight, at least, she didn't have to face this alone.

The man who waited outside for her was remarkable, she found herself thinking. He had only just met her, yet he was putting himself out in a way very few people would. Most people would have backed out of this situation just as soon as the police arrived.

If anyone had told her that a man's protectiveness could feel like a warm sable coat wrapped around her, she would have chuckled at the absurdity of it. Women, she had always believed, were perfectly capable of doing anything and everything men could do, if only they were willing to put forth the effort. She never would have imagined that she could want, could *need,* a man to stand between her and anything. Thank God nobody had told Ian McLaren he shouldn't!

"I'm ready." Stepping out into the hallway, she switched off the light behind her and let him lead the way down the stairs. That was protective, too, she realized. He was a very protective man. She wondered what he was like when he *cared.*

Wind whipped the leaves around, ghostly shadows in the night. The last of the moonlight had been swallowed by the storm clouds, and the lightning blinded more than it helped. Ian seemed to have preternaturally acute vision, however, and he guided her around the hedge toward his house as effortlessly as if it were broad daylight. For once in her life she didn't mind someone taking her elbow and guiding her. Somehow, this evening, she had lost a little of her newfound independence.

Once inside his kitchen, he locked the door behind them, and the storm was silenced. "I'm going to turn on the air-conditioning tonight," he said, filling the sudden, obvious quiet. "That way all the windows and doors will be locked and you won't be uneasy."

"You don't have—"

"No, I don't," he said. His gaze scraped over her. "Maybe I should explain that I don't do anything I don't choose to. So save your breath. I'm doing what I feel is necessary."

She hadn't misread him, then. Well, she thought as she followed him down his hallway to the foyer, and from there up the stairs to the second story, it certainly made it easier on her not to have to worry about it. It appeared that Ian McLaren was a little like a force of nature. Like that storm outside. And it seemed she was now just along for the ride, like tumbleweed caught up in a cyclone. He would do things *his* way. If that meant sheltering her and turning on the air-conditioning, then that was what he would do. She wondered if he would consult her about anything at all.

His guest room was a bare-bones affair, not too different from a cell. There was a small four-drawer dresser, a metal cot, a straight-backed chair, and nothing else. That he had this room meant he sometimes had guests. That it was decorated this way made her wonder just what kind of guests they were.

"The bathroom is down the hall," he said abruptly. "Take a shower if you like—the towels are fresh. My room is straight across the hall. If you get nervous or need anything, holler, and don't worry about disturbing me. I seldom sleep at night."

With that enigmatic and totally intriguing statement, he exited the room and closed the door gently behind him.

Sighing, Honor dropped her overnight bag on the chair and looked around once again.

It really did look like a cell. And it occurred to her that she had just become a prisoner of fear.

* * *

Across the hall, Ian McLaren stood at the closed window of his bedroom and stared out at the wild, stormy night. As a rule, he needed very little sleep, and what little he needed usually eluded him at night. That didn't prevent him from attempting to be normal, though. Every night he came up here, stripped and climbed into that narrow bed. And every night he eventually rose, dressed and pursued other activities. He had been trying to sleep when Honor's pounding at the door summoned him, and he was glad now to have an excuse to quit trying, at least for tonight.

A natural inclination toward insomnia had hardened into something nearly pathological as a result of his military experience. He had been little more than a boy when he learned that the night hours were favored for surreptitious attacks, and that night was not a safe time to trust others to remain alert. For him it was easy to stay awake and alert, but it hadn't been for his comrades. When Ian had understood that, he had taken it upon himself to keep the night watches. Now, nearly a quarter century later, he was generally able to sleep only in the daylight.

Some people might have seen that as a problem, but since Ian had little regard for other people and preferred his solitude, it was no problem at all. When he needed to advise at the base, he usually did so at unconventional hours anyway, and when he needed to do a regular nine-to-five, a quick lunchtime nap was all he required to keep him going.

From his window he had an unobstructed view of Honor's house and garage. He had noticed her occasionally in the month since she moved in, had recognized at some point or other that she worked a rotating shift, and knew she didn't pursue a social life. He knew these things because survival depended on knowing your surroundings, and while he was no longer in that kind of danger, old habits didn't die.

So he knew a little about Honor Nightingale, more than she suspected. It was nothing she would object to him knowing, but she would probably feel uneasy if she knew that he'd paid that much attention to her. Once or twice he had considered picking up the phone to request a background investigation—a BI on her, then had dismissed the idea. He was retired, damn it. He no longer needed to know everything about everyone around him.

And now she needed him. Thinking about what she had come home to, he felt a familiar stirring of anger. Anger was about the only feeling he allowed himself, and then only when someone or something violated his sense of rightness. The crud might only have been planning to rob her, but Ian doubted it. No, the intruder had had more despicable things in mind. The question was whether he had happened on her by accident or whether he had planned this. Whether he wanted Honor in particular.

Disturbed, Ian turned from the window. It wouldn't be the first time a woman had attracted the obsessive attentions of a sicko. Well, only time would settle that issue.

Deciding he wanted a cup of coffee, he stepped out of his room and began to make his silent way toward the stairs. A gust of wind rattled the window at the top of the staircase, and a sharp clatter announced the first few raindrops. Lightning flared brightly, momentarily blinding him, and he gave up, turning on the hall light. The eye's adaptation to darkness vanished in an instant before flashes that bright.

He liked the night. He liked the quiet and the solitude. He liked being able to step out his door and take long, undisturbed walks. The whole world changed at night, and a whole different set of creatures came into the ascendant. Night was the time of the predators, and the time of those who hunted them.

Ian McLaren was a hunter. And this evening he had definitely scented a predator.

CHAPTER TWO

Honor stood on the back porch of Ian's house and stared across the hedge toward her own home. The morning sun was bright and warm in Ian's treeless yard, but it failed to penetrate the shadows beneath the old oaks and Spanish moss that surrounded her house.

She had thought, when she first saw the house, only of its charm. It had the spaciousness of another age, large rooms and high ceilings, and it had solid oak floors. It had those little extras, like a built-in hutch in the dining room and huge walk-in closets, that were impossible to find in more recent construction. And the towering old live oaks and the shady curtains of Spanish moss had added romance to it all.

Now she looked at those same oaks and those same curtains of Spanish moss, and they looked ominous. The windows of her house seemed to be black and empty, holes leading into a pit. She wished suddenly that she had never set eyes on the place.

She had left her home in Seattle to escape the ghosts of sorrowful memories. Her father's long illness and death, her own failed marriage, a sense of grayness to her life, as if she were cut off behind a tinted wall of glass. The Florida sunshine had drawn her with the promise of burning away the gray fog that had swallowed her since her father became ill.

Now she looked at her home and felt as if not even the tropical sunlight were enough to banish the dark.

God!

Shivering, she turned to reenter the house and wait for Ian McLaren. He must have heard her stirring this morning, because he had had breakfast waiting for her when she came downstairs, eggs and ham and plenty of hot, fresh coffee. As soon as he had seen her served, though, he had vanished upstairs. When he came down, he'd said, he wanted to look over her house and decide what she needed to make it secure. Then they would go into town and get it, so she wouldn't have to worry tonight.

It was an awful lot of trouble for the man to go to, she thought, even if he *did* do only what he chose to. And maybe she was being too quick to trust him. But when she remembered how he had dashed out into the dark last night to look for the intruder, and how quick he had been to understand her terrors and take her under his protection, she felt guilty for even wondering about his motives. So what if his eyes were the strangest she had ever seen.

"Ready?"

She spun around at the sound of his deep voice and stared in astonishment. She hadn't expected him to appear all decked out in BDUs, the army camouflage uniform, combat boots and a red beret. Wasn't he retired? Dressed this way, he was even more overpowering than he had been last night. Bigger. Darker. More dangerous looking. And this morning those unusual cat-green eyes of his looked…eerie.

"I need to stop on the base on the way and check my schedule," he said, as if she had spoken her surprise about his uniform. "I believe I need to be in the field this weekend."

"Look," she said, hoping she sounded reasonable, not wanting to offend him, but suddenly wanting very much to be away from him, "you've obviously got important things to do, and shepherding me around is only going to get in your way. Why don't you just let me take care of this stuff?''

''No.''

No. The word seemed to hang in the humid air between them, as uncompromising a sound as any she had ever heard. No qualifier eased it; no explanation expanded it. Just *no*.

Tilting her head back, she glared up at him, then had a sudden, unexpected sense of the foolhardiness of her action. This man could undoubtedly kill her with a single blow of his powerful arm. She, who had never feared a thing, suddenly wondered if a little fear might not be wise. What did she know about him, after all? A bubble of nervous laughter escaped her. The only change in his rocklike expression was the lifting of a single eyebrow.

''Okay,'' she said, swallowing another nervous laugh. ''It's your time.''

''That's right.''

Turning, he exited his house and led the way around the hedge toward her back door. As she followed, she wondered what rank he had held before his retirement, then concluded that, whatever it had been, he was used to being followed and obeyed. It didn't seem to enter his head that anyone would do otherwise. It was an attitude she knew well; her father had been a high-ranking sergeant in the Rangers. The left hand of God, she had sometimes thought. His dicta had had the force of law.

It was still early, but the Florida sun was already burning-hot, promising a stifling September day. The normally humid climate was more so this morning, after the night's rain, and Honor wondered if she had been crazy to move here. Long ago, as a child, she had lived here, when her father had been stationed at the base. She had always remembered the Gulf Coast fondly, especially the white sand of the beaches and the aquamarine of the water. She had forgotten the heat and humidity.

Once around the hedge, they stepped into the cooler shadows beneath the trees, where the air seemed even thicker. The smell of rotting vegetation was strong here, almost overpowering, even though nothing grew in the shadows beneath the moss and the old trees. Honor shivered suddenly, despite the warmth of the air. Shadows that had seemed pleasantly cool only yesterday now seemed dank. Threatening. As if in stepping out of the light she had crossed some invisible barrier into an evil place.

Ian halted before they drew close to the house, and she halted beside him. He stood perfectly still, moving not a muscle, and she watched him curiously, wondering what he was doing.

Eventually she realized. He was allowing his eyes to adapt to the fainter illumination under the trees, but he was also taking in impressions with all his senses. His nostrils flared a little as he inhaled, and she wouldn't have been the least bit surprised to discover that he was separating out every scent and cataloging it individually. His eyes scanned everywhere, appearing to overlook nothing, and his head cocked at each sound, identifying it and locating it.

Like a hunter, she thought. Like a mountain lion. Like a jungle predator. Another shiver rippled through her, and she wondered again why she had trusted him so readily.

He stepped forward in a smooth gliding motion that made him look almost like one of the gently swaying shadows beneath the trees. "It's too dark under here," he remarked. "There are too many places to hide."

Honor looked around, wondering what it was he saw that she had missed. To her, except for the trunks of the trees, her yard looked positively barren. Grass couldn't grow in this shade, never mind bushes or shrubs that might hide someone.

"I can't do much about the shadows," she said, hesitantly. "I really don't want to cut down the trees." Although the idea was sounding more attractive by the minute. Why hadn't she noticed before just how tomblike it felt beneath all this moss? Damp, chilly, cut off.

"We might get rid of some of this moss."

Yesterday she would have been appalled at the very notion of disturbing that beautiful, graceful moss—which at this moment didn't look either beautiful or graceful. "Maybe," she said uncertainly. Lord, was she letting last night's events poison everything about her new home? But she couldn't seem to help it.

He glanced down at her. "Last resort," he said, plainly recognizing her reluctance. "Let's see to more practical things first."

She nodded and followed him around back. He didn't approach the house immediately, but instead circled the detached garage, checking out the windows and door.

"Don't park in the garage anymore," he said. "It's an obvious place for somebody to lie in wait, even in the middle of the day."

"All right." She never would have thought of such a thing. Never.

"When you have to come home after dark, give me a call. I'll wait for you and make sure you get in okay."

"But—"

A look from his cat-green eyes silenced her. "There are things out there that masquerade as human," he said intensely. "They walk, talk and look like you and me. But they're not human. They're not human at all. They get their pleasure from inflicting pain. They feast on the

suffering of others and make a banquet out of their victims' agony. The sweetest music to their ears is a tortured
cry for mercy.''

He faced her fully, impaling her on the glowing, gem-
like hardness of his gaze. Honor instinctively took a step
backward, feeling his intensity as if it were a vortex in
the very air. As if he somehow gathered energy from the
atmosphere and focused the power of it on her.

When he continued speaking, his voice was low, quiet,
but forceful. ''If one of them has set his sights on you,
it will take more than ordinary caution to protect you.
And sacrificing a little independence is a small price for
avoiding capture by a demon.''

The chill that had fallen over her in the shadows
seemed now to reach to her very bones. ''Demon?'' she
repeated hoarsely. No one talked in those terms anymore.
She wanted to believe he was exaggerating, but the look
in his strange eyes was deadly serious, disturbing. *Witch
eyes.* ''You mean like…possession?'' She whispered the
last word, hardly able to bring herself to say it.

''They're sure as hell not men.'' He looked past her,
seeing something elsewhere, elsewhen. ''They're real,
though. Too damn real.''

He turned abruptly toward the house. ''I can put locks
on doors and windows to stymie them, lady, but I can't
put locks on you. You have to exercise reasonable caution.''

''Well, of course,'' she said weakly, following him.
Maybe she was a fool to trust this man. He was talking
about demons, after all, and if that wasn't, well, *weird,*
then what was? ''Uh…Mr. McLaren? I can just have
someone come out here and install a security system—''
She broke off suddenly, the full import of his words strik-

ing her. "Wait a minute." The words were little more than a croak.

He heard them and turned. Standing there in the deep shadows beneath the moss, he settled his hands on his hips and stared at her. He looked, she thought crazily, like a being from another world, not quite mortal. He was too big, too powerful.

"Demons," she repeated hoarsely. "You're not joking."

"No." Again, that single uncompromising syllable.

"But—look. Somebody broke into my house last night. And he fled as soon as he was discovered. There's really no good reason to think he'll ever come back. Making the house more secure is simply to make me feel better, right?"

He just stared at her with eyes that burned like green fire.

"This demon business... Well, I don't believe in that kind of stuff." She managed to say that firmly, with conviction. She even sounded normal. Inside, though, her conviction was losing force, and she was beginning to feel as if the firm ground on which she had so confidently stood were turning into quicksand beneath her feet. *Abomination.* The word whispered through her brain, so strange as to feel alien. She was too tense at the moment, though, to pay it any mind.

For a moment he continued to stare at her in silence. Finally he spoke, his voice a deep rumble, like thunder in the distance. "He may not come back. You're right. There's no reason to assume he will."

Honor nearly sighed with relief. At least he could be rational.

"However," he said, shattering her moment of relief, "you really can't afford to bank on that, can you?"

Suddenly angry with the way he was trying to frighten her, she glared at him. "Perhaps not. But I don't need to start imagining ghosts and goblins in every corner, either. With all due respect to you, Mr. McLaren, I don't believe in demons."

"'There are more things in heaven and earth, Horatio, than are dreamt of in your philosophy.'" He shrugged, his expression never changing. "I don't care what you believe, Ms. Nightingale. The question is whether you want to risk meeting one in your bedroom in the dead of night." The words hung starkly in the dark, heavy air.

Game, set and match, thought Honor grimly as she walked behind him to the house and tried to tell herself that it didn't matter what he called them. He would probably say Charles Manson was a demon.

Shivering internally against the chill that had settled over her the instant she stepped into the shadows, she glanced around her yard and wondered uneasily if perhaps there *were* more things out there than she'd dreamt of.

The house still held the night's coolness and seemed just as oppressive as the shadows outside. She tried to tell herself it was just an aftereffect of last night, but the fact was, if someone had offered at that moment to take over her mortgage, she would have been packed and gone before noon.

She'd been living here for almost a month, and only yesterday she'd found herself wondering why it was taking so long for this place to feel like home. As an army brat, she was accustomed to making a new home every year or so. Nothing about this move had seemed wrenching or unusual. The only difference was that she couldn't seem to settle in. Couldn't escape the really discomfiting feeling that when she stepped in here she was stepping into someone else's home. She kept telling herself that a fresh coat of interior paint would make all the difference, yet she kept putting off buying the paint.

Ian began his self-imposed task immediately. He pulled a small memo book out of one of his pockets and handed it to her, along with a pen. "Write down the measurements as I give them to you, will you?"

"We're not going to put bars on the windows or anything, are we?" She couldn't stand the thought. It would make the house feel like a prison.

He glanced at her and shook his head. "No, but I want to get some locking bars. They'll make it impossible to jimmy the windows, even if someone breaks out a pane of glass."

The windows were multipaned, and each pane was too small to climb through without breaking the wood frame, as well, and that would make a terrible racket. Honor nodded her understanding.

"I'm especially concerned about this window, though," he said, indicating the one right beside the back door. "That's how he got in last night."

"That was how *I* was planning to get in when I got locked out of the car last night," Honor admitted. "It was the first thing that occurred to me, to break out a pane of glass and reach around to unlock the door."

"The only way to prevent that is to board up the window. Or shutter it. Could you live with a shutter?"

"On the inside?"

"Or outside. It doesn't really matter, as long as it can't be opened from the outside once it's closed."

She nodded reluctantly, unable to argue against the wisdom of it, and watched as he measured the window

and its frame, inside and out. "This isn't right," she said
a little later, as he worked his way through her house.

He looked at her, his eyes as hard as chips of jade.
"No, it isn't. But this isn't a perfect world. Your only
alternatives are to make yourself as safe as possible or
leave the area."

She really didn't need him to tell her that. She might
be only twenty-six compared to his— She glanced at him,
wondering again. Retired from the army meant only that
he had to be at least thirty-eight, but even knowing that
much, she couldn't be sure. His hair was the dark color
of teak, and the only gray in it was a startling, intriguing
slash of white that looked as if it might have come from
an old injury. Otherwise, the man was ageless. The lines
in his face had come from the elements, from the sun
and the wind, not from the years.

She followed him up the stairs, certain he was preced-
ing her because it was safer, and found herself at eye
level with his buns. Each time he flexed a leg, camouflage
fabric tightened over his buttocks and revealed just how
hard and muscled he was.

Oh, Lord, maybe she *was* losing her mind. How could
she even be noticing his buns at a time like this? Last
night someone had been waiting for her here, inside her
very own house, and only because of some ancient survival instinct had she realized she was being watched. If
she had walked up to the house and stuck her hand
through the glass to unlock the door, if she had come into
her own kitchen...

Something dark seemed to be hovering at the edges of
her mind, something dark and threatening. It soaked the
light from the room, the breath from her lungs. Suddenly
she was standing in the middle of her own bedroom, with

the hair on the back of her neck prickling as if some evil force still lingered in the house from last night.

Ian reached out suddenly. Cupping the back of her neck with one hard, callused palm, he forced her down until she sat on the edge of her bed with her head between her knees.

"Delayed reaction," he said, as calmly as if he were used to dealing with this kind of thing every day. "It'll pass in a little while. Just keep your head down for a minute."

God, was she turning into a wimp? she wondered miserably, remembering the darkness that had been closing in on her, not sure she had just been faint. But then, she told herself, she'd never had to deal with anything like this before. What did she know about delayed reactions and fainting except what she had seen as a nurse, as an observer on the outside looking in?

But now her safe little world had been invaded in the worst possible way, and instead of bucking up like the capable woman she had always believed herself to be, she was acting like a Victorian miss whose stays were too tight. Angry at herself, she sat up and waited for the brief bout of dizziness to pass.

"That's it," said the deep, dark voice of the man who seemed to be taking over her life with breathtaking speed. "Get mad. It's healthy."

He yanked the window open and leaned out to look around. Honor knew what he saw: the front porch roof, right under her window. She'd been thinking about building a small balcony there, thinking it would be a pleasant place to sit in the evenings, since a hole in the trees gave her her only real view she had, though it was only of the road leading up to the highway. Now she could think only of how easy that roof would make it for someone to get to her bedroom.

"We'll have to do something about this," Ian said, then turned in the window, leaning backward so that he could look upward. A moment later he pulled his head in. "This place is a defender's nightmare."

"I wasn't in the market for a fortress when I purchased it," she said glumly. A fortress was what she needed now, though, and the recognition of that fact rippled coldly through her. What if somebody really *did* want to get to her? Just her, Honor Nightingale. What if he came back and a few locks didn't stop him?

Ian ignored her irritation, somehow making her feel foolish. "I don't suppose you were," he said indifferently. "Let's see the other rooms. And there's an attic?"

She'd looked up there only briefly when the agent had shown her the place, and her thought had been that it could be transformed into a marvelous guest suite if she ever had the money to do anything about it. The stairs pulled down from the ceiling in the back bedroom, and she watched Ian climb them, knowing what he would see.

It was a spacious attic, and the roof was steeply pitched, giving it an almost cathedral-like quality. At both ends of the house, round windows allowed in just enough dim light to reveal beautiful lathwork and a solid plank floor. In another age it might have been servants' quarters. Now it was merely storage space, without air-conditioning or heat.

She remained below and listened to the sound of Ian's booted feet as he explored, especially around the two windows. Leaning against the wall, she looked out the window at the moss-shrouded branches of the tree just outside.

The moss took nothing from the trees, merely draping

itself from the branches to expose more of itself to the
air and humidity from which it took all its sustenance.
But it slowly killed the trees anyway, because it smothered the leaves. So far her oaks had survived, growing
upward ahead of the moss. Now all but the tips of the
lower branches were leafless hangers for the brownish-
green curtains, and only the topmost branches showed a
healthy profusion of green. At some point the balance
would shift and the tree would die.

Beautiful decay.

Suddenly cold again, she shivered and turned to watch
Ian descend the stairs. It was always cold just here at the
foot of the attic stairs, she thought. It seemed like such
a waste of air-conditioning when she didn't even use this
room. Glancing around, she looked for the duct, thinking
that she might want to cover it with plastic. No vent was
visible anywhere, though. Must be something about the
way air flowed through the house.

"The attic won't be a problem," Ian told her. "I think
we need to assume only a reasonable amount of determination if this guy comes back. He might lie in wait for
you, he might even go so far as to try to get in through
a window, but to attempt to protect against anything more
would probably cost a fortune and wouldn't work anyway."

Rubbing her arms against the chill she couldn't shake,
she looked up at him. "Why not?"

Nothing in his expression changed, and his gaze never
wavered. He dropped his bomb emotionlessly. "If this
guy is more than normally determined to get at you, there
isn't a security measure in the world that would be totally
foolproof. A man who is determined enough can get past
anything. I know, because I've done it."

And then what? she wondered. What did he do when he circumvented all those security measures?

Somehow she thought she was better off not knowing. And that brought her back to the way he seemed to be taking over with breathtaking speed.

"You really shouldn't do this, Ian. You have a life of your own, concerns of more importance—"

"There's nothing more important than this."

"Why?" She faced him squarely, making it clear that she wasn't going to settle for a brush-off.

"I've devoted a lifetime to keeping innocents like you safe from the filth of the world," he said, in a hard, harsh voice, his strange eyes boring into her. "I didn't give up that duty just because I retired. If I don't look after you, who the hell will?"

Good Lord, she thought uneasily, the man sounded like a fanatic. Nobody talked like this. Nobody thought like this. It was creepy!

His tone had been angry, but his face revealed nothing. He took her elbow and motioned toward the stairs. "Let's go."

Honor yanked herself free of his grip, annoyed by his tone and his manhandling, suddenly completely fed up with the way he was taking over her life. "You're weird, McLaren! You know that?"

"I know."

He said it flatly, as if it were an inarguable fact. The words fell harshly into the room, and the shock of their impact drove Honor's anger away, leaving her with a curious ache she couldn't have identified. And in that instant before either of them drew another breath, she saw a flicker deep in his eyes. It vanished quickly, hidden once again in the cold, hard depths, but she never doubted for an instant that she had seen the shadow of old hurts.

"Look," she said. "I didn't mean that. Not really. It's just that…that I don't know you. I was really grateful for your help last night, but you've just…taken over. And frankly, I don't know if I like having you take over without so much as a by-your-leave any more than I liked finding that creep waiting in the house for me. It's…not normal!"

He cocked his head to one side. "Normal," he said, with astonishing bitterness, "is walking away from a difficult situation just as fast as you can. Normal is avoiding involvement no matter what it costs someone else. Normal is turning your back when a woman screams for help. Normal is driving past an accident scene slowly enough to get a good idea of how bad it is, but neglecting to stop at the next telephone to call for help, because you don't have time."

Honor stared up at him, every other concern arrested as she faced the unlikely passion of this cold man. He cared, she realized. He really cared, for all that he looked and acted so hard. That caring defeated her in a way anger or hardness never could have.

"Okay," she said. "I get the picture. And you're right, of course." She had treated enough victims in the emergency room to know just how right. More times than she wanted to count, she had been appalled by the utter callousness of her fellow man.

"If you weren't alone, I wouldn't butt in," he said. "But you *are* alone. And I'll be damned if I want to live with myself if something happens to you while I'm being *normal*."

Honor almost winced at the sarcasm lacing the word. Truth to tell, she was appalled at her own behavior. Yes, it was reasonable for a woman to be cautious in this day and age, and certainly she should be cautious of strangers who acted in an unusual way, but still! To call the man weird and tell him to his face he wasn't normal, when he had done nothing at all except go out of his way to help her...well, she deserved to be slapped. "I'm sorry," she said sincerely.

"Don't be." He turned toward the stairs. "You're wise to be suspicious of me. Of any man. And just as soon as I get this place secured, I'll get the hell out of your life."

They were bombing on the range again tonight. Honor watched the eerie flashes of light as she drove home after her shift. Inside her car, with the breeze blowing through the window, she couldn't hear any sound accompanying the flashes. It was, she found herself thinking, like some kind of science-fiction film. Or like a dream. Unreal.

She hadn't called Ian McLaren before leaving work, either. The thought had crossed her mind, and he *had* insisted on it, but it had been easy, in the bright lights of the hospital, to tell herself that it would be ridiculous to call him. After all, she'd been coming home from work alone for years now, and she would be doing so for many years to come. Her reasoning had sounded good, too, until she realized she was in the nurses' locker room, changing out of her scrubs into the shorts she had worn to work, delaying her departure. Ordinarily she didn't bother.

Nor did her reasoning sound so good now that she was alone in her car. It was dark out here, moonless again, thanks to heavy cloud cover. She had left the back porch light on before leaving, so that would be some help...but not much. It would be one small light bulb in a world that suddenly seemed very dark and very threatening. And it certainly wouldn't tell her if somebody was inside the house. Not that anyone should be. Ian had done a thorough job this morning, installing deadbolts on her doors, locking bars on her windows, a steel shutter on the kitchen window by the back door. He had been mercilessly efficient, swift and silent.

She had insulted him. She knew it in her heart and felt guilty as sin. Whatever she thought of him or his methods or his manner, she had had absolutely no right to speak that way to him. He had only been trying to help, and whatever security she would be able to feel tonight in her own bed was because of him. And she had to give him his due—he hadn't let her attitude deter him from doing what he considered necessary.

But he had the strangest eyes. The mere memory of them made her feel shivery. Not too many generations ago, she thought, eyes like that probably would have gotten him burned at the stake. Something about them, about their color, didn't seem quite human.

God, it was dark! Her driveway looked like a tunnel into pitch blackness, and the back porch light must have burned out, because it was dark in her yard. Too dark. She switched off the ignition, careful this time to hold on to the keys, then sat listening to the night sounds.

Cicadas screeched ceaselessly; it was such a constant cacophony that she hardly heard it anymore. Tree frogs croaked their two hoarse notes, battling the cicadas for preeminence in the night. The offshore breeze was still strong, whispering of the night's emptiness, and the live oaks rustled uneasily.

She didn't want to get out of the car. A terrible feeling seemed to permeate the night, as if the air were a living, malevolent being. A shudder rippled down her spine, and she had to force herself not to drive away. This is ridiculous, she told herself. Her imagination was running riot, just as it had when she was four and believed there was a crocodile under her bed. Foolish imagination.

Finally she rolled up her window and climbed out of the car. Keys firmly in hand, she closed the car door and turned toward the house. There was, she reminded herself, absolutely no reason on earth to think the creep from last night had come back. None.

She had taken no more than two steps toward her door when the porch light suddenly came on. She froze, and terror trickled icily down her spine. Oh, God!

"Get in the car."

Whirling, she came face-to-face with Ian. He stood only a few feet away, Ranger knife in his hand. He wore black from head to toe and blended with the shadows. Her hand flew to her throat. "God, you scared me!"

"Get in the car and lock yourself in," he said quietly. "Give me your house keys. I'll check it out."

Her heart was hammering so loudly that she could hear it, but adrenaline muffled her initial fear. "I'll go in with you." She didn't want to wait out here alone, and she didn't want him to go in there alone. Either would be intolerable, but if she went with him, at least she would know what was happening.

"I can fight better if you're not in the way. Give me the keys and get in the car."

Instead, she headed toward the back door, finding courage in the fact that he was right behind her. This is crazy, she thought wildly, but she wasn't going to back down. Her dad hadn't raised her to be a wimp, and life as an army brat had taught her to face things head-on. If this man was going to go in there, he wasn't going alone.

Bravado carried her to the door. It couldn't, however,

keep her hand from trembling wildly as she tried to slip the key into the lock. How had he gotten inside? The question hammered at her, pulverizing any sense of security all those locks might have given her.

"Here." Ian stepped up right behind her, so close that his chest touched her back, and took the key from her hand. His touch was gentle, warm, not at all abrupt or impatient. He slipped the key in the lock, moved her to one side, then shoved the door open. "Stay behind me."

He ignored the light switch just inside the door and instead flicked on a powerful flashlight that he was carrying. Slowly, methodically, he passed the beam over every inch of the kitchen. Only then did he step inside.

"Close and lock the door," he whispered.

To prevent anyone from coming up on them from behind, she realized. Turning, she did as he asked, closing out the night sounds. But all the while some niggling feeling at the base of her skull told her the threat wasn't outside. No, it was inside. Locked in here with them.

Two doors led from the kitchen into the rest of the house. One opened on a hallway that led straight to the front door. Along one side were the doorways into the living and dining rooms. Climbing the other side was the stairway to the upstairs.

The other door opened directly into the dining room, and from an archway there it was possible to walk directly through double doors into the living room. It was therefore possible to make a complete circle of the ground floor without retracing one's steps, and Ian had evidently thought of that, because he closed the wooden door into the hallway and quietly braced a chair under the knob.

"Okay," he whispered, and opened the door that led into the dining room.

Honor stayed right on his heels, telling herself that no one could come up from behind because there was no way for anyone to get there, but feeling the back of her neck prickle anyway.

Someone was in the house. She was sure of it. She could feel it, almost as if their presence created some kind of pressure in the air, or as if some strange perfume were wafting through the rooms. Someone was here. *Abomination.* The word floated into her mind and then vanished.

The dining room was empty. Ian stepped through it and into the living room. Honor hesitated in the archway. She had never really felt comfortable in the living room. Time and again she had told herself that the feeling was simply some kind of subliminal response to the mustiness of the room, to the dingy paint and paper and the faintly moldy smell. Fresh paint and a good dose of white vinegar would clear it out, she had believed.

But now, standing there, it was almost as if a physical force held her back. She didn't want to go in there. Couldn't go in there. Ian swept the flashlight around, revealing nothing but an empty bookcase and a rocking chair. She had very little furniture, because she had planned to buy what she needed once she fixed the place up. Somehow what had seemed an innocent decision then took on ominous overtones now, as she stood there unable to cross the threshold.

Ian stepped back beside her. "Nothing. I'm going upstairs." His whisper was almost inaudible. "You go back into the kitchen and close the door until I get back."

For an instant, just an instant, her body refused to obey her brain. Then she turned and hurried back to the kitchen, her rubber soles silencing her footsteps. Her courage had vanished. She couldn't bring herself to walk through the living room or climb those stairs in Ian's wake, and somehow he had known it. He had known it even before she had faced it herself. That realization sent another uneasy shudder running down her spine.

In the kitchen, she wedged a chair under the knob of the second door and then felt around for the light switch. It was then that she realized the porch light had gone out again.

Fear locked her breath in her throat. The pounding of her heart was loud in her ears, loud enough to drown the sounds of the night outside. For endless seconds she stood frozen, her hand on the light switch, her back to the rest of the kitchen, acutely aware that someone might be right behind her. Terrifyingly aware of how exposed her back was.

She wished wildly that she could make her heart stop for just a few moments, so that she could listen and hear if someone was behind her. Then, having no choice, unable to stand the tension another minute, she spun around and pressed her back to the door, facing into the dark room.

Nothing. No one. Sobbing for breath, she felt around beside her for the switch. And then she froze again, wondering if she would regret turning on the light, afraid of what she might see. Terrified of not seeing.

Oh, God. Ian, hurry!

Then she was lanced with an ice-cold shaft of fear. Something in the kitchen had moved, making a scraping sound.

She wasn't alone.

CHAPTER THREE

That did it. The breath left her lungs, and she pawed the light switch frantically, finally managing to flip it on.

The light nearly blinded her, but even so, she saw no one. Just at that moment there was a pounding on the dining room door.

"Honor! Honor, it's Ian! Open up!"

Drawing a huge, ragged breath of relief, she hurried over and pulled the chair from under the knob. As soon as Ian heard the chair come free, he threw the door open.

"Are you all right?" he demanded.

She flew into his arms. He might be crazy, he might be weird, he might be maddening, but he also represented safety, and right now she needed, absolutely needed, to feel strong arms around her.

Without hesitation, he caught her close and surrounded her with the shield of his strength. "I got this feeling," he said gruffly. "All of a sudden I knew you needed me...."

He trailed off, as if embarrassed to admit such a thing, but Honor didn't care how he had known. If he had said the wind had whispered to him, or that he had felt her fear on the currents of the air, she would have been grateful. It was enough that he was there.

Almost awkwardly, as if unaccustomed to such gestures, Ian stroked her hair and patted her shoulder with one of his huge hands. "There's no one in the house," he told her, his deep voice a reassuring rumble. "There must be an electrical problem with that porch light."

"It went out again," Honor said shakily, relief rushing through her. "And I heard something in here. It sounded...odd. Like a scraping noise. Or a scuttling."

He tightened his hold as she started to straighten, and, grateful that he wasn't in any hurry to let go, she allowed her arms to find their way around his waist.

"A mouse, maybe," he said. "Or a lizard. Or maybe just a bug. Want me to look?"

Drawing a deep breath, she tilted her head to say something about bugs and lizards and found herself staring right into his cat-green eyes. At this distance they were unusually mesmerizing, almost glowing, and they held her gaze as if by a witch's spell.

And something deep inside her stirred. She had noticed how attractive he was, had admired his flanks and his chest and his powerful build. But not until now had she felt that long-forgotten unfurling inside herself, that strange, edgy, hopeful, hungry feeling. Every thought in her head was arrested as her attention suddenly focused completely on the man who held her, on the womanly feelings deep inside her.

His eyes darkened, as if he felt it, too. His head bowed just a fraction, hesitated. And then, as if compelled, he bent and kissed her.

Honor hadn't kissed a man since her wedding day, eight years before. Jerry hadn't liked kissing, or so he'd claimed, and had kissed her just that once, passionlessly, because it was necessary. That was before she had learned there were a lot of things Jerry didn't like when it came to sex, every one of them having to do with the fact that she was a woman. He had hoped to hide his homosexuality by marrying, and instead had managed only to confirm it for himself—and nearly destroy his eighteen-year-old wife in the process.

Telling herself that Jerry's sexual orientation had nothing to do with her hadn't helped very much. She hadn't let a man kiss her or touch her since, because she couldn't quite escape the feeling that there was something intrinsically revolting about her. Something so repulsive that it had prevented Jerry from ever consummating their union. If she ever felt that revulsion from another man, she feared, she would dive off a bridge. She couldn't handle it again.

But now here she was, clinging to this man she hardly knew, this man who frightened her in some primitive way, but who made her feel paradoxically safe. Confusion swamped her as conflicting feelings warred inside her and drove away all thought of her earlier terror.

He wasn't gentle. He took the kiss with the same unswerving determination he had so far shown in everything. He didn't coax or tease or ask. He simply opened his mouth over hers and drove his tongue into her warm depths as if he had every right to do so.

Had he done anything else, she would have tried to back off. As it was, she never had a chance. An instant deluge of feelings washed her away, sweeping her toward passion in a breathless rush. All unaware, she dug her fingers into his muscled back, clutching him closer, frustrated by the layer of black cotton between her hands and his skin.

She wanted. Oh, God, she wanted as she had never wanted before. As she had never dreamed it was possible to want. She had once craved Jerry, craved him enough to marry him despite her father's objections, but what she felt right now surpassed craving by light-years. It reached into some primitive part of her, turning her into some cavewoman who was willing to lie down on the hard ground and spread her legs just so that she could feel this man's possession, just so that she could, for a few minutes, feel his strength and hunger answer her own.

God, was she losing her mind?

Suddenly Ian lifted his head, tearing his mouth from hers almost savagely. Before she could make a sound, he pressed her face into his shoulder, hard.

"Shh!" he hissed sharply.

On the edge of screaming from frustrated need, she froze. Then, with a suddenness that deprived her of breath, she understood that he had heard something.

His hand gentled a little on the back of her head when he realized she wasn't going to make noise. After an interminable span of nerve-stretching time, he whispered, "Did you hear anything?"

She shook her head, not certain she could find air to whisper back. She was scared again. Terrified. And the back of her neck was crawling with the feeling that somebody was watching her. Watching them.

He muttered an obscenity right into her ear. She was shockproof, having heard them all over the years, so she ignored it. It was harder to ignore her feelings when he set her aside. Reality had intruded, and she had only a deep-rooted ache to tell her that she hadn't fantasized that kiss or her reaction to it.

"Let's get your things," he said. "You'll use my guest room again tonight. Tomorrow I'm going to find out what the hell is going on around here."

"But you said there's no one here."

"There isn't. I went through this place right up to the attic rafters. Lights going on and off might just be the wiring...which is dangerous enough, and I'll check it

out as soon as I have light to see. Scuttling sounds are
most likely mice or bugs…probably a damn roach or a
cicada that came in with us. No big deal. But—''

By the way he broke off, she knew he had caught
himself before he said something he didn't want her to
know. And that angered her. ''But what? What did you
hear? What aren't you telling me?''

His eyes locked on hers, and a long moment passed
before he answered. ''It's a feeling,'' he said finally,
with evident reluctance. ''A feeling I don't like.''

Hardly realizing she did so, she stepped closer to him.
''I know,'' she said, her voice little more than a whisper.
''I keep getting the feeling someone is watching.''

For long, long moments, they stared at one another.
Then Ian nodded, in acknowledgment of what she was
saying. ''Let's get your things.''

Abomination. The word whispered into her sleepy
mind, and Honor sat up abruptly, clutching the sheet to
her breast as she peered into the dark. She was sleeping
on the cot in Ian's guest room again, she remembered.
Trying to sleep despite a nervous fluttering in her stomach, despite an edginess that warned her something terrible was about to happen.

Demon. Another whisper on the edge of her mind,
almost as if someone were whispering in her ear. In her
mind. The words felt alien; they were not words she
would ever use.

Shivering against an internal chill, she lay down again
and pulled the sheet to her chin. This was crazy, she
told herself. A creep had broken into her house, and now
she was becoming unhinged, looking for sinister purpose in an electrical problem and the vagaries of an

overtired mind. Silly. Ian had planted these thoughts with his talk of demons, that was all.

Demons. Imagine it. A grown man who looked as if he didn't fear a thing—as if he didn't *need* to fear a thing—had spoken of demons. Remembering the look in his strange green eyes, she found it too easy to believe he knew what he was talking about. That he was himself personally acquainted with a few demons.

Her fingers tightened on the sheet and drew it closer. She was overreacting, she told herself. *He* was overreacting. Last night there had been some excuse for inviting her over here, but tonight?

After the horrible way she had treated him earlier— God, she still couldn't believe she had called him *weird* to his face—he had been waiting for her to come home. Waiting to be sure she got in safely. And they had both overreacted to a stupid electrical problem. A loose wire, no doubt, but they had still crept through the house looking for intruders, and afterward, hearing something, he had brought her home with him again.

They were *both* weird. He should just have said goodnight and walked away. And when he didn't, she should have insisted on sleeping in her own bed and said goodnight.

That was what they should have done. The fact that they hadn't was a mark of the depth of the threat she was feeling. Shivering again, she huddled beneath the sheet. It was more than a threat she felt, she admitted now.

It was something evil.

Sunshine bathed the world again in the morning. Honor, coming from Seattle, where people often joked that the sun was a UFO, still couldn't get over the sunniness of the days here.

When she came downstairs, she found coffee ready and poured herself a cup. Stepping onto the back porch, she looked across to her house and saw Ian busy with her back porch light. He hadn't been kidding, she realized. He meant to get to the bottom of this.

With a second mug of coffee for Ian, she rounded the holly hedge and approached him. He was standing on a cinder block, examining the light fixture. Snug, worn denim left little to her imagination, and she found herself recalling all the sensations of being in his arms last night. How hard he had felt against her. How solid and strong.

"Good morning," she said. *Witch.* The word whispered along the edges of her mind, a cold touch in the hot morning air. She ignored it.

"Morning." He glanced down at her. "Look at this." He touched the bulb and the light went on. Touched it again and it went off.

Relief was almost heady. "The wind," she said. Not a demon after all.

"Maybe." He didn't look nearly as certain as she would have liked. "The bulb's screwed in tight, though, so it must be something in the fixture or the wiring. Why don't you go throw the breaker so I can check it out?"

"Okay. Here's some coffee."

"Thanks." Bending, he took the cup from her.

The breaker box, installed at Honor's insistence as part of the deal on the house, had replaced the old fuse box in the corner beside the refrigerator. Maybe, she thought now, she should have insisted on having the wiring checked. All the breakers were labeled on little white tags in the electrician's handwriting. Kitchen 1. Kitchen 2. Upstairs. Dryer. Front.

Not certain which of a dozen breakers controlled the porch light, she threw the main and cut off all the incoming power. "Okay," she called out to Ian.

She was able to see him through the open door, and she stayed where she was, watching, waiting for him to tell her when to turn the power back on.

Hard to believe, she thought, how scared she had been in this very room only a few hours before. Hard to believe how real even the vaguest threats could seem in the dark, and how silly you could feel in the sunlight, remembering them. Remembering how scared you had been and how you had hurled yourself at a man who was practically a stranger because you were terrified of a rustling sound. Terrified of the feeling that someone was watching you.

He hadn't treated her as if she were crazy or skittish, though. And that kiss…

In spite of her intention to put all that firmly out of her mind, she found herself remembering the heat and the strength of Ian McLaren, the passion and hunger he had displayed in those all-too-brief moments. He had made her feel desired, and as one who knew too well what it was like *not* to be desired, she cherished the memory.

Yesterday she had been annoyed at the way he had barged into her life. Today she was grateful for his interference, grateful that he had been there last night when she arrived home, and grateful that he had insisted she stay with him. Because, broad daylight notwithstanding, she vividly remembered how terrified she had been last night.

But she didn't want to be sexually attracted to him.

Down that road lay disaster, as she knew all too well. So while she might stand here and admire the way he looked in an olive-drab T-shirt and snug, worn jeans, she was not going to let herself fall into his arms again. Ever. Not even for another taste of his addicting passion. Because, in the end, she would be hurt. She didn't need anyone to warn her of that. A man his age who was unattached was unattached for a reason, and a woman who had been through all she had knew just how deeply and easily a man could wound her.

But, boy, she thought wryly, common sense couldn't keep her from dreaming.

And dream she had, last night. Endless dreams of lurking shadows and aching desire. Again and again Ian had come to her in her dreams, and again and again a shadow had slipped between them, driving them apart. More than once she had awakened in fright with an aching sense of desperation.

But nightmares didn't surprise her, given the events of the past two nights. It would be more surprising if she didn't have bad dreams.

"Okay," he called through the door. "Throw the power back on."

She turned and grabbed the breaker, throwing it back. There was a funny humming sound from behind her, and then she heard a sharp crack, followed by a hoarse shout. Swinging around, she was just in time to see Ian tumble backward to the ground.

Before she even barreled through the screen door, her mind was running through all the steps for dealing with severe electrical shock. Ian was lying flat on his back in the dust, and her heart nearly stopped at the sight. As she fell to her knees beside him, though, his eyes opened. He muttered a four-letter word.

"Are you all right? What happened? No, wait, don't move until you're sure you didn't hurt something."

He stared up at her, unable to see her face because her head was silhouetted against a brilliant patch of blue sky, probably the only patch visible in this part of her tree-filled yard.

Then, suddenly, the day turned dark. The sunlight faded from the sky, and the shadows moved in, surrounding her. Threatening her.

"God!" He sat up abruptly, and the vision vanished as if it had never been. The day was suddenly normal once more...except that he felt cold inside. Deep inside. In a place he had thought he had buried more than twenty years before.

"Ian?"

He knew better, he thought savagely. He ought to just get up and walk away right now. He knew better than to get involved, because when he got too close to someone, he eventually slipped. And when he slipped, they took off, acting as if he were some kind of monster. He'd already spent too much time with her, and already he was caring too much about what happened to her. Last night, for her sake, while moving through her house in the dark, he had pried the lid off the sarcophagus in which he had buried all those...abilities. All those feelings.

And now it seemed he could not put the lid back on. Using his abominable talent, he had reached out, seeking the source of the threat to her, and he had felt malevolence. Evil. Hatred. Now it was too late to abandon her. Even yesterday, he could have walked away, but now, having felt what he had felt, he could not leave her. Not that he could do a whole hell of a lot to help, he thought angrily. A vision that said she was threatened was about as illuminating as nothing, given what had already occurred.

"Ian? Ian, what happened? Are you all right?"

He turned and looked her straight in the eyes, seeing in those blue depths a genuine caring and compassion. Well, of course. She was a nurse. Naturally she would care. The other kind of caring...well, nobody felt that way about him. They never had, and they never would. *Demon spawn.*

"I'm fine," he said finally, hoping his face hadn't betrayed any of his unusually tangled feelings. He prided himself on being unreadable. "The damn fixture and wires seemed fine. There wasn't anything wrong that I could see. Then you threw the breaker, and the damn thing arced right across my hand." He looked up at the fixture. "It shouldn't have happened," he muttered to himself. "I'm no electrician, but that shouldn't have happened."

"Did you get burned?"

He turned his left hand over, studying it curiously. A vicious red mark seared two of his fingers. "Nothing to worry about."

"I've got some anesthetic cream," she told him. "And I'll get the electrician out here to look at that thing. Maybe I need all my wiring checked."

"Skip the cream." He looked up at the fixture. Even at this distance he could see that the arc had melted part of it. That was an awful lot of current. "Yeah, you'd better call an electrician. And then let's go to the beach."

"The beach?" Her mind was so preoccupied with what had almost happened that the suggestion didn't immediately register. "Why?"

"We could use some sun and relaxation," he told her.

What they really needed to do was talk. Away from here. And he had to figure out how much he was going to tell her.

Much to Honor's amazement, the electrician came right out, so the trip to the beach had to be postponed. She was at once relieved and disappointed. Being with Ian was incredibly intense—perhaps that wasn't entirely his fault, given the circumstances—but it was almost a relief to deal with someone else. Someone who whistled cheerfully and looked perfectly ordinary. Someone who didn't seem to move in an atmosphere of darkness and mystery and...and loneliness, she added. Ian McLaren was a terribly lonely man.

Standing on her back step while the electrician examined the destroyed light fixture, she stared into the shadows under the trees and felt the loneliness in her own soul. Part of the reason she had made the big move from Seattle was to escape all the things that had reminded her of that loneliness. For the past month or so she'd been so busy packing, moving and settling into her new job that she hadn't had time to feel lonely. Now she had the time again, and the move hadn't changed one damn thing.

"This fixture is all messed up, Miss Honor," Cal Ober told her. He, too, perched on the cinder block to examine the light. "No hope of saving it."

"I didn't really think there was, Mr. Ober. I'm worried about what caused the problem, though."

"Can't tell now if it was in the fixture. All the wires are fused."

"Is there some way you can test the rest of the wiring? To make sure there isn't another problem somewhere?"

He nodded. "Sure can. First let me put up a new fixture here, then we'll check out the rest."

She followed him through the house while he checked every outlet, removing the plates to verify that the wires were secure, and testing for voltage drops with a small meter that he plugged right into the sockets. He hummed and whistled while he worked, and occasionally fell into conversation.

"You know the Sidells up the road here?" he asked her.

"I met two of the brothers, Jeb and Orville," she replied. "At the hospital."

"When Orville got bit by that coral snake. Can't figure that boy. He's lived in these woods all his life and shoulda been looking out."

"Accidents happen."

"Reckon so." He glanced up with a smile, a smile that Honor thought didn't quite reach his eyes. Then he went back to whistling.

He next spoke when they were upstairs in her bedroom. "That fella next door?"

"My neighbor, you mean?"

"Him. McLaren. He grew up in these parts."

"Did he? He didn't mention that."

"Don't reckon he wants anyone to know."

Honor bit her lip, torn between wanting to ask why and hating to gossip about someone she knew. In the end she said nothing at all, even though she knew her curiosity was going to drive her wild. She had no business listening to idle gossip, she told herself sternly. No business at all.

"There was some trouble, long time ago," Cal said some time later. "There was some talk about witchcraft and satanism. Talk of animal sacrifices. Don't know if it's true. But he left and didn't come back until a year or so ago.''

Honor's hand flew to her mouth, and she stood there, trying to reconcile what she had just heard with the man who had so carefully protected her. "I can't...I can't imagine him doing such things," she said finally, feeling sick. Animal sacrifices?

"Don't know that he did." Cal plugged his meter into another outlet and watched the needle. "There was talk, I'm told, and the cops looked into it, but nothing ever happened, so maybe there's nothing to it." He glanced up then, his dark eyes strangely opaque. "I just thought a woman living alone ought to be on guard. In case. That's all."

The wiring had checked out okay. Around lunchtime, Honor stood in her bedroom, in front of the dresser mirror, and studied her reflection. Ian would be coming at any moment to take her to the beach, and the blue maillot that had seemed so modest last year didn't strike her as modest now. Turning swiftly away, she grabbed her white shorts and blue T-shirt and tugged them on.

Witchcraft and satanism.

God! Why hadn't she stayed in Seattle? At least there the threats had been known. During the past two days, she seemed to have stepped off the edge of reality into something really...weird. Strange. Spooky.

A rustling overhead drew her eyes upward. It sounded like something moving in the attic. Bugs, she told herself. Mice. Lizards. Maybe just a branch of one of the damn trees outside. *There was nothing else up there.*

She tugged her sneakers on and picked up her beach bag, checking to make sure she had included her sunscreen and keys.

A public beach in broad daylight. She couldn't possibly have anything to fear. And why should she fear him, anyway, just because of a piece of vicious gossip about things that might or might not have happened half a lifetime ago? Hadn't he taken care of her the last couple of days? If he was any threat at all, surely she would know by now. For heaven's sake, she had spent the last two nights under his roof! Safely. If he was going to harm her, he'd had ample opportunity to do so!

A rattle at the window snared her attention, and she looked out through the glass at the bright day beyond. She had chosen this room for her bedroom because a hole in the trees provided a view of the sky and road out front. Because it didn't feel so closed in.

The rattle came again, and she darted over to the window to look out. Down below, standing far enough back to be seen over the edge of the porch roof, was Ian. When he saw her, he pointed to his watch and then held up five fingers.

He had thrown pebbles at her window to get her attention, and the silly gesture eased some of the tension inside her. He could have phoned. He could have come right to the door. He could simply have shown up whenever he was ready. Instead, he had done something fun. Feeling somehow reassured, she waved and smiled back.

Above her, something in the attic made a soft scratching sound. Just a muffled, odd little sound. She glanced up and then dismissed it. Not forty minutes ago she had been up there with the electrician. A roach had gotten into the ceiling, she told herself. Or a mouse.

She rather liked the idea of a small gray mouse.

Ian took them away from the base, out across Choctawhatchee Bay to a strip of Gulf beach that was sparkling-white and virtually empty. A few vacation houses occupied the heights of the dunes, but they appeared to be deserted today. Here and there other couples were visible, but no one close by.

The pristine white sand of the beach disappeared in the amazing aquamarine water of the shallows. A short distance from shore, the deeper water was demarcated by an abrupt change of color to royal blue. Honor had never forgotten the colors or the beauty of this coastline. It was that memory that had brought her back.

She helped Ian secure the corners of the blanket with her beach bag and towel. Then he reached for his olive-drab T-shirt and tugged it over his head. She looked quickly away, feeling somehow that the act of stripping to a bathing suit was an intimate one. Which was silly, because she had never felt that way before.

She tossed her shorts and shirt aside without once looking at him, and trotted down to the water without daring a backward glance. She didn't want to know if he was watching her, didn't know what she would do if he was. The memory of last night's kiss was seared into her brain and made even the electrician's warning seem like a dim recollection from the distant past.

The swells were too big to allow any serious swimming, so she finally found a shallow spot and sat in the water, allowing the swells to lift and drop her gently, like a baby rocking in a cradle. The sun was hot and strong, and soon baked the tension from her muscles.

Feeling calm and utterly secure for the first time in what seemed like forever, she let herself think over the events of the past couple of days. What, she asked herself, had really happened? Not much. Somebody had apparently been in her house when she came home the night before last. Other than that, there had been nothing at all. Last night had been a case of nerves from a defective light. No one had been in the house.

And the feeling of being watched, of a presence... well, that was just imagination. She had been scared, and her mind had found no difficulty in embroidering things and turning imagined threats into reality. It was easy for the mind to play tricks like that in the dark. She'd learned that as a kid, sitting around campfires with her friends. More than once, ten shrieking girls had dived for cover over something as simple as a hooting owl. Fear of bears and Bigfoot had been half the fun of those campfires.

A gloomy sigh, swallowed by the restless sounds of the waves, escaped her. The wonder of it, she decided, was that Ian could take her seriously. In retrospect, she was surprised that he hadn't just left her in her own place last night. After all, he had checked the house and found no one there. At that point, any danger had been purely imaginary.

A tingling along her shoulders finally warned her that she was in danger of burning. Reluctantly leaving the water, she walked up the beach, only to find Ian stretched out and sound asleep.

For long moments she simply stared at him, filling her eyes with his powerful masculine beauty. Little was left to the imagination by his brief black trunks, and it didn't feel as if she were invading his privacy simply by standing there and gazing at what he was so blatantly displaying.

His chest was every bit as broad, hard and powerful as she remembered, and when he was lying down like this, his flat stomach turned into a hollow. His legs were long, perfectly shaped, powerful, and dusted with golden-brown hair that looked soft. Tempting. Her palms itched with a desire to discover all those masculine textures. Ridiculous, she told herself, and plopped on the blanket beside him. Ridiculous. Tugging her T-shirt out of her bag, she pulled it on to protect her shoulders.

Oh, God, she thought suddenly, she didn't want to go home. She didn't want to go back to that house. There was no escaping it. She could sit here in the sun and pretend that all those bad feelings had been imagination, that she honestly believed she had nothing to fear, but that was all it was: pretending. Something about that house scared her the way the dark under her bed had scared her as a child. It didn't matter whether it was rational or not.

The sun still shone, but somehow the day had turned suddenly dark. Shivering despite the heat, she looked around her and wondered what had happened to the colors. The water was now more gray than blue, and choppy-looking, and the white sand, too, seemed to have lost its brilliance.

Her gaze strayed inexorably toward Ian, and she wished he would wake up. Suddenly the beach felt deserted, lonely, and the sun didn't feel quite so warm. She wished, incredibly, stupidly, that he would wake up and smile—she couldn't remember having seen him really smile yet—and that he would reach for her and pull her down into his arms. That he would give her another kiss like the one last night.

Animal sacrifices. It couldn't be true. Could it?

Suddenly Ian's cat-green eyes opened, snaring hers with their intensity. Honor had the terrible feeling that he knew what she'd been thinking, that he had been hearing every thought that crossed her mind. Crazy, she thought, even as her insides fluttered nervously. Crazy. But the feeling that he had looked inside her head wouldn't die.

Then his eyes were hooded by lowered lashes, and he sat up.

"Sorry," he said. "I didn't mean to fall asleep on you."

The innocuous, innocent comment almost startled her, when she had half expected him to mention the things that had been roiling in her thoughts. A couple of seconds passed while she gathered her scattered wits.

"I didn't mind," she said finally. "We're both a little short on rest after the last couple of nights." Now that he was staring at the water instead of her, she felt more comfortable. "Did you really mean it when you said you don't sleep at night?"

"Yeah." He drew one knee up and rested his forearm on it. "I've never needed much sleep. An hour or two here and there. I generally just nap when I need to. Like now."

"I don't think I could stand that. I love to sleep."

He turned his head and gave her a faint smile. "I do, too. I wouldn't mind doing it more often."

She smiled back at him and tried to ignore the niggling sense of unease the electrician had planted in her. No way was this man a satanist, she told herself. No way. He turned his attention back to the water, and she was free to run her gaze over his broad shoulders and powerfully muscled back. That was when she saw the scars. They were faint with age, almost invisible, but there were dozens of them, some looking like very old burns, some like knife slashes. She couldn't keep from gasping.

She couldn't imagine how he heard that small, soft

sound over the pounding surf, but he did. He didn't turn
his head to look at her, but he spoke.

"A demon caught me once," he said. "Years and
years ago. Those are his marks."

She reached out instinctively, with a woman's natural
need to offer some kind of comfort, but he had already
risen from the blanket and was striding down to the
water.

So alone, she thought, feeling tears prick at her eyes.
He was so alone.

But then, so was she.

The light became flat, unnatural, as the sky grew
hazy. There was nothing nearby to cast a shadow as
brilliant colors turned leaden and the hot, humid air
grew oppressive.

Honor felt a chill run down her spine, despite the
stifling heat of the day. It was eerie, she thought, this
sultry, flat light, the way the waves suddenly seemed to
have grown quiet. Even the eternal seashore breeze had
grown still. Turning, she looked up and down the beach
and saw not one other soul.

Ian suddenly rose from the waves and walked up the
sand toward her.

"Let's get out of here," he said as soon as he reached
her.

She tilted her head back and looked up at him. The
sky was so bright behind him that he was little more
than a dark shadow. "What's wrong?"

He squatted, bringing his face nearly level with hers.
Now she was no longer blinded by the brilliance of the
sky behind him and could make out his face. His green
eyes seemed to glow, and she suddenly understood how
tales of witchcraft might have surrounded him.

"Tell me," he said with quiet intensity, "just what you *feel* has been going on for the last couple of days. Don't tell me the facts, don't tell me what you want to think happened. Just tell me what you *feel* is going on."

Her breath jammed in her throat. Say those things out loud? Things about feeling some kind of evil presence when she was all alone? Things about hating that living room, about the odor of decay that seemed to permeate the whole house, an odor she was sure hadn't been there when she bought it. Admit that the shadows beneath the old live oaks seemed to be *alive* somehow? Seemed to be occupied by things that, though unseen, she felt right at the base of her skull? Things she hadn't even admitted to herself? Things so fanciful and impossible that she hardly dared let the thought of them cross her mind?

The hazy light, so peculiar, cast no shadows across his face, and it made him look strange, like a painting with two real, glowing eyes looking out of it. "What do you feel?" he asked again.

She wanted to look away, but somehow she couldn't. His eyes were mesmerizing; they held her. She finally spoke, words springing to her lips before she was even conscious of them. "When I was little, I thought there was a crocodile in the dark under my bed."

He nodded. "I had a bear in my closet."

Somehow that made it easier. A long breath escaped her. "I feel that way about…about the house. About the dark in the corners and under the trees and in the attic—" She shook her head, denying what she said even as she said it. "There wasn't anything under my bed when I was a kid." She looked away, feeling an almost physical ripping as she tore her eyes from his. "I feel…I feel…" She could barely whisper the words.

"What do you feel? What?"

"As if...somebody's trying to get into my head." The words spilled out of her in a long, breathless rush, taking form on the sultry air before she was even conscious of having felt such a thing. Where had that come from?

She turned swiftly, expecting to see shock on Ian's face, but he looked as impassive as always. A protest spilled from her lips just as swiftly, trying to banish the words she had just spoken. Trying to deny the reality of the awareness they had unleashed. "I didn't mean that. God, I don't know why I said that!"

"Shh..." He touched a finger to her lips, then dropped it. "It's okay. I asked what you felt. I didn't ask for reasons. Some things don't have reasons."

He looked around at the strange, flat light, at the gray water and dull sand. "Something's going on. Something...unnatural. I feel it, too."

"It's crazy!" She knew the protest was useless even as she made it.

He shook his head, and suddenly his unearthly eyes were fixed on her again. "I'm a soldier. I feel it at the base of my skull when someone's watching me. I don't question the feeling. I act on it. It's saved my life more than once."

Icy tendrils wrapped slowly around her spine. "Someone's watching." She felt it, too. Had felt it all along.

He nodded. "I thought we'd get away from it by coming out here." He scanned the beach and dunes again, evidently seeking the watcher and seeing no one. "Let's get out of here. Let's just drive somewhere and see if we can't find some privacy to talk."

It wasn't until later that she wondered about his motives. For all that he appeared to be concerned for her safety, he spent an awful lot of time scaring her even more. Instead of reassuring her, he terrified her. Instead of promising that locks would protect her, he spoke of demons.

What if he was taking advantage of the situation to terrify her? What if he was engaging in some kind of psychological warfare to scare her out of her wits? To drive her away? Or drive her over the edge?

Abomination. Witch's spawn. The words whispered through her mind again, cold and deadly. Once again she tried to ignore them. They were *not* real. They came from some buried corridor of the subconscious, stirred up by her fright, and they were meaningless.

Or were they?

CHAPTER FOUR

Ian pointed his Jeep away from the base, taking them even farther from home. Honor knew a prickle of unease, wondering if she were utterly foolish to go so far—to go anywhere—with this man. Trusting him because he was a former Ranger, like her father, was like trusting someone because of his hair color—foolhardy.

Yet she would have bet, despite all her doubts about his motives and whether he was trying to scare her half to death, that he meant her no physical harm. She *was* betting precisely that, she realized with an unpleasant lurch of her stomach as they headed into one of the more sparsely populated parts of the Panhandle. Just by being here she was betting on her safety.

Half an hour later Ian wheeled off the road into the parking lot of one of those unexpected restaurants that sometimes appeared in the middle of nowhere in this part of the world. There were several cars in the lot, though at midafternoon it wasn't likely to be busy.

"They have great seafood here," Ian told her as he parked. "Local catch, fresh daily. Interested?"

She definitely was, especially with her nerves quieting at the prospect of a public place.

Inside, a couple of men sat at the bar, sipping beer. They looked up and nodded as Ian and Honor entered. Quiet country music played in the background.

"Seat yourselves, folks," the bartender said. "Wilma'll be right with you."

By the time they'd been served a pitcher of draft beer

and a huge basket of deep-fried shrimp, Honor realized that for the first time in days she was actually beginning to relax. It felt somewhat like waking from a bad dream, or getting over the flu, to have the tension really gone. And only as it lifted did she realize just how tense and uneasy she had been.

Even Ian seemed to be relaxing in some subtle way, she realized. He was leaning back, legs loosely crossed, one arm slung casually over the back of his chair. From time to time he reached out and popped another shrimp into his mouth. The thing that struck her most, though, was the subtle change in his face. It no longer looked quite so hard or forbidding, so rocklike.

And he seemed every bit as reluctant as she to destroy the mood by discussing the very things they had come here to talk about.

Finally, though, when the shrimp were half-gone and the pitcher was half-empty, he uncrossed his legs and leaned toward her, resting his elbows on the table. His strange green eyes seemed to glow with a light of their own in the dimly lit restaurant.

"Since you don't believe in demons," he said gruffly, "I suppose you don't believe in ghosts or ESP, either."

Honor wanted to shake her head in a firm negative, but she couldn't. After a brief internal struggle, she answered. "Let's just say I'm beginning to develop an open mind."

One corner of his mouth turned up in a faint, crooked smile. "That'll do," he said.

Honor set her beer glass down, suddenly wishing she hadn't drunk anything. Her head didn't feel quite as clear as she liked it to, and now things were getting serious. Or would, if she allowed them to. "Let me guess. You're going to tell me my house is haunted." She shuddered inwardly as she spoke the words out loud. She felt crazy speaking of such things, but, after the last two days... well, she couldn't entirely dismiss them, either.

He reached for the pitcher and refilled both their glasses. "I grew up in the house I'm living in now," he told her. He glanced up, snaring her with his gaze, then let his eyes wander around the room. "So I know something about your place. There used to be an old woman living there, a Mrs. Gilhooley. She lived in that house better than fifty years, up until three years ago, when she died."

Watching his face as he spoke, Honor got the distinct feeling that this was a difficult subject for him. Since he didn't seem to have any trouble discussing demons, she wondered just what *would* give him difficulty.

Ian popped another shrimp in his mouth and washed it down with a sip of beer. "After she died, the house went to a cousin of hers, and he rented it out a few times while he tried to sell it. The last tenants moved out just about seven months ago."

She nodded. "The agent told me when he showed me the house. They left a lot of stuff behind that I made the owner clear out before I bought it."

Ian wrapped both his hands around his mug. The mug was large, but his huge hands nearly swallowed it. Honor stared at those hands, remembering suddenly how gently they had held her last night. How awkwardly they had patted her and stroked her. Those same hands, she had no doubt, could kill with swift, merciless efficiency. The dichotomy gave her a fractured sense of the man who sat across from her, a contradictory picture of Ian the soldier and Ian the man.

He spoke. "Did the agent also tell you that the last

tenants left in the middle of the night? Only ten days after they moved in?''

Honor's heart thudded uncomfortably. ''Uh…no, she didn't. Why did they do that? Do you know?''

He looked her right in the eye. ''They heard things. The kids hated the place. But what happened that last night is anybody's guess. They were gone before dawn, leaving most of their stuff behind.''

Honor was aware of the deep, slow thudding of her heart, an uneasy rhythm. ''Some people scare easily,'' she said. ''Some people attribute every sound to something unnatural. Once a person gets spooked…'' She let her words trail off, wondering why she heard her father's voice speaking those same words in her head. As if he had once said such things to her. But it was irrelevant to the moment, so she tucked the question away for later.

Ian ignored her comments. ''I understand they weren't the only tenants to leave abruptly in the middle of the night.''

Her mouth felt as dry as straw. Sipping her beer, she wrestled with uneasiness and a growing sense of danger. A ghost! ''Well,'' she said finally, ''a ghost is nothing but a pain in the neck. I mean, sure, it can annoy you, I guess, if you let it, but what can it possibly *do* to you? If that's what's going on, I guess I'll just quit worrying about it.''

She looked up at Ian then and realized he didn't agree with her. Something in his cat-green eyes and granite features told her that he didn't think a ghost was something to dismiss. That he wasn't thinking in terms of a jolly poltergeist or a veiled lady who didn't realize she had died. What he had in mind was very different.

He opened his mouth just a fraction, then closed it, evidently thinking better of whatever he had been about to say. Instead, he swallowed half a mug of beer, then ate another handful of shrimp.

Damn it, she thought. He kept scaring her half to death, and then, when she had the gall to argue with him, he clammed up and left her dangling, wondering what he had been driving at. Irritation pushed her past caution.

"What is it with you?" she demanded, keeping her voice low. "All this talk of ghosts and demons... Are you really a satanist?"

As soon as the words popped out of her mouth, she would have given almost anything to snatch them back. Ian froze, every muscle in his body going as rigid as stone. For the longest time he didn't even seem to breathe. Only his eyes appeared alive. Green, glowing, intense, they held hers almost by force, somehow forbidding her to look away. She glimpsed, in those moments, the hunter in him. With a deep sense of dread, she realized he would be implacable.

And then he let her go. All he did was shift his gaze from hers, and she felt as if she had been released.

"That's old gossip," he said. "What else have you been hearing?"

She felt at once horrified by what she had blurted out and defiant. She hardly knew the man, after all. Surely she had a right to wonder about him and question his trustworthiness? Even so, she couldn't bring herself to mention the other accusation. A moment later she was wondering if it had been written across her forehead and had the worst feeling that he had plucked the words right out of her mind.

"Animal sacrifices," he said, in a low voice. He turned his head to the side and swore softly.

An ache bloomed deep in Honor, and something in her heart shifted. Her mind kept telling her that she didn't know this man, not really, and that she would be wise to be cautious and careful. Her heart wasn't listening. Instinctively she reached out and covered his hand with hers, wanting to comfort him, sensing somehow that she had opened a very old wound.

Slowly he turned and looked straight at her. "You don't believe it," he said quietly.

Her hand on his acknowledged it. Honor tried to smile, and failed. "My mind keeps telling me I don't know you at all." She shrugged. "No, I don't believe it. Not where it counts."

He lowered his gaze to their hands, then slowly turned his over to clasp her fingers gently. "I was never a satanist," he said. "And I never sacrificed or tormented an animal. I never would." Slowly he looked up at her. "I'm no saint, not by a long sight. But I'd never do anything like that." One corner of his mouth lifted up a fraction, giving the impression of a sad smile. "To tell you the truth, I generally like animals a whole lot better than people."

Somehow that didn't surprise her. The ache in her deepened, and she had to draw a deep breath to ease it. This man, this hard, dangerous, isolated man, carried deep scars, she realized. And against every grain of common sense and every ounce of caution, she wanted to comfort him. Unconsciously she tightened her fingers around his.

Something leapt in his eyes at that, something scalding. Something sensuous. Her heart began to hammer a heavy rhythm in response. No, thought her battered and scarred heart. Not that. That was too dangerous. It would be too easy to get hurt.

Ian ran his thumb over the back of her hand in a gentle caress. Then he released her and reached for his mug.

"About the house," he said, as if he hadn't just been looking as if he wanted to devour her.

Honor drew her hand back, wondering if he had sensed her sudden uneasiness. Maybe. She liked to think she had a poker face, but this man was beginning to make her feel as if she were an open book. "The house," she repeated.

He nodded, his green eyes scraping over her face as if trying to read an oracle. Suddenly he leaned over the table and touched her cheek with his warm fingers. "You're very pretty," he said, almost roughly. "Soft, warm, fresh. And so damn young. I don't know what the hell is happening at that place, but I'd hate it like the devil if anything hurt you."

"But what can a ghost do?" she asked, feeling somehow bereft when he drew his hand back.

"This may come as a shock," he said after a moment, sounding almost gentle, "but I really don't know. You probably think I'm into all sorts of occult stuff because of my remarks about demons." He shrugged a massive shoulder. "The truth is, I've never had any experience with ghosts or any interest in the subject. But there's something going on in that house. I can *feel* it."

An icy little shiver ran down her spine as she considered just what it would take to cause this man to make such an admission—unless, of course, he was deliberately trying to scare her. But no. Right here, and right now, she didn't think he was. Right now she felt that his concern was genuine, and that he had crossed a difficult barrier to tell her he *felt* something was wrong.

"You're saying there's a difference between a ghost and a demon?" Was she really talking about this?

"A demon is physical," he said baldly. "I told you. He walks and talks and looks just like a human being.

But he isn't human. When you run into one, believe me, you know it. Cops talk about it, Honor. I've heard them. They talk about the *eyes*. There's something there that I—'' He broke off abruptly and looked away. ''Once you've seen it, you never forget it. And you can't mistake it, if you have any idea what you're looking for.''

Again that ache settled into her chest, filling her with a yearning to reach out and somehow wipe away his anguished memories. But she couldn't. She didn't have the right, and she was sure she didn't have the ability. ''You would know,'' she said finally.

He nodded briefly, and after a bit he looked back at her. ''But I don't know ghosts. All I know is there's something wrong. And it worries me.''

Honor spared a moment to wish she'd never even thought of leaving Seattle. Then she squared her shoulders and looked at the big man with the granite face who was waiting for her reaction. ''Well, I'm stuck,'' she said. ''My savings are tied up in the property, and my credit rating is riding on the mortgage. I'll just have to tough it out. Honestly, I just can't see what a ghost could do, other than scare me. The worst I've read about poltergeists sounds annoying but not terribly threatening. Anyway, I'm not even sure I have a ghost.''

Something flickered in his unusual eyes, and then he nodded. ''Okay. It's your call. But remember, I feel it, too. So don't you ever hesitate to call on me for help.''

The sultry haze had turned into threatening storm clouds by the time they emerged from the restaurant. The leather seats in Ian's Jeep were hot and sticky, and he spread out a towel for Honor to sit on. She still squirmed uncomfortably, because her bathing suit wasn't quite dry beneath her clothes and there was sand in it. Suddenly she was eager to get home and into the shower.

And that thought, for some odd reason, had her turning her head to look at Ian.

She was torn between the sense that she ought not to trust him so quickly and the sense that she could trust him implicitly. Worse, all that confusion was tied up in a knot of sexual desire such as she had not felt since before her marriage. Nor could she tell herself it was just wishful thinking. Not after that kiss he had given her last night. This man had the power to set her ablaze.

Which was a good reason to avoid him, never mind anything else. But her mind kept straying that way, and she wondered why she couldn't have met him at a time when she might have felt freer to explore her feelings. But at another time, she acknowledged, he never would have noticed her. He was very self-contained and solitary, and the only reason he had spent this much time with her was because he felt she needed him. Last night's kiss had been an aberration, and she seriously doubted it had affected him at all…because if it had, surely he would have tried to kiss her again.

Just more proof, she thought glumly, of how utterly unattractive she was. Oh, Lord, listen to her! Drowning in self-pity again. Disgusted, she forced herself to look away from Ian. She was just tired from the stress of the last few days, she assured herself. Just tired.

Now, if only the house would let her take a nap.

It didn't strike her until much later just how odd that thought was.

Thunder cracked loudly just as they pulled into Ian's driveway. A gust of wind blew up the red dirt road, driving small dust devils ahead of it, and causing the long curtains of Spanish moss to sway slowly.

"Looks like it'll be a good one," Ian said as he pulled his keys from the ignition. "I'll walk you over."

She didn't argue. She didn't want to argue. Looking over at the dark, swaying shadows beneath those trees and the dark, fathomless windows of that house, she knew only that she didn't want to be alone in there.

"Why don't you join me for dinner tonight?" she heard herself say. "I've got the graveyard shift tonight, so it'll probably be around nine before it's ready."

He paused in the act of climbing out of the Jeep and faced her. She got the distinct impression that he was both shocked and pleased. And that was when she realized that this was the very first overtly friendly gesture she had made to this man. Shame burned her cheeks at the thought.

"I'd like that," he said. He didn't quite smile, but the feeling of it touched his face. "What can I bring?"

"Yourself." She smiled at him, wishing he would smile back. "Come in an hour or so, if you want. You can keep me company." Keep the shadows at bay, keep the loneliness away.

There was nothing quite like a slightly damp bathing suit full of sand, Honor thought as she peeled hers away with relief. She threw it into the tub and then climbed in with it beneath the hot spray. Oh, did that feel good after so many hours in the damp, chilly suit! It felt so good, in fact, that she stayed under the spray until she had used the last of the hot water.

Squealing at the change of temperature, she turned off the water and yanked the shower curtain open to grab a towel.

Her heart climbed into her throat.

The door to the hallway, which she had closed to prevent a draft, was standing wide open. Beyond it was only empty, echoing darkness.

A crack of thunder caused her to start and gasp. The hair on the back of her neck was standing up, and goose bumps broke out all over her. Reaching out with a shaking hand, never taking her eyes from the open door, she snatched a towel from the rack and wrapped it around herself.

Oh, God. Oh, God.

Maybe, she tried to tell herself, she hadn't closed the door all the way, even though she thought she had. Maybe a draft had just nudged it open. Maybe the door wasn't hung right and had just swung open. Maybe it was nothing at all. But her ears strained, listening intently to the silence, alert for any sound that might betray another presence.

A minute passed. Then another. She could hear nothing from the hallway beyond. Thunder cracked again, and the wind banged against something, but those sounds all came from without. Within the house there was no sound save her own ragged breathing and the hammering of her heart.

Finally, much as she had done when she was a child in the dark with a crocodile under her bed, she screwed up her courage and made a mad dash down the hall to her bedroom. There she slammed the door and leaned against it, gasping for air, wondering how she could be so foolish as to believe she had locked anything out.

But she did. Somehow she did. Somehow she felt safer here. Safe from what, she had no idea. Beyond her window, lightning flashed brilliantly, and thunder rolled in a hollow boom. The rain had not yet started.

And from overhead came the odd scratching she had heard earlier. Slowly she looked up at the ceiling. Please, she thought. Oh, please, let it be a mouse.

Ian, hurry! Please hurry!

Another flare of lightning drew her attention to the window. Ian wasn't due to come over for another half hour or so. She could get dressed, she thought, if she could pry her back away from the door and take the chance that something might come through it. She could get dressed and climb out the window onto the porch roof and shimmy down one of the columns. She could get out of here that fast. That easily. All she had to do was move away from the door and get dressed.

But she couldn't. Oh, God, she couldn't move. The sense of something on the other side of the door was growing past all reason, a sense of dark menace pressing inward, trying to slip past the door....

Oh, God, was she losing her mind?

And then, as if someone had flipped a switch, it was gone. Completely.

Shivering, Honor stood with her back pressed to the door, unable to believe that the horrifying presence had left, waiting for it to return. But it didn't. It was gone. With it had vanished the dark pressure in her mind and the fear at the base of her skull. In the blink of an eye, the world had returned to normal.

The suddenness of the change convinced her, as nothing else could have, that this was no figment of her imagination. What had been there had *really* been there. And now it was gone.

The afternoon grew darker and more threatening, but still the rain didn't fall. Honor dressed and stayed in her bedroom until she heard Ian knock at the back door. Then she flew down the stairs through the shadowy house and threw the back door open. At the last second she managed to avoid flinging herself into his arms.

"Hi," she said instead, summoning up a smile. Stepping back, she invited him in.

The back door had been locked, she realized, feeling a sudden compulsion to check the front door. What if somebody had actually been in the house? What if it hadn't been the "presence" at all, but a real person? The man who had been waiting for her the other night?

Suddenly her knees turned to water and her heart stopped dead. She hadn't even considered that possibility. Not once.

"Honor?" Ian frowned at her. "Honor, what's wrong?"

She blinked and managed to focus on him. "I, um...I need to check the front door."

Turning, she hurried down the hallway, not caring what he thought. She *had* to know if that door was still locked. She *had* to know the dimensions of whatever had been in this house with her.

The door was locked. She almost collapsed against it in sheer relief until she remembered the windows. Turning swiftly, she nearly bumped into Ian. He caught her gently by the shoulders.

"Honey, what's wrong?"

"I...just want to check the windows. Make sure everything is locked up." She couldn't bring herself to look up into his strange green eyes. The compulsion to check locks was almost irrational, and completely overwhelming. Then his choice of words struck her. Slowly she raised her gaze to his. *Abomination.* "I'm not your honey."

At once he stepped back, and something in his face grew tight.

Honor turned from him and headed into the living room to check all the windows. God, how she hated this room! *Witch boy.* The bars were all in place there and in the dining room. She wasn't worried about the upstairs, because only her bedroom was accessible from the ground without a ladder, and no one had been in her bedroom.

Back in the kitchen, she suddenly felt as if somebody had pulled her plug. She sank bonelessly onto a chair and put her head down on her arms. She heard Ian pull out the chair across from her and sit.

And suddenly, with a crawling sense of shame, she remembered her behavior of the past few minutes, the way she had spoken to him. Oh, God, what had come over her? How could she have been so rude? She had acted like a crazy person, not like herself at all.

Slowly, reluctantly, she lifted her head and looked at him. He was regarding her remotely, much as he had the first time they met, from across a chasm of emotional distance. That look, that chilly, distant look, made her realize just how close she had felt to him earlier that afternoon. And how rude she had just been.

Lightning flared brilliantly, so bright that for an instant Ian was nothing but a dark silhouette against the kitchen window. Thunder rumbled, long and low, vibrating the table beneath her arms.

"Something…something was in here," she said. "Before you came. I…was in the shower, and when I pulled back the curtain, the bathroom door was open."

His eyes never flickered. Not a muscle on his face moved. She forced herself to continue, needing him to understand.

"I...couldn't hear anyone. I ran down the hall and...hid in my bedroom. With the door closed. I...I don't think I've ever been so scared in my life!" The last words burst from her on a rising note.

Seconds ticked away in silence as he stared at her, unmoving. Finally he spoke. "What then?"

"It was gone," she said hoarsely. "Just like that, it was gone. As if it had never been."

Lightning flashed again, and thunder cracked deafeningly. The overhead light flickered and went out.

"Hell," said Ian. The room was dark, illuminated only by the flashes of lightning outside.

Moments later the light flared on again. Honor stared at Ian, feeling trapped in ways she couldn't have begun to explain, and wondering how she was going to get out of this. He couldn't help her. He had done so much already; what more could he possibly do? What could anybody do against something that even locks couldn't keep out?

She longed just to leave, but for financial reasons she couldn't do that. And even the thought of turning tail shamed her. She wasn't her father's daughter for nothing. *Face it head-on,* he'd always said. *Don't let anything get the best of you.*

But how could she face something she couldn't see? How could she stand up to something she couldn't touch? Earlier, she'd asked what a ghost could do except scare her. Now she knew that being scared was quite enough. She couldn't live in a state of terror, and she couldn't reason it away.

She returned her gaze to Ian's impassive face and wondered what he was thinking. *Witch eyes.* Why did she keep thinking these things about him? Witch eyes. Where had that come from? And the other stuff. Demon spawn.

Abomination. Lord, she'd never used words like that in her life!

She shuddered, then nearly jumped when a deafening crack of thunder sounded overhead.

Suddenly Ian reached across the table and captured one of her tightly clenched hands. "Easy, lady," he said. "Nothing's going to happen to you while I'm here."

But what about later? she wondered miserably.

The storm continued to rumble angrily without raining throughout the evening. Ian seemed to have put her rudeness behind him, though there was a reserve in his actions that had nearly vanished earlier. There was distance between them again; they were not-quite-strangers thrown together by circumstance.

Since she had so little furniture, they were essentially confined to the kitchen. Ian had brought a bottle of white wine, but she decided not to have any, because she had to go to work later. He never opened the bottle.

He offered to help with the meal, but she insisted he just keep her company. She needed to be busy, and the work was a good excuse to keep going.

"You need a TV," he said. "Or a radio. Something to make noise in this place. And you should keep up with the weather, anyway, this time of year."

It would probably help, she thought. It would keep her from hearing things. Just as pulling the blanket over your eyes could keep you from seeing things. As if not seeing or hearing made things go away.

Dinner was simple: steak, salad and bread. She drank milk. Ian asked for coffee. For a few minutes, things seemed normal. Almost. She wondered if anything would ever truly seem normal again.

Looking at the hard, ravaged face of the man who sat

across from her, she tried to imagine the roads he must have traveled in his life. Most men didn't stay with the Rangers throughout their careers. Most soldiers spent a few years there and then went on to join other units, where they were the seeds of a better, harder, tougher fighting force. Those who did stay were...special. Unique. The kind of men you would definitely want on your side in a fight. But not the kind of men any woman in her right mind would want to give her heart to.

They were too hard, she thought. Too toughened. Too devoted to honor and duty and country. Anything else took a decided second place. A man like that would turn his back on his own wife if ordered to. The way her father had turned his back on her mother.

Suddenly a door yawned open in the depths of her mind, and she felt herself tumbling backward into the past, like Alice falling down the rabbit hole.

Her father stood over her, a tall, intimidating presence in camouflage. He was big, so big, and she was small, so very small. And so very frightened.

"I told you to cut out that nonsense, Honor. You're a big girl now."

"Cleve, just let her be," said her mother from somewhere behind him. She sounded worried. Frightened. "She can't help these feelings."

"She sure as hell can," her father said sharply. "It's just her imagination, and I'm getting damn sick and tired of her getting hysterical in the middle of the night because we have ghosts, for God's sake! As long as we keep pandering to this crap, she'll never quit it."

"Cleve, she's only five. She can't help being scared."

"But she can help talking about ghosts! She can learn to handle her fear the way the rest of us do."

"But she's so little!"

"And that's the whole damn problem, Sheila! You keep excusing her because she's so little. How the hell will she ever grow up?"

"Oh, my God," Honor whispered, forgetting where she was, wondering how she could ever have forgotten what had happened when she was five. Trapped in a terrifying corridor of memory, she closed her eyes and remembered being locked in the closet all night long so that she would learn to face her fears. Learn to control her wild talk of ghosts. Learn to deny what she heard, what she saw, what she felt.

Night after night after night...

Ian felt her slip away. He had resurrected his terrible talent for this woman's sake, and it was not something he could switch on and off now, like a light. He felt her slip into her memories, and he felt anguish grip her.

And around him he felt the gathering evil. Whatever had earlier scared her was strengthening again, growing, little by little filling the house with its dark presence. Gathering its power.

He instinctively looked up, toward the ceiling, but what he felt wasn't located there. It was everywhere, throughout this house. Thunder rolled deeply outside, and lightning continued to flicker, and even the force of the storm seemed like a small thing compared to the evil he felt growing here.

He looked over at Honor, and the expression on her face pierced him, pierced all the granite walls he had built for protection. He needed to help her. And because of his need, he reached over and touched her mind, forgetting that it was an invasion of privacy of the worst kind.

He went into the locked closet with her, and without

a thought he tried to comfort the five-year-old girl who was trapped in the dark with no companion but terror.

"Oh, my God!" Honor gasped the words, and her eyes flew open. She had felt, unmistakably, a touch, an indescribable touch, in her mind. How could such a thing be? One moment she had been alone in a locked closet, reliving a horrible childhood memory, and the next she had not been alone. "Oh, my God," she whispered again, wondering if this was what it felt like to lose one's mind.

Ian watched her with those strange, cat-green eyes of his. He looked, she thought warily, as if he had felt something of her pain. She couldn't stand this anymore, she realized. She couldn't stand feeling these things and then keeping them all locked up, even if it was what her father had expected of her. Would expect of her. She needed desperately to know if someone else thought she was crazy, or sane. And Ian was the only person she could turn to.

"You won't believe this," she said, almost hoarsely.

He continued to regard her steadily. "Try me," he said quietly.

But just then she felt another pressure in her mind, a dark, sinister touch, like icy, wet fingers. She shivered and looked around, almost as if she thought she could find its source. And then she looked into Ian's eerie eyes. *Spawn of demons. Witch boy.* How could she trust him? she wondered wildly. What if he was the evil thing she felt?

Abomination.

"Let's get the hell out of here," Ian said suddenly, harshly. "I'll drive you to work."

She was startled, and the icy touch in her mind vanished. "But I don't have to leave for an hour yet."

"Good. We'll stop and get coffee someplace. We need to talk. There's…there's stuff I need to tell you."

A touch of stubbornness flared in her. "I thought we talked earlier."

"That wasn't everything. There's more. A lot more."

She opened her mouth to argue that they could talk right here, but before the words escaped, she felt it again. The presence. The dark thing that loomed in this house. It was strengthening. Growing.

She had to get out of here. Now.

She looked at Ian. "I'll get my stuff."

At the foot of the stairs, she froze, not wanting to go up there. Ian was suddenly beside her, touching her elbow. How did he know?

"I'll go up with you," he said. "You don't have to face it alone anymore, Honor."

Face what alone? she wondered. And wondered even more at the way his words dovetailed with the memory from her childhood. Her father had insisted she face it alone. Ian said she didn't have to.

It was all too weird. No one would ever believe…

At the top of the stairs, she looked back at the dark, hard man who followed her so protectively. *He* would believe her, she thought.

And she wondered why that thought didn't comfort her at all.

CHAPTER FIVE

Lightning flickered among the trees as they drove down the two-lane highway toward town. Pines and oaks crowded the shoulders of the road, dark shadows in the headlights. It was a relief, Honor thought, to be away from that house.

A half-hour later they reached the edge of town and Ian pulled into the parking lot of a brightly lit all-night hamburger place. Air Force uniforms were visible at a number of tables. A couple of guys in Ranger uniforms nodded to Ian as he guided Honor to a table in an out-of-the-way corner.

People. Normal, ordinary people. How wonderful they looked after a day like today.

"Coffee?" Ian asked. "I'll get it."

"Please. Black."

There was something so wonderfully normal about this place, the bright lights, the gleaming floors, the buzz of quiet conversation, that the past couple of days seemed like a movie nightmare. Almost.

When he returned with the coffee, Ian slid into the booth across from her.

"How are you going to manage to stay awake all night?" he asked her, surprising her. "You've had one long day."

"I'll be okay. Adrenaline usually does the trick."

"I'll come to get you in the morning. Seven-thirty?"

Honor nodded. "I might be a few minutes late, though."

Ian shrugged. "No big deal."

A few more minutes passed while they sipped coffee in silence. Finally, looking about as happy as a man facing a firing squad, Ian came to the point.

"I don't want you being alone in that house anymore."

The first thing to hit her was a tidal wave of overwhelming relief. Then reality intruded.

"I can't afford to move out," she said flatly.

"I realize that. What we need to do is see if we can't get rid of this...whatever it is. There's got to be some way to fight it. Exterminate it."

She thought of the movies and spoke the word with difficulty, rebelling at the whole idea. "Exorcism?"

A strange thing happened then. It almost seemed to her that Ian's gaze slid away, as if he were uneasy with the subject. As if the word had struck him personally somehow. And that brought the rumors about him being a satanist racing to the forefront of her mind.

"No." He said it sharply, flatly, in a low voice, a commanding voice. "No. Don't even think that."

"What? Think what?"

"That I'm afraid of an exorcism."

"I wasn't—" She broke off, realizing that she had been on the verge of thinking exactly that, that a satanist would be terrified of such a thing. "What the hell do you do? Read minds?"

His mouth compressed into a tight line. "I'm not afraid of it," he said, ignoring her question. "I've been through it."

Through it? He'd been *through it?* She sank back against the vinyl-padded bench and just stared at him. In all honesty, she wouldn't have guessed that anyone in this part of the world could even perform such a ceremony. And certainly not that someone she knew might actually have been through it.

"Why?" she said finally. "When?"

"When I was a kid," he said. The words came roughly, as if they were extremely difficult to force out, but his face never changed. "I was just six. Mrs. Gilhooley—the woman who lived in your house—had a goat. Damn animal was as old as Methuselah. Anyhow, I told her the goat was going to die. I don't even remember why I said it. Probably because it was so old. And damned if the goat didn't drop dead on the spot."

"Oh, my," Honor breathed, finding it not at all difficult to envision the progression of events. Just imagining it made her ache for the boy he must once have been.

"Mrs. Gilhooley accused me of witchcraft or being possessed or something," Ian continued. "I don't remember much of it very clearly. The preacher performed an exorcism on me. I mainly remember being locked up for days while people prayed and sang over me. I wasn't allowed to eat or drink, and sometimes they'd slap me silly, trying to drive the demon out."

He shrugged again, as if it no longer mattered, but Honor wasn't quite buying that. "How awful," she said softly. "Why would she ever accuse you of something like that? You were just a child!"

A child who saw things he shouldn't. Who heard the thoughts of others. Ian looked at her, but he didn't answer, because if he told her why Mrs. Gilhooley had hated him so much, she would be scared to death of him. And that wouldn't help at all right now. Instead, he lied by omission. "I don't remember much about the whole thing...except you'll never persuade me that exorcism is worth a whole lot."

She guessed she could understand that. For a moment

she simply sat and looked at him, thinking that they both had childhood scars. It made her feel closer to him. "Did they think they had cured you?"

"For a while, at any rate." He picked up his cup and sipped. "Something like that sticks with you. Like the smell of skunk. When folks think you were possessed once, they're always on the lookout for it to happen again."

Honor nodded. "That must have given you a rough time for years." Even as she spoke, she realized that for him it had never been over. Just today the electrician had brought the subject up again, even though more than thirty years had passed. "Why did you come back here, Ian? Some of these people..." She hesitated. "Well, some of them evidently haven't forgotten."

His eyes bored into her. "It's my home," he said.

Honor shook her head slightly. "Being an army brat, I've never felt that way about any place. And I don't think I'll ever get to feel that way about *this* place. I like what you said about getting rid of this—this whatever-it-is—but how can we possibly do that?"

"I don't know yet, but I intend to find out. I'm going to check out the base library this morning. If they don't have anything, there's an occult bookstore downtown." One corner of his mouth lifted a little, just a faint suggestion of humor. "Maybe all we need is a garlic necklace."

A rusty laugh escaped Honor, and it struck her that she hadn't laughed in two days now...and ordinarily she was quick to laugh. "Nothing in my life has ever been that easy."

"Or mine."

He went to get them some more coffee, and Honor watched him, noting how easily he moved, like a man in complete command of his body. He was used to being in command, that much was obvious. Faced with a ghost— or whatever awful thing was in that house—he considered himself quite capable of dealing with it. All he had to do was discover what needed doing. She liked his attitude and wished she could be so confident. All of *her* self-confidence was limited to nursing.

Turning her head, she stared past the reflections in the window glass and saw that the night was still storm-tossed, though it hadn't yet begun to rain. Odd weather, she thought.

She had very nearly forgotten being locked in the closet as a child. Her father had meant it to toughen her and to stop her from seeing things in the dark. It might have toughened her, but now she was seeing things in the dark again. And in broad daylight, for that matter.

Looking back at those endless nights of terror, when she had cried and shrieked and begged for hours to be let out of that small, dark closet, she wondered if they hadn't contributed to her mother's decision to divorce her father.

What struck her most now, though, was that this was not the first time in her life she had had a brush with...with the occult, for lack of a better word. Time had rendered her memory hazy, but she vaguely remembered lying awake in her bed, hearing sounds in the night. Footsteps, when no one was there. Voices, sounding distant and garbled, when no one was talking. Sights...

She caught her breath and stiffened. Oh, Lord, she had *seen* something as a child. A figure. Something. It had terrified her, and when her father had locked her in the closet, it had been there, too. There had been no escape.

"Honor?"

Ian slid into the booth beside her and wrapped a powerful arm around her shoulders. "Shh…" he said softly. "It's all right. It's all right."

Accepting without question that he somehow knew she was feeling scared and frightened, she turned toward him and buried her face in his strong shoulder. The terror was a memory, she reminded herself, an old memory. She was reacting to something that no longer threatened her.

But oh, how good it felt to be held. He even smelled good, like laundry soap and man, and the cotton of his olive T-shirt was soft against her skin. But she couldn't afford to notice things like that, she reminded herself. And this was certainly not the time or the place, anyway.

"I was remembering," she said. "I'd nearly forgotten…."

"Tell me."

"You'll think I'm crazy."

"Who, me?"

A weak chuckle escaped her then, and she eased back from his shoulder. He released her at once, and she wished he hadn't let go. Looking up almost shyly into his hard face, she found he was smiling faintly. Something about that smile made it possible to confide in him.

"When I was a kid, I saw and heard things in our house. My dad thought it was my imagination and locked me in the closet to break me of it."

Ian frowned. "He'd be arrested for that nowadays."

"Maybe. I don't think he meant to be cruel. He wasn't a cruel man. Just a hard one. What's important, though, is that…well, I've been through something like this before. If it's not my imagination—"

"It's not," he said, interrupting her. "I feel it, too. You're sensitive, that's all. I suspect some people wouldn't feel a thing in that house." He gave her another, very faint smile. "Some very *dense* people might not feel anything," he amended. "Whatever it is, it's strong."

"And getting stronger," Honor whispered, battling a sudden urge to look over her shoulder. The idea appalled her.

"Maybe not. I mean, if your father locked you in the closet to get you to suppress your sensitivity, it might just have taken a while for your awareness of this...thing to penetrate your barriers. It may have been this strong all along." He shrugged. "We're just speculating now, in any case. I suggest we wait until we find some useful information to base our theories on. In the meantime..."

Honor waited as he frowned thoughtfully, looking down at his coffee.

Here she was, sitting around talking of ghosts and other things that went bump in the night, and wishing that Ian McLaren would kiss her again, so that she could find out if the feelings she remembered from last night were real. Stupid. Incredible. But adrenaline had funny effects like that, she reminded herself. So maybe it wasn't stupid that she was thinking about sex when she ought to be thinking about how she was going to save her house from whatever was occupying it. Of course, maybe she was just overloaded. Maybe she just needed a break, and thinking about her attraction to Ian was a great break from other things.

It might be a dangerous attraction, she found herself thinking. What did she really know about him...except that as a child people had thought he was possessed? Well, with those eyes...

Suddenly those eyes were fixed on her. "We've got a little time yet. Want to take a walk?"

Walking at night was something she had nearly given up doing, because it just wasn't safe for a woman alone, and she'd seen too much in the emergency room to remain ignorant of the hazards. Walking with Ian, all six-foot-five and two-hundred-plus pounds of him, made her feel completely safe. She was able to throw back her head, enjoy the stiff breeze and the smell of the sea. The storm had moved far enough away that she didn't think lightning was a real danger...though it still flickered off to the northwest.

They walked away from the bright lights and onto the athletic field of a nearby school. There they could see the silver-lined storm clouds when the moon occasionally peeked through.

"Some night," Ian remarked, "we'll have to take a walk on the beach. When the moon is full."

"I'd love that." Amazed that he was planning such things for them, she turned and peered up at him. He looked even more mysterious than usual in the uncertain light. Lightning flashed to the east, causing the shadow on his face to shift strangely. Even in this poor light, his eyes seemed to glow.

Surely, said a faint little voice in her head, she ought to be afraid of this huge man she hardly knew? But she wasn't. Not at all. Not at this moment. What she felt—*all* she felt—was an urgent desire to be kissed by him.

He read minds. She became almost convinced of it when his strong arms suddenly closed around her and drew her against him. Suddenly aware of the nerve-exciting textures of man, muscle and denim, she felt her knees turn soft.

"Me too," he said huskily. "Me too."

She wondered what he meant, but then she didn't care, because he lifted her right off her feet and brought her eager mouth to his. Strong. He was so strong. He made her feel small, delicate, fragile...and for once she didn't mind.

Caution was swept away on a riptide of long-buried passion. All the things she had denied herself, all the things she had thought she would never know, were suddenly within her grasp. Her arms wrapped around broad shoulders, and she reveled in the powerful flexing of his muscles as he held her effortlessly above the ground. Such a large, strong man. Every cell in her body responded to his potency.

And every wounded cell in her heart responded to the unmistakable evidence that he desired her.

He held her with one arm around her waist, as if she weighed nothing, and allowed his other hand to roam. Downward it swept, slowly, along the slender line of her back, the soft curve of her hip, to the silky skin of the back of her thigh. She gasped against his mouth at the exquisite sensation of his callused palm on her sensitive skin and tightened her arms unconsciously, trying to get closer still.

With steady, gentle pressure, he brought her leg up to his waist, and suddenly she was pressed with breath-stealing intimacy against his arousal, while his tongue pillaged her mouth in a blatant imitation of mating.

She had never...not in her wildest dreams... Her fingers dug into the corded muscles of his shoulders, and she tore her mouth from his, throwing her head back in surrender as she abandoned herself to sensations beyond imagining. An extraordinary tension filled her, a wild expectancy that made everything else seem insignificant in comparison.

She wanted. Blindly, heedlessly, instinctively, she wanted this man.

How did he do this to her?

The thought flashed in her brain like a warning beacon. This was too fast, too hot, too wild. Unnatural. *Abomination.*

A groan erupted from the chest of the man who held her, the man who had mesmerized her, bewitched her and turned her into flame. Suddenly she was on her feet, free of him, except for the hands that steadied her gently. Then, when he had made sure she wouldn't stumble, he turned his back to her.

Stunned by what had just passed between them, and by the abrupt change, Honor simply stood and stared at his back. She could feel it, she thought crazily. She could feel the control he exerted now as he stood with his hands on his hips and his head thrown back and waited for his own needs to subside. She could feel it as surely as she could feel her own body shriek its disappointment and its hunger.

She hurt. He hurt.

What had happened?

Abomination. The word twisted coldly through her mind, as repulsive and disturbing as a clammy touch. Alien. Not hers.

Troubled, frightened, she wrapped her arms around herself, feeling cold despite the muggy heat of the Florida night. Thunder rumbled distantly, an edgy reminder of a storm that had not yet broken.

"Ian?"

She said his name softly, in a voice that was barely more than a whisper, but he heard her and turned to face her.

"I...need to get to work."

After a moment, he nodded. "Let's go."

He dropped Honor off at the emergency room entrance and watched her cross the twenty feet of concrete, her cute rump an incitement in those white shorts she was wearing. His palm remembered in exquisite detail just how the smooth skin of her thigh had felt, and the rest of him remembered with excruciating accuracy just how she had wrapped herself around him.

He was spending too much time with her. Getting drawn in too far. He'd slipped badly tonight. Very badly. She'd almost caught him out twice.

He had felt her yearning for him as strongly as he had felt his own for her. He wanted her. She wanted him. It should have been enough—except that he was…an abomination. She had sensed it, too, tonight. He had felt her alarm. Felt her recognition that something was unnatural. She just hadn't realized that it was *him*.

He couldn't afford to get close to her like that. Couldn't afford to slip. Didn't think he could stand to see the revulsion and fear on her face if she discovered his secret.

He had plenty of experience in keeping a safe distance, and the few relationships with women he'd allowed himself over the years had been chosen because they would preserve that distance. And always, always, if he felt that distance begin to erode to even a small degree, he'd left before the woman could discover what he really was.

It would be a damn sight more difficult to recover lost distance with his next-door neighbor. If he had half a brain, he would leave her to deal with her ghost by herself, let her get driven out of the place like all the other tenants.

Evidently he didn't have half a brain. When she was safely inside, he turned his Jeep out of the lot and headed back down the highway toward home. He was going to check out that damn house. Tonight. While she wasn't there to add to the psychic confusion in the place.

The wind was picking up again by the time he pulled into his driveway. A new storm was moving in, this one more restless than the last. Lightning flickered in sheets, and thunder growled hollowly.

When he had put the deadbolts on Honor's doors, he had kept a key for himself—another in the long list of his transgressions in life. The problem with security, he had realized years ago, was that if you made it nearly impossible for someone to get in, you might pay a price for being unreachable. People burned to death in homes with barred windows. Medical help couldn't reach you quickly if no one could break in.

So he had kept a key. And now with it, he let himself into her house. He didn't bring a flashlight, because there was nothing he wanted to see. He stood inside her front door and closed his eyes.

And waited.

It was nearly dawn before he felt it. At first it was like a soft stirring of the psychic breeze, just a whisper of shifting shadows in the living room. Instinctively he turned toward it, though he would never see it with his eyes.

It strengthened slowly, as if waking from a long sleep. From a shifting in the shadows, from a whisper of movement, it grew. Dark. Roiling. Hateful. Evil.

Ah, God, so cold! It seemed to soak the last heat from the room, leaving a cold so intense it froze the soul. Oppressive. Suffocating. Like cold, oily smoke.

Aware. It was aware of him. It was gathering itself, gathering its strength and its hatred, and it knew him.

Reaching out with icy tendrils of hate, it touched the edges of his mind and caused him to recoil helplessly.

Hunkering down and wrapping his arms around his knees for protection against a blast of cold that threatened frostbite, he waited it out. He needed knowledge of his enemy, and there was only one way to get it. Cautiously, he reached out with his mind.

And nearly died.

In an instant he was back in the pit that haunted his worst nightmares. Tied ankle and wrist with wire that cut to the bone. Helpless to protect himself. Helpless against the demon who tortured him. Naked to the eyes of his enemy. Knowing his every stifled scream of agony gave pleasure, because he could feel it with his abominable talent, could feel the pleasure of the men who tortured him. Wanting to die with a passion that beggared description, because it was his only way out.

No!

The word exploded in his head like a thunderclap as he grabbed for his self-control and refused to allow the vision power over him. Heedless of the cold that flayed his skin, he rose in the dark and faced his invisible tormentor.

No. By sheer effort of will, he forced his mind into the present, forced it to bury again what had happened in the past. He had been there. He refused to allow a mere memory to wield that kind of power over him.

He was shivering violently now, from the cold that had swallowed all the heat, and he still hadn't found what he needed. Hate. It was full of hate. Rage. Bitterness. But nothing he could use against it.

Then, suddenly, something shifted. Something changed, a new scent on the wind. The cold withdrew a little; the direction of the hate turned a little.

A change of focus.

Seizing the opportunity, Ian reached out, seeking a clue, a weakness...anything.

What he found was another presence. Outside the house. Drawing closer. Bent on murder.

Turning, he dismissed the evil inside the house to concentrate on the threat outside. Cold breath brushed his neck, making his scalp prickle, but he ignored it, concentrating on the new threat, instead.

Fractured images filled his head, battlefield nightmares, the worst of the things he had ever seen in his life, as the hateful thing in the house assaulted his mind. Dismembered bodies, screaming friends, dead buddies. With a monumental effort of will, he ignored the visions that always haunted him, refusing to give a toehold to the thing that would use them against him.

He was still cold, but sweat broke out all over him, soaking him, as he wrestled for supremacy over his own mind. And the thing outside drew closer. It had been summoned.

Grabbing the doorknob, he twisted it and pulled the door open. The real threat was outside, and he had to face it.

But suddenly he froze, as the cold touched the edges of his mind again. And buried deep in that cold and hate and rage, he thought he felt the touch of something...not exactly familiar, but something he had touched once before.

Before he could latch on to it, though, it vanished. Thunder cracked deafeningly, and the wind moaned around the corner of the house, reminding him where he was. When he was. The darkness in the living room shrank a little, pulling away from him.

And the thing outside was almost here. Swinging the

door open the rest of the way, he stepped out into the wild darkness. The storm was right overhead now, and the old live oaks groaned before the buffeting of the wind.

A fork of lightning zigzagged downward, striking a tree farther up the road. The concussion made his eardrums hurt, almost distracting him from the awareness that something was watching. From out there. From across the road.

Keeping low, Ian hurried down off the porch and around to the side, so that he could circle around and come up behind whoever—or whatever—was over there.

Across the road, though a few scrubby pines grew tall, for some reason the vegetation was nearly tropical. Palmettos and ferns that had never been disturbed by man grew thickly. Running on silent feet, crouching to keep a low profile, Ian hurried fifty or sixty yards up the road and then crossed over. Behind him, he felt the presence in the house fade a little, weakening. As if it had used all the energy it could. Or as if its attention had turned elsewhere.

And then he discovered why he'd considered this threat worse than the one in the house.

Thunder cracked loudly, and lightning flared, illuminating the night. Then there was another sharp crack, an unnatural one.

Pain seared his side, and he went down. He'd been shot.

Thunder growled like a hungry beast at bay. Lightning slashed jaggedly toward the horizon from heavy clouds that hid the early-dawn light. On a clear day, the sky would be brightening by this time. Today it was a dark, leaden gray.

Ian didn't show up at 7:30. By eight, Honor was feeling impatient and irritated. This was why she hated to depend on someone else for transport.

By 8:30 she was beginning to worry about him. He didn't seem like an undependable sort of person, whatever else he might be. She called his house and received no answer.

By nine she was wondering if she could call the police. Something was wrong. She felt it in her bones.

Just as she was turning from the door to go back to the pay phone, she saw his Jeep pull into the hospital parking lot. Grabbing her purse, she trotted out to meet him.

"Sorry I'm so late," he said as she climbed in beside him. "I was unavoidably detained."

There was sarcasm in the statement, along with something else she couldn't quite define. She turned to look at him, really look at him, and gasped. "What happened to you?"

He looked pale under his tan, and his eyes appeared sunken. Running a professional eye over him, she realized for the first time that his olive-drab T-shirt had given way to a green hospital shirt. "Ian?"

"I thought we'd grab a quick breakfast and then hit the base library. That okay?"

She knew that tone of voice. Her father had often used it to indicate that a subject wasn't open for discussion. Instead of arguing, which was what she wanted to, she decided to bide her time. Things had a way of coming out if you were patient. "Okay," she said, and fixed her attention out the window.

He needed a shave, she thought as she stared out at the scenery. He looked like hell, he needed a shave, and something was very, very wrong. Once or twice she heard him mutter an oath as he took a corner.

They grabbed biscuits and sausage at a fast-food place, and large cups of hot, fresh coffee. They ate outdoors at a stone table, away from the other patrons, who were wisely avoiding the humid morning heat.

"Is it going to clear today at all?" Honor asked as she looked up at the leaden sky.

"I haven't heard the weather."

"I came down here for sunshine," she remarked. "I feel cheated when I don't get it."

It was a stupid, inane conversation, but it kept her from asking why he was moving so strangely. So stiffly. And why his mouth tightened at times, as if he were in pain. Not that she needed him to explain that he'd gotten hurt somehow. She did wonder, though, *how* he'd been hurt. And how bad it was. Instead, she talked of something else. Anything else.

"Do you really think we'll find anything useful at the library?"

He looked up from his third biscuit. "We're hardly the first people in the world to be faced with this problem."

"Well, no." Not likely. Not when she remembered an earlier encounter just in her own life. Tens of thousands of other people must have experienced such things.

One corner of his mouth lifted in that faint smile she was beginning to find familiar. "The way things are, if two people have experienced something, one of them will have written a book about it."

She almost laughed then. He was right, of course.

"Even if we don't find something useful in terms of getting rid of the thing," he continued, "every bit of knowledge we can gather is potentially useful. And in the meantime, I want you to stay at my house."

She blinked, startled by both the suggestion and her own response, a swift upsurge of mingled relief and yearning. "I don't think—"

"Look," he said, "don't get all coy and prissy on me. You know damn well you're not comfortable in that house. Do you really think you'll be able to close your eyes and go to sleep there after what you tell me you felt yesterday? Are you just calmly going to ignore it and get into your shower again?"

Ice slid slowly down her spine. Inwardly she admitted he was right. She wasn't going to be able to ignore the presence in the house. No amount of arguing with herself would change the fact that she would always be on edge, listening, waiting.

"But it can't hurt me," she said, making one last protest.

His answer was uncompromising. "Oh, yes, it can," he said grimly. "It sure as hell can."

It was early afternoon by the time they returned home, bringing more than a dozen books with them. After the library, they'd gone to the occult bookstore, as well, and found a couple of additional volumes.

When Ian climbed out of the Jeep, he stood in his driveway and stared across at Honor's house. Silent, unblinking, motionless, he reminded her of a cat with its eye on a bird, its nose lifted to scent the breeze. He was a hunter.

"Let's get your stuff now," he said abruptly.

Honor was feeling as tired as she had ever felt, and her only desire at the moment was to curl up somewhere and sleep. Anywhere. Even in that damn house she had bought.

"Look," she said. "Why don't I just go home and catch some sleep? I can bring my stuff over later."

"No."

No? He'd spoken that single syllable in that uncompromising way of his, and it suddenly occurred to Honor that of all the things she disliked about this man, this was the one she disliked most.

"Damn it, McLaren, will you quit trying to run my life?"

Turning to face her, he yanked up the loose green surgical shirt and showed her ten inches of taped stiches in his side. "See that?" he said harshly. "It damn well *can* hurt you, and I'll be doubled damned if I'm going to let your stubbornness make you an easy target. We're getting your stuff. Now."

He started to tug the shirt down, but Honor stopped him by touching the skin below the wound with gentle fingertips. At her touch, a tremor passed through him. "Oh, Ian," she said shakily. "What happened?"

"I'll tell you later," he said. "For now, let's just get whatever you need for a couple of days. Now. While it's…sleeping."

"Sleeping?" A chill touched the back of her neck, and goose bumps rose on her arms, despite the day's heavy, suffocating heat. "What do you mean?"

He shook his head. "I meant while it's quiet. It's quiet now." God, he was slipping, slipping badly. He could see it in her eyes. It was almost as if some evil genius were driving him to betray himself.

"How do you know that?"

He looked down into her soft young face, into her concerned, frightened blue eyes, and wondered why he couldn't have been just a normal man. Wondered why he had been so savagely cursed all his days.

"Later," he said. "We're beat. We need to sleep. We

can talk about everything later. Let's just get your things.''

Something had flickered in his cat-green eyes, something that her heart recognized as anguish. Compassion rose in her and washed away her irritation. ''Okay,'' she said. ''Okay. But I don't want you carrying anything, not with those stitches.''

He looked down at her, and then, for the first time in years, he laughed. It was a rusty sound, almost unrecognizable, but it lightened the shadows in his eyes. ''Lady, you're a born dragon.''

She would have bristled, except that she nearly lost her breath at a sudden glimpse of this man as he might have been, given a happier road in life. ''I'm a nurse,'' she managed to say. ''And from the look of it, they should have kept you in the hospital overnight.''

He shook his head and turned toward her house. ''The nice thing about being retired is that the base hospital can't call my commander anymore. They couldn't make me stay.''

She could well believe that, Honor thought, following him. She could well believe that.

CHAPTER SIX

Come home, Honor. It's all right. There's nothing in the house to hurt you. It's the man you need to watch out for. He's the one who's threatening you.

She awoke slowly in the early evening, stale air-conditioned air stirring in the room around her. Ian's guest room. The narrow iron cot.

She turned over and drifted, half in and half out of a dream. Her house was welcoming her, making her feel at home. The dark threat was gone, a figment of her imagination. She smiled and snuggled into her pillow, liking the sunny yellow of the kitchen.

She turned to smile at Ian, and her contentment shattered like exploding glass. He held a knife and was moving toward her, and there was murder in his strange green eyes.

Devil's spawn.

She sat up, suddenly cold and very much awake, and clutched the sheets to her.

God! What an awful dream!

Moments later, wrapped in her short cotton robe, she padded barefoot down the hall to take a shower. She needed to shake off the last of the strange dream, and this seemed the best way to do it.

It was certainly getting to her, she thought as she stood under the hot spray and let it beat the tension out of her muscles. She had stopped having nightmares years ago, but now she seemed to be having them almost incessantly.

And maybe, she found herself thinking uneasily, maybe there was something to the dream. Maybe her subconscious was trying to get through to her. Maybe she was looking at things from the wrong perspective.

Back in the cell-like room, she dressed swiftly in white shorts and a red tank top, then sat on the edge of the bed to buckle her sandals. What, she found herself wondering, had *actually* happened?

There had been someone waiting for her when she came home the other night. That much she was sure of. After all, she'd heard something fall. But other than that, what did she have? A feeling that someone was watching? A feeling that someone was in the house?

And what had Ian done, except encourage her in the belief that there was something in her house? He had added to her fear, hadn't he?

Sitting on the edge of the cot in the bare room, she rested her elbows on her knees and wondered what was going on. Was she really feeling something? Or was Ian taking advantage of her suggestibility? Why would he want to do that? What could he possibly hope to get out of this?

Or were they both caught up in some kind of folie à deux, feeding one another's delusions?

But no, she reminded herself. Yesterday, all alone in her house in the late afternoon, when she'd been thinking of nothing but cooking dinner and going to work, she had found her bathroom door open. Had felt the cold touch of something…something *other.*

If that was imagination, she never wanted to imagine anything again. She couldn't blame Ian for that, could she?

Or could she?

Witchcraft and satanism. Some people believed in

those things. Believed it was possible to cast spells on other people. To make them see and hear things.

Abomination. Those eyes of his were…strange. Unnatural.

Suddenly shocked by the direction her thoughts were taking, Honor shook her head and stood up. No way. The man had done nothing but try to help her. He was a little strange, to be sure, but strangeness was not a hanging offense. Time to think of something else, she told herself. Time to think about something normal.

Twilight was just beginning to settle over the land when Honor remembered that she hadn't collected her mail. Feeling a little homesick, hoping one of her friends back in Seattle had written, she told Ian she was going out to the mailbox. Even with the fading of the day, the air was still too warm and muggy for comfort. In a little while, though, the breeze would start up, causing the trees to rustle and sway, and the tree frogs would begin their nightly chorus.

Stepping into the road so that she could reach the front of her mailbox, she saw the flattened carapace of an insect that had to be at least ten inches long. Were there really bugs that big around here? The largest she had seen so far were the tree roaches, and they were only a couple of inches at their biggest. Horrified, she stared at the bug and tried to tell herself it was something else.

"Miss Honor?"

Startled, she swung around toward the voice, then smiled as she recognized Orville Sidell, a ten-year-old boy who lived farther up the road, deeper in the woods. He had been one of her first patients, brought in by his older brother and sister after being bitten by a coral snake. She had seen him several times since, and as usual he was wearing only a dusty pair of shorts and a grimy T-shirt. "Hello, Orville. How's your leg?"

"Jes' fine." He held it out briefly for her inspection. The tissue damage had been minimal, she saw with relief. Only a small pit marked the death of muscle. "That really looks good."

He nodded, then put his bare foot back down in the dust. "I brought you some squirrel."

"Squirrel?"

"Yeah." He brought his hand out from behind his back and held out two dead squirrels. "Shot 'em m'self."

"You did?" Honor had a feeling this wasn't the time for her to react as she would have in Seattle. "You must be a good shot."

Orville nodded. "Ma's got more'n she needs. Said you might like 'em."

Honor looked from him to the pathetic-looking squirrels he dangled by their tails. "For what?"

He grinned suddenly, amused by her stupidity. "Eat 'em, Miss Honor. They're good."

"Oh." She regarded the squirrels uncertainly. "What do they taste like?"

He shrugged. "Like squirrel."

"How do I cook them?"

"Any way you like."

She guessed she was going to have to do this. She certainly didn't want to offend Orville. "Tell you what, Orville. If you would be so kind as to clean them for me, I'll give it a try." She gave him an apologetic smile. "I've never had to skin a squirrel. I wouldn't know where to begin."

"Okay." He started to turn away, apparently satisfied, but then he paused and faced her again. "Miss Honor, my ma says you oughta be careful of that man."

"Which man?"

The boy's brown eyes slid past her. "Him," he said. "The army man."

Once again Honor felt a chill trickle of unease run down her back. "He seems like a perfectly nice man, Orville."

"Ma says he's got the evil eye."

At any other time, under any other circumstances, Honor would have been hard-pressed not to laugh. Right now, all she felt was a crawling sense of unease. "Well, he hasn't done anything to hurt me," she told Orville. "He's been very helpful. You can tell your mother I said that."

Orville simply stared at her, clearly nonplussed.

"Hey, Orville!"

Honor looked down the road and saw Orville's older brother, Jeb, wave the boy over. Jeb had been with Orville the night he came to the emergency room. He was an extremely big, slow-witted man who made a living at manual labor, and there wasn't a doubt in Honor's mind but that he loved his younger brother dearly.

"Comin'!" Orville shouted back. He started to leave, then glanced over his shoulder at Honor. "Ma says the old preacher used to shun him."

"Shun him? Who?"

"The army guy." Then he was off and running, the squirrels dangling from his hand.

Honor stared after them until they disappeared around a bend in the road and were hidden behind the dense foliage. *Shunned.* What on earth had he done to deserve that?

Damn it, now she was going to demand some explanations. He was still avoiding the question of his injuries, with his nose buried in all those books he'd gotten today.

Surely she deserved some answers. Surely she deserved
to know a little about the man whose roof she was sharing?

Clutching her mail, she turned toward the house and
again noticed the huge squashed insect. Why hadn't she
stayed in Seattle?

Ian was still seated at his kitchen table, with books
spread all around him. Photos purporting to be pictures
of apparitions stared up at Honor from several of the
opened volumes.

"Find anything?" she asked.

"Plenty, but nothing that looks really useful yet." An
hour's nap seemed to have nearly restored him. When he
looked up at her, his eyes didn't appear nearly so sunken.
"You must be getting hungry. I should make dinner."

"It can wait. How's your side?"

"Sore."

The sudden intensity of his gaze left her wondering if
he had somehow sensed her determination to tolerate no
further evasions. Feeling nervous, she pulled out a chair
facing him and sat. "I've been waiting all day for an
explanation," she said, refusing to chicken out, even
though he had never looked more forbidding or more
terrifying than he did at this moment. "How did you get
hurt?"

For a moment, he didn't answer. He stared at her with
those odd eyes of his, looking as if he could see past her
surface to deeper things. Deeper feelings. "What," he
asked, "makes you so sure you're entitled to any explanation at all?"

Honor gasped, as stunned as if she'd been struck. The
man was incredible, she found herself thinking. She'd
never met anyone like him for sheer, uncompromising,

unapologetic rudeness—when he felt like it. Then she got mad. "What makes me think I deserve an explanation? How about you yanking up your shirt earlier to show me twenty or thirty stitches and then telling me that…that thing could hurt me? How's that for a reason?"

He gave an infinitesimal nod, but she was too wound up to register his agreement. "How about the fact that you're insisting I live under your roof? How about the fact that you keep telling me I need to be protected, but you won't tell me what from? How about—"

He laughed. Amazingly, incredibly, astonishingly, he laughed. The sound instantly halted Honor's diatribe, and she stared at him in utter amazement. He looked so… different when he laughed. So attractive. So nice. So warm. So…sexy. So damn irritating.

"What is so funny?" she demanded. "Why are you laughing at me?"

Still grinning, a wonderfully attractive expression on his face, he answered on a chuckle. "I'm not laughing at you. You just surprised me. I can't remember the last time anybody yelled at me."

"Well, of course not," she said sharply. "I imagine everyone is too terrified of you."

His smile broadened a shade. "Probably. But you aren't."

The casual statement struck her forcefully, reminding her afresh of how big he was, how powerfully built. A much smaller, weaker man with his Ranger training would be dangerous. A man like Ian McLaren would be lethal with very little effort.

His smile faded, almost as if he had sensed her renewed uneasiness. In the blink of an eye, he once again became the dark monolith she had first met, the extraordinarily powerful, solitary man who needed nothing and no one. The man who wore loneliness like a concealing cloak.

"I'd never hurt you," he said roughly, looking away. "But I can see you're not going to believe that."

"Ian..." She felt the need to say something, but what? From moment to moment, she was constantly unsure what she felt about this man, what she thought of him. Sometimes she longed to reach out and wrap her arms around him in hopes of easing the loneliness she sensed in him. Other times she was unsure she should trust him at all. What did she really know about him, after all?

"I was shot," he said abruptly.

"Shot?" All her other concerns scattered. "How? When? My God, how bad was it?"

"It was just a graze."

She had helped patch together a lot of gunshot wounds in her career; it was an inevitable experience in a city emergency room. She didn't lose her cool over such things.

Except that this time, the man who had been shot was someone she knew. Someone she...cared about. Her stomach twisted, and she pressed her fingers to her mouth, seeking self-control. "Oh, my God," she whispered, knowing too well what could have happened if that bullet had hit him dead-center. "Oh, my God."

"It wasn't that bad," he said, his deep, dark voice pitched soothingly. "Honey, it was just a graze. Not much worse than a cut. I put a pressure bandage on it and drove to the base hospital."

This time she didn't jump all over him for calling her *honey*. Instead she thought of him bandaging his own wound and then driving to the hospital. About what you would expect from a Ranger, she thought with amazing bitterness. An ordinary person would consider it a major achievement to have phoned for help. Not a Ranger. They weren't ordinary mortals. They were superhuman, or they were nothing.

If he'd had to, he probably would have sewed the wound himself. Look at him sitting there, treating it as if it were all in a day's work…which it was, for him, she reminded herself. So he wouldn't want any fussing or concern. He wouldn't want her to reach out.…

But somehow she did anyway. Somehow she was bending over him, with her arms wrapped tightly around his broad shoulders and her face pressed to the warm, fragrant curve between his neck and his shoulder.

For an instant, he seemed frozen; then his arm lifted to curl around her waist to make her welcome. He tugged gently and pulled her down so that she was perched on his thigh.

"It's okay," he murmured.

"You could have been killed." She barely whispered the words, hardly daring to voice the possibility. Everything inside her felt as if it were twisted out of shape, as if she were trying to find some kind of equilibrium in a world gone mad.

"But I wasn't." She was wearing her hair down, and of its own accord his hand burrowed into the silky strands. He didn't want to think about how long it had been since he had risked letting a woman come this close. Right now he felt a very normal, very human, need to give in to some very normal human urges. He couldn't, of course, and he wouldn't. But, damn it, he could be forgiven for stealing just a few minutes of warmth.

After a few moments she gave a tremulous sigh and straightened. Looking at that slash of white in his dark hair that must have resulted from an injury, thinking about the scars on his back that spoke of great suffering, she ached for this man. Subjected to an exorcism as a child of six, slapped and shouted at for days. Shunned by his own church. He lived inside a concrete emotional bunker, she thought now. Letting no one come close. How sad. How lonely.

And wasn't she doing the same thing?

Lifting an unsteady hand, she pressed her palm to his cheek, felt the warmth of his skin, the prickle of his stubble. Masculine textures that made her ache deep inside for things lost, for a naïveté that had been stolen from her by deceit. Jerry had crippled her, but this man had come dangerously close to making her forget that.

Something cold seemed to touch the base of her skull, and she shivered. "I'm glad you're okay," she said, then rose from his knee. "Why don't I make supper while you tell me what happened, and why you think the ghost had something to do with you being shot? I mean, ghosts don't carry guns. Do they?"

"No, ghosts don't carry guns." He was perfectly capable of cooking their meal, but he sensed that she needed the activity, so he simply told her where everything was.

A short while later, as she shaped a hamburger patty, she faced him. "What happened last night, Ian?"

Something in his face shut down, and that was when she began to grow distinctly uneasy. Whatever he told her now, she realized, wasn't going to be everything. Not by a long shot. How could she trust him if he was withholding information? But how could she be positive that he was? The chilly touch at the base of her skull returned.

"I was checking out your house last night," Ian said finally. "I...get these feelings sometimes. I've mentioned them before."

He had, so she nodded. She knew about those intuitive

feelings; she'd had them all her life, and she knew it didn't pay to ignore them. She just hoped the uneasiness she was feeling right now wasn't intuitive.

Turning, she set the patty down on a plate and started making another one. "What happened?" she repeated. His reluctance to talk wasn't making her feel any better. This man, after all, was the guy who could say no with all the finesse of a sledgehammer. The thought of him tiptoeing around something, anything, wasn't reassuring.

"I kept a key to the new lock I put on your front door," he said flatly.

Honor spun around and stared at him, aghast. "Why?"

"Because, damn it, when you lock everything out, you lock yourself in. If you needed help, how was anyone going to get in? The fire department. EMS. The cops. Think about it."

Slowly, reluctantly, she nodded, remembering a couple in Seattle who had arrived too late in the emergency room, killed by carbon monoxide in their home. The husband had called for help, realizing something was wrong with his wife, but the windows had been covered by iron bars, and the doors had been securely bolted. By the time rescue personnel had managed to break in, it was too late. "You should have told me."

"You're right. I should have told you." But his expression never changed, and she remembered him telling her that he always did whatever he considered necessary, regardless of what others thought.

"I realize you don't give a damn what I think about anything," she said tautly, "but I would appreciate being informed when you take any action that affects me."

He gave a brief nod that told her nothing, his strange green eyes never wavering from her face.

"So you went into my house last night?" she asked. "Why?"

"To see if I could learn anything about what you've been feeling. What I've felt in there."

"And did you?"

"Yes," he said.

Honor looked down at the hamburger patty she had been making and realized she had squeezed it between her fingers. Did she really want to hear what he had learned last night? The icy touch at the base of her neck grew stronger, and she had the worst urge to flee, to just say to hell with it all, ditch the house and file for bankruptcy.

As soon as she thought it, she felt ashamed. Her dad had raised her to be tougher than that. You didn't run from these things; you faced them. The alternative was being locked in the dark closet of fear. Her father had been right about that, even if his methods had left something to be desired.

"What happened?" she asked finally.

"Just an hour or so before dawn, it came."

It came. The words were like ice water running down her back. "It? You felt it?" *It.* Oh, God, the word gave form to the thing. Made it more than a feeling. Turned it into an entity. A being. *It.*

"It's...pretty hard to describe," he said slowly. "But you felt it, so I guess I don't have to. It...seemed almost to gather itself. Like a storm. As if it's not there all the time and has to be triggered by something."

Honor sank slowly into a chair, the hamburger forgotten in her hand. "It has to be," she said quietly. "Otherwise I'd feel it all the time, and I don't."

He nodded briefly. "That's what happened this morning, anyway. It...gathered, for lack of a better word. The house grew really cold, as if it were sucking all the heat out of the air. All the energy.''

Honor felt her scalp prickle as she thought of that cold spot at the foot of the attic stairs. "Oh, boy."

"Anyway, then I felt something from outside."

"Outside?" She stiffened. "You mean there's more than one?"

"No. It was…well, whoever was out there was human. It was no phantom that took a shot at me. But I think he might have been influenced by the thing in your house."

Honor closed her eyes. "Oh, no…" she breathed. "Didn't I tell you I felt like something was trying to get into my head? Didn't I tell you?" Her eyes opened in time to see Ian nod. "So you think this thing influenced somebody to shoot at you. Do you know how crazy that sounds? Why the hell do I believe it? But I do! I do!"

She jumped up and put the squashed hamburger down on the plate in front of her. "It was bad enough when I thought some spook was trying to scare me out of the house, but this is worse. This is incredible. Unbelievable. Guns!"

And if it could influence somebody to shoot at Ian, it could influence Ian.

The thought chilled her to the very bone. She would have given a great deal not to have even thought of the possibility, but now that she had, she couldn't ignore it. And it made the threat so much worse. So very much worse.

Outside, night had descended. Through the window she saw flickers that might be lightning or might be the bombing on the reservation. A hundred yards away was her house, in the possession of some…*thing*. Some evil thing that had tried to hurt Ian. That might well have been trying to kill him.

"What do I do?" The words escaped her as little more than a whisper.

"I'm going to keep reading," Ian answered. "Maybe I can find something. In the meantime, you're safe here with me. Absolutely no one and nothing is going to get to you without going through me first. That much I can guarantee."

She looked down at the raw hamburger meat and felt her stomach twist. But how, she wondered, would it get through him? By killing him?

Or by turning him to its purposes?

It wasn't until much later in the evening, with another thunderstorm breaking over their heads, that Honor recalled what Orville Sidell had told her.

Looking up from the book she was reading, she studied Ian's bowed head in the lamplight. They had moved into his living room, into worn but comfortable overstuffed chairs, and were reading the books he had gotten that day.

So far, all the books had done was give her a much more frightening idea of just what ghosts could do. Poltergeists, it seemed, had occasionally been known to set fires. She *did* have fire insurance, but she wasn't sure she wanted to be sleeping in a house when a ghost started a bonfire. And if it could do that, then it could do other things.

Ian looked up, the lamplight gleaming on his gray streak and glimmering oddly in his eyes. "Problem?" he asked.

"I was just having some unhappy thoughts about the fact that poltergeists have been known to start fires. And I haven't found one useful thing about dealing with them. Everything I've read so far just seems to indicate that these things eventually go away by themselves. The question is whether I can wait that long.''

He pointed to the book he held. ''This one suggests trying to tell the ghost it's dead.''

Honor thought about what she had felt, about what Ian had earlier told her had happened to him. ''Great. And hopefully it won't tell somebody to shoot us while we're arguing with it.''

A smile cracked the frozen landscape of his face. ''There *is* that problem. But a human agent can be locked out.''

Instinctively she turned toward the window when a particularly loud crack of thunder startled her. ''Yeah,'' she said after a moment. ''And you think it's really going to listen?'' Suddenly she wished she had to work tonight. She was off for the next three days, and while ordinarily she thoroughly enjoyed her breaks, this one loomed in front of her seemingly endless. Between ghosts and Ian McLaren, she would rather work the ER during a natural disaster.

''No.''

Again that single uncompromising syllable. Honor looked at him. ''It won't listen?''

''It didn't feel like a confused soul to me. It felt…'' He hesitated, clearly reluctant to go on.

''Evil,'' Honor said. ''I know. I felt it.'' She wrapped her arms around herself, feeling chilled. The wind rattled the rain against the windowpane. ''I didn't always believe in evil,'' she remarked. ''It's easy not to believe until you run into it, impossible not to believe once you've seen it.''

She glanced at him and found him nodding in agreement. His eyes looked even eerier than usual in the lamplight. ''Why were you shunned?'' The words were out

of her mouth before she was even aware that she was
going to speak them. Shock at her own temerity trickled
through her. She expected some kind of reaction from
him—shock, surprise, anger. Anything. But like the
Sphinx, he betrayed nothing.

"What else did Orville tell you?" he asked.

"How did you know it was Orville?"

"I saw you talking with him," he said dryly. "What
else did he tell you?"

Honor hesitated only a moment before plunging ahead.
They might as well clear the air, she thought. "He said
his mother said I ought to avoid you. That's all."

"Annie Sidell." He nodded. "I went to school with
her. She was a thorn in my side all along, but that was
hardly surprising, considering old Mrs. Gilhooley was her
mother. The woman had it in for me."

She studied him in silence, wondering why she had to
feel so drawn to someone she wasn't sure she could trust.
Wondering why she felt compelled to question him about
things that she suspected had scarred him. She couldn't
imagine anyone becoming as remote and removed as this
man without a damn good reason. People were social
animals, and instinct generally led them to reach out. This
man must have powerful reasons for being so isolated.
So unnatural.

Abomination.

Honor shrugged the cold whisper away as if it were
nothing but an annoying insect. Whatever was working
on her to drag such words out of her unconscious, she
wasn't going to pay any attention to it. Not right now.

"There must," she said finally, "have been more to it
than a goat as old as Methuselah."

The silence grew long. Heavy. Rain and wind rattled
at the windows, a cold sound.

"There was."

She swung her head around to stare intently at him, having heard the tension in his brief statement. And the way he had spoken those words warned her it was not some minor, long-forgotten transgression. She waited.

With a suddenness that was jarring, he slammed closed the book he held. "I'm getting some coffee," he said roughly. "Want some?"

"Ian..." Surely he wasn't going to leave her dangling without an explanation?

"Look, lady." Suddenly he leaned over her. Loomed over her. She shrank back a little in her chair, unable to look away from his oddly glowing eyes. "You're asking questions about things that happened thirty-five years ago. Things I never talk about." His voice was a thunderous growl. "You're just going to have to let me do this in my own way. In my own time. It's the least you can do when you ask somebody to bare his soul."

"I didn't—"

"Oh, yes, you did," he said, almost savagely, spacing his words emphatically. "I've never told anyone what you're asking me to tell you. Never." Abruptly, he stepped back. "Now, do you want that coffee?"

Stiffly she nodded an affirmative. What, she wondered, had she unleashed? What had she asked? She had known it had to be more than a goat, but she hadn't envisioned anything so awful that he hadn't spoken about it in thirty-five years.

A strong gust of wind splattered rain against the window, and she looked toward it, thinking what a miserable night it had turned into. If she were working, she could have been sure of seeing a number of auto accidents. Right now she wondered if that wouldn't have been easier to face.

What a morbid thought! Dismayed because she ordinarily wasn't in the least morbid, she told herself that the lonely sound of the rain and wind was getting to her. She hadn't really been herself for a couple of days now. Not since the night she had come home to find someone—or something—waiting in her house.

"Here." Ian had come soundlessly into the room, and he was putting her coffee on the table at her elbow before she even heard him. Fresh coffee. Its aroma was homey, welcoming, a marked contrast to the man who had brought it. He returned to his seat in the chair across from her, then put his heels up on the scarred coffee table.

Looking around her now, it suddenly occurred to her that this was probably the same furniture he had grown up with. This room probably hadn't changed at all.

"So you want to know why Mrs. Gilhooley hated me," he said. His voice was low, rough. Reluctant.

"Well, she might have been crazy," Honor said, "but you have to admit, it's rather extreme for an adult to hate a child as much as she must have hated you to accuse you of being possessed."

Ian lifted his mug to his lips, then put it on the table beside him. "First I was possessed. Later I was a witch. Finally I was—" He broke off. His jaw worked visibly. It was the first genuine sign of distress Honor had ever seen him show. The ache she felt for him deepened, and she wished there were a way to erase bad memories for people. To just take them away and make them vanish.

"What set her off," he said. It was not a question. "Her husband died. I remember it was August. Hot. Nobody had air-conditioning then, and we just endured the heat, the humidity, the bugs. I was just a kid, though, and it didn't bother me too much. When all the adults were indoors, staying as cool as they could, I was usually out playing.

"This one afternoon, I came around the rear of the Gilhooley house and saw old man Gilhooley flat on his back. He'd evidently been on a ladder, and the ladder fell over. I looked up and saw Mrs. Gilhooley standing in the open attic window, looking down. He was dead. I knew that right off. And I knew she had pushed the ladder over."

Honor shivered, seeing the scene so clearly in her mind's eye. "How did you know that? How *could* you know that?"

He ignored the question. "Being only six, I didn't have the sense to keep my mouth shut. I told my parents. I told the policemen who came to investigate. Nobody listened."

He reached for his coffee mug. "Except Mrs. Gilhooley. She listened. It wasn't long after that when she claimed I was possessed."

"But why would anyone listen to her? Why would anyone believe such a thing?"

Thunder rumbled, a deep, low sound. A gust of wind rattled the house.

"Given the beliefs of the church to which both my parents and the Gilhooleys belonged, it wasn't unheard-of. Or even difficult to accept."

"Did your parents believe it?" The ache she felt for him was growing stronger, as she considered how bewildering and frightening all this must have been for a six-year-old boy.

"Of course."

"So they performed an exorcism."

He nodded once, slowly, never taking his eyes from her.

"Didn't that put an end to it?"

"No. I told you, that kind of thing sticks like the odor of skunk. Nobody ever really trusted me after that. I shut up about the old woman killing her husband, but that didn't make her feel any more secure, I guess. She kept muttering about me being unnatural. Demon spawn, she called me." Now he did look away, as if he didn't want her to glimpse the pain in his eyes.

Demon spawn. She had heard that before, Honor thought, as a chill crept down her neck.

"Finally," he said, "her muttering got me shunned by the church members. My parents kept dragging me anyway, probably hoping some kind of sanctity would rub off on me. I don't know. They'd drag me, and then I'd have to sit in a special chair. No one would talk to me or look at me or even come near me. Made it kind of hard to forget what they thought of me."

"How awful," she murmured. She wanted to reach out to him, but she stopped herself. Nothing she could do now would ease the pain of what had happened to him so long ago. "How could your parents do that to you? How could they let you be treated that way? Why didn't they look for another church?"

Slowly he turned his head to look straight at her. "Because they believed it, too."

"My God." She breathed the words, hardly able to conceive of such a thing. "They believed you were— were demon spawn? A devil? Evil?"

He gave a slight nod.

Indignation swept through her, so hot and furious in its strength that she could no longer sit still. Leaping to her feet, she paced the lamplit living room. "That's awful. That's terrible! I can't imagine *any* parent feeling that way about a child. Oh, I know some parents are terrible, but—I can't believe it!''

"You were locked in a closet," he pointed out.

"Yes, but—" She broke off, realizing that his parents had probably justified themselves in exactly the same way her father had. "They did it for my own good."

"Exactly." Ian shook his head. "It didn't do me any good." One corner of his mouth lifted in a faint, wry smile. "About the time I was ten, I quit going to church at all. Nobody could make me. My dad whipped me half to death for it, but I refused to go anymore. I used to slip out of the house before everybody woke up and hide. And I was getting too big for him to force me. Finally he gave up and left me alone. And Mrs. Gilhooley married again and left me alone. For a while."

There was more. She knew there was more, because they still hadn't covered the events the electrician had referred to. So far he had said nothing to explain why he had been accused of witchcraft.

She stopped pacing near the window and looked out at the stormy night. It was so dark outside that she couldn't make out her house, or the trees and moss around it. They might have been alone in the universe, floating endlessly through empty space.

Then she caught sight of a glimmer, high up in the direction of her house, as if a distant light had been reflected on glass. Probably a headlight from the highway, she thought, that had somehow pierced the gloom and rain. As she watched, it flickered and was gone.

Then it appeared again, in the same place. And this time it looked…orange. More like…

Fire.

CHAPTER SEVEN

Fire.

Almost as soon as she spoke the word, Ian was at her side, looking out the window. He saw it, too, and swore. "Looks like it might be in the back bedroom." But with nothing visible in the darkness except the orange glow, it was impossible to be sure. "I'll check it out."

"I'm going with you."

"No."

She turned and grabbed his arm. "Ian—"

He shook free, glaring at her. "One, if I don't come out of there in ten minutes, I want you to call for help. If you're in there with me, you might get into the same trouble, and then we'd both be done for. Two, this might well be an attempt to get you back there."

Get her back there? "Why? Why would—?"

But he was already heading for the kitchen, so she followed him, trying to reframe her question. She stood back as he bent to the cabinet beneath the sink and pulled out a large fire extinguisher.

"Look," he said as he straightened, his strange eyes as opaque as jade. "Maybe it wants to hurt you. Maybe it just wants to scare you so bad you'll never come back. Maybe it wants to influence you somehow. Damn it, Honor, how would *I* know what it's up to? Just stay clear so it can't succeed!"

Once again she reached out and grabbed his arm, acutely aware of the strength of the muscles beneath her clutching fingers, well aware that he could fling her away with no more difficulty than if she were some trouble-some gnat. But he held still beneath her touch, accepting the restraint...for a moment.

"I could say the same for you," she told him. "What if it wants to hurt *you?*"

He stared down at her, not a muscle in his face flickering, not the slightest movement of his eyes betraying his thoughts. "Then it's going to get its chance right now."

Then he was gone, leaving her in the silence of the kitchen. Through the open screen door, she heard the steady hammer of the rain, the low rumble of the thunder, saw the flicker of sheet lightning. The cicadas were quiet for once, and only a few hardy tree frogs kept up their nightly chorus.

Wasn't it only a few nights ago that she had stood in this same kitchen in the dead of night, scared out of her mind, while he went next door to check things out?

Ten minutes, he had said. Ten minutes. Lord, she didn't know if she would be able to stand it that long. Ten minutes was an awful lot of time. Long enough for that fire to get out of control. Long enough for terrible things to happen.

What if it wants to get you over there?

She shuddered and pushed open the screen door to stand on his back porch. Her ears strained for every sound, listening for any warning that Ian was in trouble. Through the rain and the heavy Spanish moss, she could still see the faint orange glow, but not clearly enough to tell if it had spread to any other window. By now Ian must be inside and climbing those stairs.

Ten minutes was too long, surely, for him simply to discover what was wrong. Of course, he meant to put it out if it was a small fire...but how long could that take?

She waited, holding herself so tightly that she was sure she would have bruises on her upper arms from her own fingers. Why would that thing want her back, if it was really trying to drive her away?

What if it was trying to get Ian over there? Not to hurt him, but to influence him. To make him help get rid of her?

The thought twisted into her mind as sinuously and smoothly as the serpent must have undulated into Eden. He had said he had gone into her house last night. Had kept a key without telling her—an action that hardly inspired trust, no matter how he explained it. He claimed he had been shot by someone who was influenced by that thing in the house, but how could he know that? He could have been shot by anyone, for any reason.

She glanced again at the luminous dial of her watch and shivered. Six minutes. Four left. She wondered if she could stand it.

What if—? She hated to let her thoughts stray in that direction, but she had been raised to ask tough questions and face unpleasant ideas. What if that thing in the house—she could no longer deny its reality, not after what she had felt yesterday—what if that thing *were* to use Ian against her?

She had wondered before at the way he seemed to be bent on scaring her even more. Now this idea of someone shooting at him because of that *thing*…well, it could have been anyone, for any reason, couldn't it? Maybe it had only been an accident, someone like Orville out hunting birds or squirrels….

Oh, God, wasn't he ever going to come out of there? She glanced at her watch again and was appalled to realize that only one more minute had passed.

Maybe all this tension was getting to her, affecting her

objectivity and ability to judge things. She didn't want to believe such horrible things about Ian. And on the face of it, he had only looked after her, hadn't he? Offered her a place to sleep when she was scared to stay in her own bed, kept her company… Hell, he'd taken her in. How could she even suspect such awful things?

It's foolish to trust unquestioningly.

Well, of course, she thought, as the back of her neck prickled from a cold touch. She wasn't trusting him unquestioningly. She just didn't want to leap to wild conclusions.

Abomination.

She shivered again and glanced at her watch. Eight minutes. A gust of wind blew rain under the porch roof, and she felt the cold spray against her cheek and bare leg. Damn it, where was he?

His own family had thought him unnatural. He had admitted as much. Maybe they'd had a reason. A good reason. And maybe she ought to be a lot more cautious of him.

Suddenly, over the hammering rain and rumble of thunder, she heard rapid footsteps. Moments later Ian trotted up onto the porch. He was soaked to the skin, and his T-shirt and jeans were plastered to him. To every muscular inch of him. Something in Honor responded to all that masculinity, even as she warned herself to be more cautious of him.

"Did you find it?"

He shook his head.

Instinctively she turned toward her house again and tried to pick out the orange glow. It was no longer there. "Then what was it?"

"I don't have any idea." He shook his head sharply and sent water flying. "I went in there expecting just about anything, to tell you the truth. There was nothing. No fire, no spook, nothing.''

She faced him. ''I didn't imagine it.''

''Hell, no. I saw it, too.'' He reached for the screen door and pulled it open. The springs protested crankily. ''Come on. I could use some more coffee. There's sure no point standing out here getting soaked.''

But she stayed where she was. She heard the cupboard door slap shut as he put the fire extinguisher away. Then a clink as he set the coffee carafe back on the warming plate.

He was really going to go in, dry off and settle down with a cup of coffee as if nothing had happened!

Making an irritated sound, she turned sharply and stared toward her house again. Something had happened over there, and she couldn't stand not knowing what it was, couldn't stand the feeling that things were happening that were beyond her control. Couldn't stand now knowing how to deal with this threat, whatever it was.

Couldn't stand the idea that something had taken over her house. That some evil had moved in and forced her out.

Why had that light flickered up there? If it was some kind of ghostly manifestation, what had caused it, and why? She definitely had the feeling that it had wanted to draw attention. Hers? Or Ian's?

What had happened while Ian was over there? He'd seemed awfully quick to deny having found anything, especially when he had been there for nearly ten minutes. It was hard to believe the ghost had manifested some kind of light and he had felt nothing. Not when he claimed to be sensitive to it.

The screen door squeaked, and she swung around, startled. Ian poked his head out. His hair had been toweled, and he had changed into dry jeans and a black T-shirt.

"Why don't you come in?" he asked. "If that thing wants to get our attention again, I'm sure it'll manage."

"You're probaby right about that." After glancing over her shoulder one last time, she moved toward the door.

And wondered if she was stepping inside with the very thing she was trying to evade.

Her malaise lingered all through the evening. Sitting in the living room with Ian, she found herself unable to concentrate on the book in her lap, gruesome and frightening though it was. Her gaze kept straying his way as questions taunted her.

He hadn't told her the entire story of how he had come to be accused of witchcraft. Why not? He knew she wanted to know, and since she was aware of the charge, shouldn't he want to put the record straight? What if there was no way to put it straight? The thought sent another shiver coursing along her spine.

Then there was this business of how he could know that his assailant had been influenced by the entity in her house. How could he claim that, then say he had no idea what the thing might be up to, as he had earlier? It didn't add up.

Nothing added up. Nervous, she rose from her chair and paced to the window again, looking out at the stormy night. From behind her came the sound of a page being turned. One thing she envied him was his evident ability to ignore all unanswered questions and concentrate on finding an answer to the real problem—how to get rid of a ghost. At least, she thought he was concentrating on it.

Maybe he was just sitting there pretending to read?

He spoke unexpectedly, causing her to jump and turn

swiftly around. "I don't know how much help these books are going to be. So far, I've found ghosts who don't know they're dead, and ghosts who've left something undone and are hanging around worrying about it. Neither one seems right for your specter."

"Hey, it's not my ghost!"

He surprised her with a real smile, small though it was. "It's your house, and the ghost seems to be attached to it. That gives you proprietary rights."

"No thanks." Again that icy river ran down her spine. She didn't want to own a ghost, and she didn't want to make jokes about what she had sensed over there. She doubted any man could understand her sense of violation at finding her bathroom door open yesterday. At knowing some unseen watcher had invaded her privacy like that.

And then the feeling in her mind of something trying to get inside, of...what? There had been alien touches, of that she was sure. Those words that seemed to pop up out of nowhere sometimes felt as if they had come from outside. And sometimes she could almost have sworn someone else was inside her head, experiencing her thoughts.

She shuddered and kept quiet. Paranoia. Saying things like that out loud was enough to get you committed. But then she thought, no, it wouldn't get her committed. Not here. Not in the company of a man who had already announced that he thought that the thing was able to influence people.

"It keeps trying to get into my head," she said.

"I know. You told me yesterday, at the beach." His expression never changed as he stared at her and waited.

After a moment she decided to plunge ahead and watch his reaction. Certainly something ought to startle him. "Sometimes it feels as if it puts thoughts in my head.

Oh, man, does that sound weird!'' She was hugging herself again, feeling cold when she really wasn't. And feeling so, so alone. ''Other times it feels like somebody's in there just listening. Just...reading my mind.''

He looked away, and she figured he was embarrassed by her confession. She gave a little laugh. ''Classic schizophrenic delusion.''

That brought Ian instantly out of his chair. Before Honor even guessed what he was about to do, he had taken her into his arms and was holding her with surprising gentleness against his hard, broad chest. ''No,'' he said quietly. ''Don't even think it. These things that are happening are so far from normal that they seem crazy. But they aren't. I feel it, too.''

''You feel like someone's trying to get into your head?''

He hesitated. Too long, she thought, but just as her distrust of him began to revive, he bent his head and kissed her, driving everything else out of her mind.

For a moment, just a brief instant, she resented him for being able to do that to her. Then she gave herself up to the reckless heat he stirred so easily in her, gave herself up to the escape he offered. She'd lived long enough to know that it was highly unlikely she would ever meet another man who could do this to her. Wary as she was of him, she needed his heat. Needed the feelings he stirred in her. Needed to taste the passion she had never before felt.

This time it wasn't quite so explosive, wasn't quite so fast. He held her with such care, as if he were afraid she might shatter. His tongue slipped past her guard easily, but without force, promising soft seduction rather than fury. It was as if he were saying, For this little while, forget. For this little while, don't be afraid.

She let her head sag backward under his gentle assault and let go of every worry, every concern. His tongue stroked hers as if he were thirsty for her, as thirsty for her as she was for him, she admitted. He had cast some kind of spell over her, because despite all her doubts and all her fears, she wanted him past reason. Past caution. Past thought.

His hand slipped slowly upward, finding its way beneath her blouse. At the first touch of his warm fingertips on her soft skin, she shivered in pure pleasure. And arched like a cat being stroked. Ribbons of fire plunged downward to her aching core, and instinctively she pressed closer. Wanting more. Needing more. Forgetting every painful lesson she had ever learned.

Gently, gently, his fingertips stroked across her midriff, as if they enjoyed the warm satiny feel of her. No higher did they climb, though she wanted it and began to will him to move his hand, began to will him to find her breast with those tantalizing, tempting touches. Raising her arms, she looped them around his neck in invitation.

A muffled sound escaped him, rising from deep within. She felt the vibration in his chest, and the sound thrilled her. Then he shifted his hold, turning her a little to the side and bending her over his arm.

Her eyes fluttered open when his mouth left hers, and she found herself looking straight into his strange green eyes from a distance of only a couple of inches as he bent over her. They glittered almost like polished gems and held her gaze prisoner as his hand, slowly—oh, so slowly!—eased upward.

Honor caught her breath and kept perfectly still as anticipation filled her. No one had ever... Oh, she wanted his touch so badly! Suddenly unable to bear his stare any longer, she turned her face into his shoulder, buried her eyes and her nose in the soft warmth of his T-shirt and filled herself with the good scent of him.

He murmured something rough and sensual right into her ear, sending chills of pleasure racing along her nerves. Then his hand found her, at first with a gentle, almost comforting touch, as if he knew this was new and might scare her.

But it didn't scare her; it electrified her. It was better than her wildest imaginings, and unconsciously she dug her nails into his shoulders, encouraging him.

"Damn," he whispered unsteadily as he squeezed her breast. "Oh, damn."

A helpless moan escaped her. More. She wanted more. Much, much more.

Almost impatiently he found the clasp of her bra and uncovered her. Honor caught her breath, suddenly aware of him, of herself, of all her inadequacies, imagined or real.

But then he smiled at her, right into her eyes, with an expression of such warmth that she never would have imagined this man to be capable of it. "Beautiful," he said roughly. "Perfect."

She squeezed her eyes shut against an almost painful wave of emotion, then shivered with sheer pleasure as he closed his callused palm over her. Slowly, sending exquisite sparks to her core, he rubbed her hardening nipple with his thumb.

And then, utterly depriving her of breath, he bent and drew her nipple into his hot mouth. A low moan of pleasure escaped her, and he made a rough sound in answer as his lips and tongue taught her pleasure beyond her wildest imaginings.

He's seducing you.

The thought penetrated the pleasurable haze of desire

like a cold whisper. A minor irritant. Another tug of his mouth on her nipple banished it. Helpless against her own long-denied hungers, she lifted a hand and tunneled her fingers into his soft hair, tugging him closer.

He's manipulating you.

The cold chill of that thought came to her just as his mouth moved to her other breast and spread the growing conflagration. A gasp escaped her, and she arched upward, begging for more. Not caring any longer whether he was using her or pleasing her, not caring about anything except finding the answer to the mystery of her womanhood.

Suddenly she was lying on her back on the couch. Ian knelt beside her, cherishing her with his mouth and hands in ways she had only dreamed of before. She clutched him closer, prepared to surrender everything to the relentless need he was building in her.

Remember Jerry.

In a flash her arousal vanished. Suddenly she was filled with the crawling sense of shame that had been Jerry's legacy to her. The feeling of inadequacy, of downright repulsiveness, he had given her. The fear. The paralyzing fear of a man turning away from her in disgust. Oh, no, what was she doing?

"It's all right, it's all right," Ian murmured thickly. Lifting his head, he caught her face gently between his hands and looked down at her with eyes made heavy-lidded by passion. "Oh, baby, how could you think such a thing? You're not repulsive. He was the one who was wrong, not you."

Everything inside her stilled, and the chill that washed through her didn't spring from memories. Her heart seemed to stop beating, and the rush of blood in her ears became deafening. And as he stared down at her, his expression slowly changed, too. No longer did he look sleepy and aroused. He looked as he had when she first met him, remote and hard.

"Honor..." His voice trailed off, as if he had no words.

She didn't want words, anyway. It was too late for words. There was only one way to explain what had just happened, because she had never, ever told him about Jerry or the scars from her marriage. Never.

Slowly, afraid that if she moved too fast she might provoke him in some way, she sat up and pulled her blouse over her naked, aching breasts. "I...I think I'll go to bed," she said. She felt exposed, raw, invaded. Violated.

And scared.

How could you hide from a man who read minds?

If he could read her mind, then he could very definitely plant thoughts there, as well.

Huddled beneath the sheets on the narrow cot in Ian's guest room, she tried to organize her thoughts, tried to cope with her feelings, tried to figure out a rational course of action.

Not that anything about this incredible mess was rational. How could you react rationally to things that defied logic? How could you react rationally to things that were...paranormal? Supernatural?

What if there was no ghost in her house? What if all of that had been done by Ian? What if he was responsible for every feeling of being watched, every feeling that someone else was there?

If he was, he could have no innocent motive. He could only intend harm.

She had to get away. But how could she flee him when

he could read minds? He must know every thought in her head.

She shuddered and pulled the blanket to her chin. No, she decided, he didn't read every thought in her head. If he did, he wouldn't have time for any thoughts of his own. It must happen sporadically, perhaps unpredictably.

And that gave her a chance to escape.

But first she had to sleep. To lull him. With a skill perfected by years of nursing, she set her internal alarm clock for four in the morning. It was the time when men were at their lowest ebb, least likely to be alert. By then he would consider her asleep for the night. He wouldn't be expecting her to slip away.

The storm had blown over. The night beyond the closed windows was quiet, still, in the predawn darkness. Even the offshore breeze had died.

With her shoes in her hand, her keys and wallet in her pocket, Honor crept down the stairs, taking care to set her foot down at the very edge of each riser so as not to cause a telltale creaking. She had tried, on her way upstairs, to note which steps were noisy, but she was damned now if she could remember which ones they were.

As soon as she got out of here, she was going to get in her car and drive far enough away that she could feel safe from mental eavesdropping and invasive thoughts. Until she felt that her mind was free of violation. Then she was going to try to figure out what in the name of heaven she could do about this mess.

Twice on the stairway she froze, her heart in her throat, thinking she had heard something. Both times the darkness mocked her with perfect silence.

Adrenaline increased her need for oxygen, and she

fought to breathe silently when she desperately wanted to pant. Her own heartbeat grew nearly deafening in her ears. Step down. Again. Another step.

Finally she was at the foot of the stairs. A shaft of moonlight poked through the curtains covering the window on the front door and illuminated the hallway. Quietly she inched her way back to the kitchen, wanting to be as far as possible from the stairway, and thus as far as possible from Ian, when she opened that door. The lock was bound to make noise; the screen door certainly did.

Once in the kitchen, she paused, listening, and heard nothing. Finally some deep fear of the evil that had touched her caused her to take a butcher knife from the block on the counter. In case, she told herself. Just in case.

That's right. Protect yourself.

The kind of person who could try to make her believe in ghosts, who could wantonly invade the sanctity of her mind, probably wouldn't hesitate to hurt her.

Don't let him stop you. He intends you harm.

Yes, she thought, opening the door slowly. Obviously he intended her harm. That was very clear now.

Outside, the night held its breath. Only the irritating background chatter of insects disturbed the dark, motionless air. In the pale, watery moonlight, the Spanish moss turned into shadowy giants, looming figures made of living darkness.

Keep moving. You don't want him to find you. He'll hurt you.

She hesitated on the porch step, and something in her squeezed with a tight, dry grief as she thought of what she was losing. All unaware, in the last few days she had given part of her heart to the cold, lonely man she had sensed in him. Even while she had been uneasy about him and his motives, some part of her had yearned toward him. Some part of her had become his.

Now all that was hopeless. Just another source of pain. But maybe she was wrong about him....

No! He violated your mind. Invaded the most private place you have. Exposed your secrets.

Her hand tightened on the knife handle, and she stepped off the porch. She had to get away. Had to.

By the time she reached the end of the holly hedge that separated their yards, she was sure she was going to make it. Relief eased the rapid pace of her heart. Now all she had to do was get into her car and drive into town. She would be free, and she would be able to think, able to come up with some kind of plan.

"Going somewhere?"

Gasping, she whirled around and came face-to-face with Ian. The moonlight caught him from the side and made his face look like a carved mask, made his eyes glitter.

"Damn it, Honor," he said, "you could get hurt out here! I just got shot last night!"

He reached out toward her. She panicked.

Protect yourself! Stop him!

Instinctively, without conscious thought, she raised the ten-inch butcher knife in self-defense. "Stay away!" she gasped. "Stay back!"

But he shook his head and continued to reach for her. With an agonized cry, she lunged at him with the knife.

What came next happened in a blur, so fast that the next thing she knew she was being held hard against him, her hands firmly captured behind her back. The knife was gone. For a long moment she strained against his hold, trying to break away, panting almost wildly. He held her effortlessly, painlessly, moving with her struggles and preventing her escape.

And then realization washed through her in a tide so cold she felt chilled to the bone. She had tried to hurt him. Had tried to stab him. Oh, God, she was losing her mind!

"Shh…" he said, shifting his hold to a gentler one as he felt her sag in shock. "Easy, honey. Shh… It's okay."

"Oh, God," she whispered into the soft cotton of his T-shirt. "What was I doing?" His heart was racing as hard as hers, she realized. Adrenaline filled them both, unsatisfied by the abortive fight. She tipped her head back and looked up at him, tangled feelings pulling her in a dozen directions.

Passion, never far from fear, surged suddenly. She felt it as an almost physical change in the atmosphere, and then his mouth was on hers, his tongue plundering her hot depths as if treasure were hidden there. As hungry as he, wild with the need for something human and warm, she tugged her hands free of his grip and dug her fingers into the hard muscles of his upper arms. Heat. She needed his heat, needed his hunger, needed to find reality in his strength and his passion.

Suddenly he tore his mouth from hers. Another gasp escaped her as he effortlessly lifted her into his arms, reminding her of his vast strength, reminding her that he could probably snap her in two with his bare hands. But his hands, though hard as steel, didn't hurt her. They touched her flesh with exquisite care.

He carried her back to the house with long, impatient strides. His breathing never even deepened as he mounted the stairs with her in his arms. There wasn't a doubt in her mind as to what was coming now. The fires they had ignited between them had never been doused, and fear and anger had fueled the blaze with adrenaline.

Nor could the primitive cavewoman he had first awakened in her protest. Only a couple of days ago she had wanted to lie on the hard ground and take him into her without thought, without caring, without affection. Now, however much she distrusted him, she cared, and caring made the need so much more intense. So much more undeniable.

He set her down on his bed, an iron cot hardly wide enough for two. It didn't matter. Lying over her, his leg pinning hers, his arms holding her tight, he plundered her mouth with a kiss so hungry, so needful, that it forced everything else from her mind. She became woman at her most basic.

There was little tenderness, a lot of eagerness and some roughness. He stripped her clothes and his own away with equal impatience and molded her flesh with touches that just missed being painful. She didn't care. How could she care when this man made her feel so *wanted?* Oh, how she needed to be wanted!

His mouth closed on her nipple, sending spears of longing straight to her womb. His hand stroked the smooth skin of her hip, and then dived impatiently between her thighs, seeking her heat, her moisture, her life-giving core. Wildly she arched, an inarticulate cry escaping her. She was caught in a storm, with no desire to escape. Whatever he took was rightfully his.

Raising his head, he muttered guttural words of encouragement as his touch lifted her higher and higher. Too fast, too fast, she thought dizzily, and then stopped worrying as he took her closer and closer to the brink she dimly sensed was waiting.

"So sweet," he growled in her ear, sending another

river of excitement pouring through her. "Come on,
honey. That's the way."

When her hands clawed for purchase, tearing at the
sheets and him, he guided them up to the headboard and
wrapped them around the iron spindles. "Hang on," he
said roughly, and settled between her legs.

Gasping for air, she clung to the headboard and looked
up at him from eyes that were dark with arousal. He
loomed over her in the dark, so huge, so powerful, so
strong. She'd never thought, never dreamed, never imagined, that anything could be so overwhelming. Every cell
in her body was begging for him, for completion, for the
answer to the screaming ache he had awakened in her.

He touched her. Gently, finding that delicate knot of
nerves, he lifted her higher and higher until she hung
suspended in exquisite agony and nearly screamed his
name.

"Now!" he said hoarsely. Slipping an arm beneath her
hips, he lifted her to him and took her in one swift, deep
thrust.

If there was any pain, she was past noticing it. The
precipice was close, so close, and his every movement
drove her nearer the edge. Letting go of the headboard,
she grabbed his shoulders, digging her fingers into
smooth, muscled flesh, drawing him down, needing his
weight as she had never needed anything. Needing him.

"Let it happen," he growled in her ear. "Damn it,
Honor, let go!" and then, with a single long, deep, twisting thrust of his hips, he pushed her over the edge.

And moments later, his face contorting, he arched into
her and followed her over.

It occurred to her that she could curl up into a tight
little ball and pretend to be catatonic. She could deny all

knowledge of the woman who had just lain beneath this man and acted like a wild thing. She could fake a multiple personality and blame the last fifteen minutes on someone else.

It had been hot, swift, and very, very basic. Nothing romantic about it. Sighing, she turned onto her side and buried her face in his warm shoulder and decided not to deny anything. Her mind could never have conceived of such a thing, but now that it had happened, she admitted she wouldn't have missed it for anything.

He drew her closer, squeezing her. "You okay?" He sounded gruff.

"I'm fine."

"Good. I don't usually come on like gangbusters, but…"

She covered his mouth with her hand. "If you apologize, I'll get embarrassed. If you don't mind, I'd prefer to skip that part."

A low rumble of laughter rose in him, and then he astonished her by rolling to his feet and sweeping her up into his arms. The first time he had picked her up with such ease, she had been uncomfortably aware of how dangerous his strength could be. This time she felt confident that he wouldn't use it against her.

At least not right now.

In the bathroom, he set her on her feet and bent over to turn on the shower. Taking the opportunity to look at him in the light, she trailed her gaze from his broad shoulders to his narrow waist and hips…and saw blood. As a nurse, she knew about these things, knew that she certainly shouldn't be embarrassed by anything so perfectly normal and natural—but she was anyway. Somehow it was different when it was her blood. She closed her eyes.

"You should have told me," he murmured huskily. "I could have hurt you."

"I thought you could read my mind," she said weakly, grabbing his shoulders as he lifted her into the shower.

"Only when you broadcast at top volume. Never purposely. We'll talk about that later, I promise."

Slowly she opened her eyes and looked right up into his. At this moment they looked almost...tender. His hands moved over her carefully, soaping her with exquisite care. Her heartbeat grew heavy, and she drew a deep breath.

"Is that why you ran?" he asked. His hand slipped between her legs, washing her oh-so-carefully.

"Is this an interrogation technique?" She gasped and dug her fingers into his powerful shoulders. "When you knew how I felt—" She broke off abruptly, unable to continue. "I don't know exactly what happened. When you knew that, I thought...well, I thought you might be responsible for that feeling I get sometimes. Like someone is in my mind."

His eyes darkened, and he turned her suddenly so that the shower spray rinsed her.

"Come with me," he said harshly. "Let's get out of here. Let's go somewhere away from that...thing."

She hesitated, remembering her fear of him and the fact that he had looked into her mind.

"I promise I'll tell you everything," he said. "I swear. Let's just get out of here. Come with me."

Turning her head, she looked up at him, and some part of her realized that she was committed to riding this train to the end of the line, wherever that might be.

"All right," she said. And acknowledged that if Ian McLaren was the villain, she was going to curl up and die.

CHAPTER EIGHT

They drove past Fort Walton Beach and nearly to Pensacola before Ian pulled over at a motel and took a room. One room.

The sun was up, and the curtain was open. Ian stood in a puddle of golden light as Honor looked around and finally sank onto the edge of one of the double beds.

"I'll go rustle up some breakfast for us," he said. "And then we'll talk."

She nodded. "How far do you have to go to escape a ghost?"

"Damned if *I* know." He came over and squatted before her, taking one of her hands. "If you get any urges to run, or anything like that, fight them."

She stared at him, absorbing the meaning of his words. "You...you think that when I...that I..."

He squeezed her hand. "You don't strike me as the kind of person who reaches for a knife too readily. And you definitely don't strike me as the kind who would lunge at me with one. It would be more like you to try to evade me."

She nodded slowly. "I know. I can't believe I did that. I can't believe that was *me*. It was like being caught in a dream of some kind. A bad dream."

And maybe that was exactly what it had been. Alone again while Ian went out to find some food for them, she curled up tiredly on the bed and thought about what had happened. She still didn't entirely trust him, but she no longer felt as endangered as she had last night.

And that was the creepy thing, she thought. That *thing* had affected her mind. Had made her feel emotions that perhaps hadn't been entirely her own. In retrospect, now that she was free of the dark feelings that had haunted her last night, she found herself far more disturbed by the thought that the ghost might have planted thoughts in her head than by the idea that Ian had read her mind. It was far, far less distressing to have someone know what she was thinking than to have someone—or some*thing*—make her think things.

A sudden shiver passed through her, and she curled up into a tight ball. There was no doubt that she had been manipulated. No doubt. And the thought was horrifying. The question now was who, or what, had done it?

"Are you reading my mind right now?" Honor asked him while they ate eggs and biscuits and drank hot coffee at the small table by the window.

"No." Ian put down his plastic fork and leaned back in his chair, looking at her. "I never did it purposely. Never. But sometimes…it's as if you broadcast. Or shout. It's impossible not to hear."

"*Could* you do it on purpose?"

"Yes."

"Damn," she said, putting down her coffee. "I hate the way you do that."

"Do what?"

"Those single unvarnished syllables. No. Yes. Either way, it drives me crazy. Elaborate, why don't you?"

He almost smiled. She caught the glimmer of it in his eyes. "Yes, I can sometimes read minds on purpose. It's something I avoid doing, for obvious reasons."

She shook her head. "Not so obvious to me. And what do you mean, *sometimes* you can do it on purpose?"

He really didn't want to discuss this. It was apparent in the way he turned his head to one side and fiddled with a plastic spoon.

"It's a wild talent," he said finally, his voice rusty with suppressed feelings. "When I was little, it just happened sometimes. It wasn't something I did consciously, or that I was actually aware of doing. I think the first time I knew there was something different about me was when Mrs. Gilhooley killed her husband."

He tilted his head back and closed his eyes, and there was something about the way he did it that told Honor how difficult it was for him to remember these things.

"I *saw* it," he said after a moment. "I saw it in her mind, just as she saw it standing at the attic window. I saw it from inside her, saw her push the ladder away from the wall. She pushed hard. Really hard. It was no accident."

Her scalp prickled, but then, almost before she thought about how creepy that was, she thought how terrifying it must have been for a six-year-old boy to witness. Worse, to witness it from inside the head of the murderess.

"I remember...I remember how scared I was when no one believed me, because I knew Mrs. Gilhooley was furious with me and was planning to get even. I had nightmares about it for weeks."

Imagine, she thought, how terrifying it must have been for a six-year-old boy to know such things. To know that someone capable of murder wanted to get even with him.

"How," she asked, "did you ever stand it?"

He shrugged slightly. "You get through things because there's no alternative."

It was as if he had spread out his life before her and let her see the gray, bleak world in which he had lived. You get through things because there's no alternative.

She had felt like that at times. Occasionally there was no other way to feel. But she had the sense that this man had lived his *entire* life that way, and sadness tightened her throat.

"Was this, um, before or after the goat?" she asked, hoping he didn't notice how her voice had thickened.

"Before. The goat was the last straw, I guess. My memory of events isn't too clear, because I was so young, and because I wasn't part of a lot of it. I don't know what she did, what she said or why she was believed. All I know is, not too long after the goat, they tried exorcism on me."

Again she felt the impulse to reach out, but she stifled it. He kept evading her gaze, as if he were afraid she might read emotion in his eyes. He would hardly appreciate her touch, or her overt sympathy.

"Anyway," he continued after a moment, "after three or four days, the preacher decided the exorcism was a success. After that I screwed up a few more times. I just...sometimes I just knew what people were thinking. And I was young enough not to know how to conceal the knowledge. I slipped. Again and again. After a while, I was shunning other people as much as they were shunning me."

He rose from his chair and went to stand at the window, looking out at the sun-drenched day, as if the light could drive away the darkness inside him. He shoved his hands into the back pockets of his jeans, and for a long time he didn't speak.

"It was...like it was with you," he said eventually. "I slipped. I don't know if you can understand, but for me it's the same as hearing you say something. I react to it in the same way, and even if I'm on guard, sooner or later I say something or do something that reveals the fact that I know something the other person doesn't think I should. It's just about impossible in retrospect for me to distinguish knowledge gained one way from knowledge gained the other. So I slip. Or I get involved so deeply in what's happening that I slip. And nobody on earth likes to be around a telepath.''

He was silent for so long that Honor felt he was waiting for some kind of response from her. She wasn't sure what she felt about what he was telling her. He was a telepath. An exceptional one, to judge by what he was telling her. And, yes, it was unnerving to have someone read your mind. She wasn't sure she liked the idea at all.

But something else had also gotten into her mind. Something evil. And that was worse by far. Shuddering inwardly, she shook away the memory of last night and tried to focus on Ian. He needed something from her right now, and she wasn't sure what it was. Or even if she could give it.

Finally he spoke again, his voice low, tense. ''The business about the witchcraft, well—'' He broke off abruptly and shook his head. Honor couldn't see his face, but she didn't need to. The difficulty of this for him was apparent in his tension, in his voice.

''I was seventeen,'' he said flatly. ''Mrs. Gilhooley had two daughters. Annie—Orville's mother—and Maggie. Maggie was fifteen. She…got herself pregnant by…um…by her stepfather, Bill Gilhooley.''

''Mrs. Gilhooley remarried?''

''Yes. I guess I forgot to tell you that. She married Bill Gilhooley about eight months after she buried her first husband. Anyhow, Maggie claimed I was the kid's father. Said I'd, uh, witched her and had my way with her.''

''Oh, my God!'' Honor scarcely breathed the words,

horrified and aching for him. Such terrible, terrible things to have lived through. "Nobody believed that, surely!"

He gave a snort, but he didn't look at her. "Oh, yeah, lots of people believed it, even when it was proved that I was somewhere else the night she claimed all this happened. The cops investigated, but they didn't bring any charges, because there wasn't any evidence. Some folks believe that was witchcraft, too. Then…then one night Maggie called the cops and said she'd taken poison, and that she didn't want to die with a guilty conscience. Said I hadn't touched her. She died and…everybody believed I'd done that, too.

"So I left. Joined the army and left."

And left the human race, too, Honor thought, staring at his unyielding back. How awful. How unspeakable. No longer restraining the impulse, she rose and went to him, touching him gently on the arm, aware that he might reject her touch.

But he turned suddenly and faced her, and there were no secrets left. There, in the anguish stamped on his face, in the redness of eyes that could not weep, she saw just what it had cost him to tell her. Just how deep his scars were.

"Oh, Ian," she whispered on a broken breath. Stepping toward him, she wrapped her arms around his waist and held him close.

At first he remained rigid and unyielding, as if he were resisting her concern with all his might. As if he had forgotten how to open himself in even this small way. But then, with jerky reluctance, he wound his arms around her and squeezed her closer.

For a long time neither of them spoke or moved. Honor absorbed all that he had told her and suspected that he was reconstructing the inner walls behind which he had

probably entombed all those memories. How awful, she
thought. It was a miracle he had survived such a childhood.

"Come on," he said after a while, his voice calm and
expressionless once more. "You haven't finished your
breakfast, and you need to get some sleep before we go
back."

She tilted her head and looked up at him. "What are
we going to do?" As soon as she spoke the question, she
wished she hadn't because there didn't seem to be any
answer.

He didn't answer, just shook his head. "Eat," he said.
"Then sleep. When we've had some rest, we'll brain-
storm."

Honor had fallen asleep almost as soon as her head
touched the pillow. Ian, cursed with insomnia, lay wide
awake in the next bed, his hands clasped behind his head.

Years ago he had done his best to bury his abominable
talent, and until a few days ago he had succeeded, rela-
tively speaking. It was possible for any skill to atrophy
through lack of use. His telepathy might have been born
of genetics, but it was also a skill that could atrophy.

And it had. But not nearly as much as he had thought,
and he was recovering it more quickly than he would
have dreamed possible. He hadn't tried to read Honor's
mind—he'd been telling the absolute truth about that—
but it was getting so he was receiving flashes from her
all the time. Never before in his life had that happened
with anyone to this extent. It made him uneasy.

Even now, the flashes of her dreams were dancing
around the edges of his mind. Just random snatches that
told him she was having a mild nightmare about some
inchoate threat. If she started to get really frightened, he

would wake her...or would that be an invasion of her privacy?

The thought had troubled him ever since he'd grown old enough to be concerned with such things. If he couldn't help doing it, how could it be an invasion? But perhaps he should leave the illusion of privacy intact, for the sake of the person he was eavesdropping on?

He didn't know, and he wasn't sure he even cared anymore. In his adult life, he'd had a couple of intimate relationships. Each time he had carefully chosen a woman in uniform, one who would understand the demands of his job, the fact that he might leave without warning and offer no explanations when he returned. Someone with whom the army provided enough impersonal topics of conversation that he could avoid getting too intimate, too involved.

And each time, eventually, he had slipped in a way they could not ignore. Each time he had seen horror in their eyes. Uneasiness. Condemnation. He was an abomination.

Mrs. Gilhooley had first called him that, and the word had been echoed by many in his childhood. Away from the atmosphere of his parents' church, the epithet had changed, but not its meaning. *Weird* was the word he'd heard most often. *Creepy* was another one.

Lifting his head a little, he looked over at Honor. She was still dreaming, and a little more anxious now. He wondered how long it would be before she turned from him in horror again. She had last night. He'd known the instant when she realized that he had looked into her mind. He'd felt her horror and fear.

That seemed to have faded considerably since their lovemaking, but he never for an instant doubted it would

return. He'd grown up hearing that he was some kind of
unnatural genetic accident. A mutation. An abomination.

And nothing in his life since had convinced him that
he wasn't.

Honor woke slowly, feeling more comfortable than she
had in a long time. It was as if she had reached some
kind of resolution in her sleep, as if some internal equilibrium had finally been established. Or maybe, she
thought drowsily, it was just a protective reaction to all
the stress of the past few days. At the moment, she didn't
care. It was enough that, for right now, the tension had
let go.

For now the looming black shadow was gone.

She opened her eyes and looked straight into Ian's cat-
green ones. He was on the next bed, just three feet away,
but suddenly Honor felt he wasn't close enough. She
wanted him here, beside her. Touching her. Exploring
some of the incredible possibilities he had opened up for
her last night, in those all-too-brief moments when they
had lost control together. It was as if some fire in her had
been ignited last night and only slightly damped down
by fulfillment. As if a craving had been planted in her, a
craving that could never quite be satisfied.

He saw it. Read it. Perceived the yearning, however it
was that he did such things. And this time she didn't
mind. There was only a momentary uneasiness that
quickly fled.

"Yeah," he said, and sat up. Crossing his arms before
him, he tugged his olive T-shirt over his head and bared
his chest. "I hear you," he said roughly. "I feel you.
I've never been so in tune with anybody in my life. I
don't know if this is good or bad, but I'm through pre-

tending it isn't happening. This is the way I am, lady. If you can't handle it, let's find out now.''

He stood and unbuttoned his jeans, never turning away, just watching her steadily, waiting for some objection. She didn't object. Instead, she held her breath as expectancy grew heavy at her core. He shoved his jeans and briefs down together and kicked them aside. Then he stood there and looked down at her, waiting. He was completely exposed to her, completely vulnerable to whatever she might say or do to him. He was making himself as vulnerable to her as she felt to him. As vulnerable as he could make himself. Her throat tightened at the understanding.

Whatever her mind might be broadcasting to him, she realized, he was going to wait for her to say yes or no. He understood that her desire for him might not be something she wanted to acknowledge or give in to. He was granting her the right to decide, regardless of what she was thinking and feeling. And that eased her discomfort a little more.

And, oh, he was magnificent! Honed to a peak of physical perfection in every respect. And so perfectly male. Slowly she lifted her arms and reached for him.

He sank down beside her on the bed and wrapped her in his arms, drawing her flush against him. The layers of her clothing were only a small impediment as she felt the strength of sinew and muscle against her.

''I can hear you,'' he murmured roughly, touching her tousled hair. ''I can feel what you want. Do you want me to pay attention? Or do you want me to try to ignore it?''

Her breath caught a little, and she gave a moment's serious thought to the degree of intimacy he was talking about. Making up her mind proved surprisingly easy.

"Listen," she said. "You're right. If I can't handle it, let's find out now."

He nodded and closed his eyes. For a moment her heart stopped beating as she realized he was listening to what was going on inside her, to her scattered thoughts and powerful yearnings. To every barely formed desire.

And then he caught her chin gently in his hand and took her mouth in a breath-stealing, soul-searing kiss. His tongue plunged deeply, roughly, coaxing hers into erotic play. And, as always, just his kiss was enough to ignite her smoldering hunger.

He broke away from her mouth long enough to tug away her shirt and shorts, just long enough to pull away her bra and panties. Then he rolled half over her, pinning her to the bed with a thigh between her legs, and his chest against her aching breasts.

And then he caught her face between his hands and stole her breath by the simple act of whispering her name as if it were torn from the depths of his being.

"Honor…"

Her eyes fluttered open, and she gazed into the depths of his. And saw into his soul. Saw loneliness. Terrible, terrible loneliness. And a yearning. White heat. Hunger.

"Touch me," he whispered. "I need…"

She understood, though she didn't know how. Even as her own hungers made her restless, she felt his needs in her heart. Touch him. He hadn't been touched in so long, hadn't allowed himself even that very human contact. He had held himself aloof, and now he was asking her to shatter his isolation. She spared one last hope that this wouldn't prove to be the biggest mistake of both their lives.

Then she gave herself up to the blossoming heat and touched him. Her hands stroked down his shoulders to the small of his back, enjoying the incredible smoothness of his warm skin, thrilling to the way he shuddered at her touch. Then her hands traveled lower, finding his muscular buttocks and instinctively digging her fingers in.

Finally, driven by a restless hunger and a need to possess this man in whatever way he would permit, she shoved gently, urging him onto his back. Without a murmur, he rolled over, offering himself to her eyes and hands.

There was something incredibly seductive about holding a man like this captive to her hands, her whims. Something even more seductive about the feel of steely muscles bunching beneath her palms as she swept them over him. Something thrilling about the restless, helpless movements he made in response to her touch and his rising heat.

Slipping her hand downward, she skipped over his silky length to tender, delicate, private places. When she cupped him, he shuddered and went perfectly still, drawn taut as a bowstring. The man who seldom suffered another to touch him now permitted her to trespass. Needing her touch more than he needed safety. Trusting her to do no harm.

The weight of him filled her palm, a promise of life, strength and virility. His submission to her touches was the most erotic experience of her life, and her own body responded with a flash of heat and dampness. Licking her lips, breathing raggedly, she ran her fingers teasingly up his length.

He groaned and was suddenly galvanized. Reaching for her, he turned her onto her back, lying over her and driving his tongue into her mouth again. He found her breast with his hand, kneading fire into her every cell.

Rivers of burning lava poured through her, causing her to arch upward against him and clamp her thighs around his. She heard herself moan his name, heard him groan in response. She needed more. More. Much more.

And he knew it. Dimly she was aware that his hands and mouth moved to answer her every wish, her every ache, her every desire, no matter how fleeting or unformed. From her mind he took the least of her impulses and wove them into an erotic fantasy around her, at once satisfying her and deepening her need.

And somehow, as he answered her every whim, she felt the longing in him, the need to be cherished in return. His life had been so lonely, so empty, and for so long he had been on the outside, held at a distance by hatred and fear.

Tears prickled in her eyes even as her body arched upward in passion and begged him to finish it. Even as she reached for the sunburst within, she reached out to wrap him in the first human warmth he had known since childhood. With arms and legs she surrounded him and tried to shelter him, with heart and soul she yearned to give him ease.

And he felt it. A great shudder tore through him, and he opened his eyes, hiding nothing from her, not the shimmer of unshed tears, not the agonizing need for acceptance. He kept them open as he settled between her legs and slowly drove his flesh into her, claiming her body with his.

And when he was buried deeply in her warmth, he cradled her face gently in his hands and gave her a tender, almost reverent kiss. Then, with slow, deep, satisfying thrusts of his hips, he carried them both up and over.

Afterward she wondered how she could ever have been so naive as to think anything would change. Ian stayed beside her, holding her while the cool air dried their damp skin, but he had withdrawn in another way. He had let her see his vulnerability, had let her glimpse the lonely man who yearned to belong to someone, and then he had pulled back inside himself, as if he really didn't care at all.

Unconsciously sighing, she tunneled her fingers through the soft, dark hair on his chest and savored the warm skin beneath. Maybe, she thought, he was feeling uncertain because he had revealed so much and wasn't sure how she would react. Whether she might use it in some way. He had said, after all, that he couldn't read every thought in her head. Maybe he had no idea what she was thinking right now.

And maybe she owed him some of the same honesty he had given her. He had revealed his past at her insistence, had exposed painful wounds to her. Didn't she owe him the same trust in return? A secret for a secret, so that no one felt at a disadvantage?

"Ian?"

"Mmm?" The sound was a deep rumble in his chest. She loved the way his low voice vibrated inside him. It was one of the many very masculine things about him, things that affected her in ways that were hard to explain, but that drew her to him.

"Are you reading my thoughts right now?"

"No."

No. That damn word again. "Not at all?"

"Not a thing. It's not constant, not infallible, and it sure as hell isn't reliable. You're a closed book right now. Completely private."

And maybe that was part of his problem, she thought. She was closed to him, and he couldn't tell what she thought and felt about what had just happened. About him.

Tilting her head back, she looked up at him. "We're going to need to discuss that thing in my house before we go back."

He nodded, looking watchful. That wariness hurt her a little, after all that had just happened between them, but she understood it now that she knew about his past. And the best way to deal with that was to tell him something equally private about herself and her past. To offer him her emotional vulnerability.

"Do—do you remember last night?" she asked, her mouth going dry and her voice growing a little unsteady. God, this was hard! "When…I was afraid I was repulsive, and you said I wasn't?"

"Yes."

She couldn't force herself to look at him. "Do you know why I felt that way? Or did you just pick up on the feeling?"

"Just the feeling." He shifted his hold on her, and then astonished her by tucking her closer and stroking her back soothingly. "Who made you feel that way? Tell me what happened."

"I got married when I was eighteen." Her heart was beating a nervous, rapid tattoo, and she was sure he must be able to hear it. "My…Jerry was a really nice guy, and I think he was just seriously confused. I honestly don't think he meant to hurt me. It's just that…well, he was homosexual. And…he couldn't have sex with me. So I—" Her voice broke, and she couldn't continue.

"Got to feeling inadequate and repulsive," he finished for her. "Got to feeling maybe you were responsible for his problem."

Slowly she lifted her gaze to his face, and she was

astonished by the incredible amount of understanding there.

"It's okay," he said. "You're not repulsive. You've been driving me out of my mind since I first laid eyes on you. And now that I've got you right where I want you, I think I'll take advantage of you one more time."

The look in his eyes right then seemed to reach deep inside her and untie some old, aching knot. Free of its constriction, she felt as if she could draw her first unfettered breath in years.

They showered, dressed and went looking for a restaurant for dinner. They'd spent the entire afternoon making love, talking little, but as evening approached, they both knew they were going to have to face the horror lurking at home. The interlude was over.

And with the return of reality came the return of Honor's uneasiness. What did she really know about this man, except that he had had an unfortunate childhood, and that he had taken her to the moon, proving that all those romantic old songs weren't lies?

But he had distanced himself again, almost as if his earlier exposure of himself and his feelings had left him raw and unable to bear any closeness. What if he had only used her? What if she had just been convenient?

The restaurant he selected served everything from steak to seafood casserole. When they had ordered, he turned his strange green eyes on her. "We have to talk about what we're going to do. If it could manipulate someone into shooting at me, and you into trying to stab me, there's no telling what else it can do."

Just like that, the last lingering glow from the afternoon was gone. Honor leaned forward, resting her forearms on the table, and absently drew a pattern on the

Formica with her fingertip. "I don't see what we *can* do, to tell you the truth. You didn't find anything useful in those books, did you?"

"Actually, I think I did, indirectly. After reading about all those lost ladies and murder victims and all the rest of it, it occurred to me that most of them had one thing in common—unfinished business. If we can figure out what your ghost—"

"It's not my ghost," Honor told him, suppressing an unhappy shudder. "God, I wish you wouldn't keep saying that. It makes me feel...cold. Like someone walked on my grave."

"Okay." He gave a little shrug. "*The* ghost. We need to figure out what's holding the ghost here."

"Of course!" Honor couldn't keep the sarcasm out of her voice. "Just walk up and ask it, right? I'm sure it'll sit down with us and explain..." Her voice trailed off as understanding struck. "No," she said hoarsely. "You can't. I won't let you. That thing could hurt you. It could get into your mind and do terrible things. Ian, no!"

He reached across the table and captured one of her hands with his. "What's the alternative?" he demanded quietly. "You can't live in that house. You can't afford to live anywhere else, and even if you stay with me, you're obviously at risk, to judge by what happened last night."

She wanted to look away from his eerie, haunting gaze, but she couldn't. A small shiver passed through her, and she felt her fingers return his clasp. As if she trusted him, even though right now, to be truthful, she wasn't sure she did.

"Honor, we've got to get rid of that thing."

She nodded. "I know." There didn't seem to be any alternative. "But, Ian, that...that thing has twice caused someone to try to hurt you. What makes you think you can just open your mind to it and come away unscathed? What if it provokes *you* into hurting someone? What if it turns *you* into a criminal? People could get hurt, and you could wind up in prison for the rest of your life!''

Something in his gaze grew chilly and remote. He had gone away to some place so deep inside himself that she was almost sure he had forgotten where they were. Had forgotten he was not alone. And then, after a long moment, his green eyes focused on her, and he spoke, his voice low, intense.

''No one can control me,'' he said levelly. ''It's been tried by the masters. I don't break, and I don't kneel.''

Hell looked out of his eyes then, just a glimpse of the anguish of the damned, before he turned away and leaned back to allow the waiter to serve them.

When the waiter left, Ian faced her again and held her gaze unwaveringly. ''Trust me,'' he said quietly. ''In this, just trust me.''

Famous last words, she thought grimly, and looked down at her plate of steamed oysters. ''I don't know if I can,'' she said finally. ''I honestly don't know if I can.''

Another storm was gathering as they drove east toward home. Honor didn't remember this much rain from her years here as a child, and she commented on it.

''Late afternoon thunderstorms frequently blow up over the Gulf and move inland at this time of year,'' he answered. ''It'll get better.''

Leaning her cheek against the headrest, she watched him drive and thought about all that had occurred between them in the past twenty-four hours. Part of her desperately wished she could savor the change in her, practice her wiles and give herself up to the wonder of having Ian McLaren for a lover. Another part of her, though, whispered warnings and cautions, reminding her that she certainly ought to know by now that very little was what it appeared to be.

"When do you go back to work?" he asked.

"Thursday morning." Two days.

"That'll give us time to move whatever else you might need over to my place. In addition to what you brought yesterday."

She stiffened a little, not sure what he meant and how she should react. He turned and looked at her from those incredible eyes of his, and a faint smile curved one corner of his mouth. She realized with a twinge of discomfort that he was hearing her thoughts again.

"It's okay," he said. "As much or as little as you want, Honor. I swear. I just don't want you trying to live in that house until we take care of this thing."

"And what if we can't? Take care of it, I mean."

"Then we'll think of something else." His jaw squared as he stared down the long, winding ribbon of wet pavement that stretched before them. "We'll think of something else."

Five more wet miles passed before he spoke again, startling her. "I knew your father."

She twisted on the seat and looked at him. "I wondered." Both men had been Rangers, after all.

"I was First Battalion, out of Fort Stewart." Georgia.

"He was Second Battalion." Fort Lewis, Washington.

"I know. But years ago...years ago he saved my life. He led a team in to rescue me and a couple of my men after we were...captured. Maybe he wasn't a perfect dad to you, but he sure was one hell of a soldier."

"It was his whole life," she said. "His *whole* life."

"No room for you?"

"He made some after Mom died. I'll give him that.

He ran me like one of his troops, though. Why did you bring this up?''

"Because I owe your old man. I want you to know that, if you start to get scared of me again. I owe him. And if the only way I can pay him back is to look after you, I will.''

"Why didn't you tell me this before? Didn't you think I needed to know?'' She didn't know whether to be annoyed or frustrated with him.

"I wanted…'' He hesitated, then forced the words out with evident effort. "I just wanted you to accept me for what I am. Since that's out of the question…'' He shrugged and let the words trail away, appearing not to care one way or the other.

Honor knew better. *Out of the question?* Suddenly she wasn't wondering what she should feel. She knew; she was mad. "Who said it's out of the question? And if you think I'm going to trust you just because you say you owe my father—'' She broke off sharply, spluttering.

And suddenly, catching her utterly by surprise, sorrow pierced her with a sharp ache. He had just wanted her to accept him for what he was. Without trading on old relationships or old obligations. Just him, Ian McLaren, what she knew of him. Was that so awful? Was that too much?

"I don't want your pity,'' he said harshly.

He had picked up on her feelings again, but he had read them wrong. "Believe me, I'm not feeling any pity. You're not in the least pitiable. And if you're going to read my mind, at least do it right.''

His head jerked a little, as if she had caught him by surprise. Then he asked, "It doesn't bother you?''

"It's bothering me a lot less than I thought it would,'' she admitted. "Maybe because I don't have any real secrets. Certainly none after…'' She felt herself coloring and let her words trail away.

He laughed softly and reached out, snagging her hand and holding it on his thigh. ''I loved it,'' he said. ''Believe me, I loved it.''

''But you must have—'' Embarrassment smothered the words. She couldn't really be asking this, could she?

''Never,'' he said gruffly. ''Never before. I never let myself. I never dared to.''

''I wish…I wish I could read your mind.''

''I wish you could, too. And sometimes I think you almost do.''

She thought back over the day and realized that sometimes she felt she could tell what he was thinking, what he was feeling.

''There have been a couple of times,'' he continued, ''when I've been almost positive you're a latent telepath. When we first met. And today. Most definitely today. You read me like an open book.''

''Not an open book. You'll never be that.'' Another mile passed, then another, and she realized they were almost home. And then she remembered something he had said, something she had wanted to ask him about.

''Ian?''

''Hmm?''

''What did you mean, you were captured by a demon?''

Suddenly he slammed on the brakes, turning off the two-lane highway onto a muddy dirt road so sharply that the wheels skidded briefly. He brought them to an abrupt, rattling halt. For a long moment there was no sound save the quiet rumble of the engine, the whoosh of the air conditioner and the patter of rain on the hood.

''God, Honor,'' he said finally. Just that.

She wondered if she should apologize for bringing up the subject, but that didn't seem right, since he had told her about it when they'd been nearly strangers. Maybe, she thought, maybe she had just caught him unawares by dredging up deeply buried memories. Painful memories.

Spurred by her concern, she released her seat belt and slid closer to him, ignoring the stick shift. He let go of the steering wheel immediately and wrapped her in his powerful arms. A shudder ripped through him as he released a long, ragged breath.

"Sorry," he said gruffly.

"No, I'm sorry. I shouldn't have brought it up."

She felt him shake his head, and his arms tightened. "I just...don't like to think about it. If it catches me off guard, like just now, I...react kind of strongly."

Pressed against his shoulder, she inhaled his rich, musky scent and wondered why she had never before realized how good another person could smell. How comforting that aroma could be. But there were more important things to think about now. She tipped her head back and tried to see him clearly. "You've buried a lot of things, haven't you?"

"A few."

Well, she understood that, she guessed. Imagine her having forgotten being locked in that closet when she was so little. Imagine having forgotten that kind of terror. Imagine terror so great that you *had* to forget it.

Ian unleashed another sigh, cupped the back of her head in his hand and gave her a soft, quick kiss. "It was that time I mentioned before, the time your father led the rescue team. I took a patrol on a reconnaissance into...never mind. We were taken prisoner and... tortured. Only three of us were still alive when your father arrived."

Honor held him as close as she could and waited, willing him to feel how much she cared.

"The worst...the worst of it," he said raggedly, "the worst was knowing what that guy was thinking. Knowing how much...pleasure he got out of the screams. He was—he was getting off on it."

Something inside Honor grew silent and still, grew cold and empty as shock filled her. As a helpless anger was planted in the soil of her caring. As she wondered how anybody could survive such a thing. Turning into him, she held him as fiercely as she could, trying to tell him what words never could.

"I didn't scream," he said, in an oddly calm voice. "Not once."

It had been his victory. His only victory in that hell. Honor stifled a sob and blinked back tears as she came to understand. He didn't break. He didn't kneel. He endured.

And now, for her sake, he was going to face the evil and hatred in her house.

CHAPTER NINE

Her house seemed to brood in the shadows beneath the trees. Honor watched it draw closer as they drove slowly down the road. And when they pulled into Ian's driveway, an overpowering sense of impending doom seemed to fall over her.

"Let's get out of here."

He turned to look at her as he switched off the ignition. "I feel it, too," he said. He looked over at her house.

"It's...worse." Far worse, if she was feeling it over here. It hadn't rained here yet, she noted vaguely. The ground looked dry.

"I'll take you to a motel," Ian said decisively, reaching for the ignition key. "It's...angry. I don't want you around here."

Honor reached out and stopped him. She felt his muscles tense beneath her fingers, felt how he was still reluctant to be touched. Even by her. It hurt. "Are you coming with me? Or are you coming back to face it alone?"

He didn't answer, which was an answer in itself. "Forget it." She shoved open the door of his Jeep and climbed out.

Ian jumped out his side and came after her. "What the hell are you doing?" he demanded.

"I'm not leaving you to face this alone." She turned, setting her hands on her hips and glaring up at him. "I'm not sure I trust you, sometimes I don't even think I like you, but I'll be *damned* if I'll let you face this alone!"

He scowled at her. It was a look that had terrified dangerous men. She never flinched. "Damn it, Honor! There's not a damn thing you can do that I can't do just as well. Or better."

"Yes, there is! I can make sure you're not alone!" She started to turn away, then paused and looked up at him again. When she spoke, her voice wobbled, betraying things she hadn't said. Things she wouldn't say, because she didn't yet trust him enough. "You've been alone long enough."

He swore. Violently, viciously, savagely, he swore. Then he snatched her up in his arms, lifting her feet right off the ground and holding her as close as he could without hurting her.

She hated it when he did that, hated the way it made her feel small and helpless against his larger size, but before she could say something nasty, his hold on her gentled, grew tender and cherishing. And instead of yelling at him, she ached in response, her chest growing heavy with feeling, her eyes prickling with unshed tears. She wrapped her legs around his hips, pressed her face to his warm neck and hugged him back.

"Okay," he said. "Okay."

Thunder growled threateningly overhead, and rain started to fall warningly. Holding her close, he carried her into the house with him.

In the kitchen, he set her on the counter, but stayed where he was between her legs, bringing her mouth to his for a kiss filled with tender savagery.

"God, what you do to me, woman," he said huskily. "You've got my head as scrambled as my hormones. Honor, honey, I couldn't…handle it if something happened to you."

"I couldn't handle it if something happened to you,"

she answered back. "Looks like you're stuck with me, McLaren."

He was pressed snugly to her womanhood, and she felt his answering hardness against her. All around them shadows were gathering in the air, looming with threat, making it impossible to truly forget what they were facing. That thing was angry. Furious. And neither of them could guess what it might be capable of.

Which just added desperation to the explosive passion between them. Ian rocked his hips against her, slowly, deeply. Groaning, Honor closed her eyes and threw her head back in an ancient surrender, in a timeless invitation. Wrapping her legs around his thighs, she held him to her and pulled him closer.

He lifted his head and looked down at her, just as lightning flashed outside. "You sounded an awful lot like your father just now." His voice was rough, like grating gravel, and his hips ground into hers once more.

She gasped, never opening her eyes, and dug her nails into his powerful shoulders. She had to force the words out. "He did most of my raising." He'd called her his little soldier and demanded she behave like one. Bravely. Honorably.

"It shows." His hands were at her waist, holding her to him, but now they slid slowly upward, taking her T-shirt with them. All of a sudden she felt the touch of cool air on her nipples. They puckered eagerly, just in time to receive the heated caress of his callused hands. Lightning zapped through her, rivaling the storm outside.

His next words came out roughly, brokenly. "I haven't told you…how pretty…pretty breasts…"

She hardly heard him. She was tugging his T-shirt up, needing his skin beneath her hands as desperately as she had ever needed anything. She clawed the shirt up to his

shoulders, and then his hands came to her aid, yanking
the cotton over his head. Then he bent, arching his lower
body away from her so that he could suck her tender,
yearning nipples to ecstasy.

She left marks on his back; she was sure of it. Never
had she felt so desperate, so needy, so violently hungry.
Her nails raked him as she writhed, trying to bring his
hips back to hers to answer the throbbing ache he was
feeding with his mouth at her breast.

She felt the button on her shorts pop, heard the rip of
the zipper. Then his hand was inside, gripping her buttocks as he lifted her and yanked away the shorts and her
panties. Then he was back, pressed to her, denim rough
against her tenderest skin. She loved it.

"Here," he muttered. "Here." He drew her mouth to
his own nipple, and she took the invitation with wild
delight, tonguing him, nipping him, sucking him, listening to his deep groans, then groaning herself as his fingers found her. Unerringly he found the delicate nub
where she was most sensitive. She was so slick and so
wet already that his fingers filled her easily, and she
groaned again as he worked his magic. It was almost
enough. Almost.

But not quite. Blindly she reached for the button of his
jeans. And suddenly everything grew still.

Something in her quieted. Something in him quieted.
They both looked down. He withdrew his hand from her
and stepped back, just a little. Slowly she released the
button. Slowly she drew the zipper down.

And released him.

He was hard, thick, ready. When she curled her hand
around him, he groaned and shook from head to toe, as
if barely able to restrain himself. "Yes," he whispered.
"Yes..."

Guided by the same primitive instincts that always drew her to this man, she lifted her heels to the counter, opening herself as never before, opening herself as she had never imagined doing. Then, slowly, watching every incredible moment, she drew him to her and watched him take her. When he was buried deeply, she lifted her blue eyes to his face and found that he was watching her. Watching them. And the look in his eyes…

He whispered something awed. Something reverent. And she knew she would never be the same again.

"Now," he whispered, and kissed her. His tongue plunged into her mouth in a rhythm that matched the lunging of his hips, making her feel totally and completely possessed. Totally and completely wanted. The ache grew, the power between them thrumming almost audibly.

And then everything inside her exploded in a cataclysm of pleasure so intense that it hurled her beyond thought.

He held her close for a long time, while their breathing slowed, and their bodies cooled and dried. Little by little she became aware that her T-shirt was bunched up under her arms. That his jeans were tangled around his legs. The realization brought a silly smile to her lips, and as she rubbed her cheek against his chest, she wondered if it would always be this way between them—quick, hot, hard.

"God, I hope so," Ian murmured roughly.

Not minding at all that he was reading her thoughts again, she tilted her head back and smiled. "Yeah," she whispered. "Yeah."

And then they both felt it, something chilling, like a

soundless howl of rage. Ian's head jerked, and he seemed
to be listening intently.

"What is it?" Honor asked after a moment. "Ian?"

He shook his head. "If we don't do something, *it's*
going to. We'd better get in gear, honey."

Honor nodded. She suddenly felt cold. So cold, as if
an icy wind had blown out of eternity.

"Did you bring some jeans over? I'd feel better if you
wore something that would give you some protection
against...scrapes and things. And better shoes. Sandals
aren't very stable if you have to run."

If she had to run? What was he expecting to happen?
Upstairs, she changed quickly, feeling more nervous than
she had in a long time. Her hands shook, fumbling with
the buttons on her long-sleeved shirt, having trouble tying
her jogging shoes.

Downstairs, she found Ian waiting, dressed in camouflage and combat boots. On his hip he wore his sheathed
survival knife. He looked ready for anything.

But how did you prepare for a ghost?

"All I'm going to try to do," he said, "is figure out
what it's up to. What it wants. I want you to stand back
and keep watch for...anyone else, I guess. If the entity
calls the person who shot at me, we could be in big trouble. So you keep watch and yell if you see anyone. *Anyone.*"

She hadn't thought of that. Her heart slammed in her
chest, and she bit her lip. "Okay." And he had been
planning to do this alone, while she huddled safely in a
motel? She suddenly scowled up at him and poked him
in the chest with her finger. "Damn you, Ian! You need
a reality check! You're not indestructible! How could you
ever have suggested doing this without help? You would
be completely exposed! Vulnerable!"

He shook his head. "No."

No. She wanted to scream in frustration. He must have picked up on it, because he suddenly bent and kissed her lightly on the mouth.

"If you weren't with me, I'd just keep part of my attention focused outward. I would have stayed alert. With you there, I'll be able to concentrate harder on finding out what's going on."

"Thank you," she said with dignity.

"For what?"

"For explaining."

He amazed her then with a crooked smile that was astonishing under the circumstances, a smile that forced itself past the tension that gripped them both. "I could feel you were ready to pop your cork."

A soft, rueful laugh escaped her. "Yeah. My temper tends to get short when I'm scared."

"Everyone's does." He turned toward the door, but stopped when she touched his arm.

"Ian?"

He faced her fully, looking down at her worried face.

"What if—what if it influences *me?*" The thought had occurred to her while she was changing, and it kept piercing her, like a stiletto.

"It might try," he said after a moment. "But I don't think you'll let it."

She nearly gasped in her amazement. "But it did last night! And look what I tried to do to you! How can you be so sure?"

He simply looked down at her, as impassive as the damn Sphinx. "I trust you," he said.

Oh, great! she thought as she followed him out the door. Oh, great. He trusts me.

She sure as hell didn't trust herself anymore.

* * *

The rain had stopped, but thunder still growled like an angry beast at bay. The shadows beneath the Spanish moss were nearly as dark as night.

And alive, Honor thought as they approached. They were alive. Crazy as it sounded, she was convinced there was something in those dark places, something formless that was created out of shadow. Something evil.

Perhaps Ian felt it, too. He certainly picked up on her uneasiness. Pausing, he wrapped an arm around her shoulders. "I can take you out of here," he said quietly. "I'd be glad to do it, babe."

"I'm not leaving you alone." No amount of terror could make her do that. She would never be able to forgive herself for such cowardice.

He dropped his arm and took her hand. "All right."

The butcher knife that he had knocked out of her hand the night before still lay in the dirt, already showing signs of rust. Honor shivered when she saw it. Last night, when she had picked it up, it had looked barely adequate as a defensive weapon. This evening it looked wickedly dangerous. She hated to think how badly she might have hurt Ian if she had succeeded in stabbing him just once.

It crossed her mind to pick up the knife in case she needed to protect herself, but she immediately squelched the notion. It was horrifying to realize how little she could trust herself, but it would be foolhardy to forget what had happened last night. A weapon in her hands could be dangerous to Ian.

And he trusted her. Unconsciously she shook her head.

Beneath the trees, the leaden gray light of evening became a near-dark gloom. If, Honor promised herself, *if* they managed to get rid of this ghost so that she could live unmolested in this house, that moss was definitely going to go. The romance of it was gone forever.

The air beneath the trees was dank and carried the cloyingly sweet scent of rotting flesh. As soon as she smelled it, Honor halted.

"It's just a dead rat or a mouse," Ian said.

They entered the house through the front door. Inside, the air was stale, and stench of rotting flesh was even stronger. Something must have died in the crawl space beneath the house, she thought, hoping desperately that that was all it was.

Ian had stepped inside first, blocking her view with the breadth of his shoulders, but suddenly he stepped aside. Lying in the middle of the hallway, in a line leading back to the kitchen, were open packages of meat. Chicken, beef, fish, everything that had been in her freezer.

"Well, that explains the smell," Ian remarked.

"Do you...think the ghost did it?"

"Or the ghost's accomplice."

Honor started forward instinctively to clean up the mess, but Ian stopped her. "Leave it for now," he said. "Just keep your eyes and ears open while I see if I can sense it."

"But why would it do something like that? What's the point?"

Ian shrugged one shoulder, looking grimmer than usual. "Maybe that's just its way of saying we're going to be dead meat."

Honor's heart skipped a couple of beats. Oh, God, what a thought!

Ian turned and threw the deadbolt on the door, locking them in securely. "You stay right here," he said. "Keep an eye on the road in case anyone approaches."

"Where will you be?"

"Right here. This is where I felt it last time. It seems to be attracted to the living room, for some reason."

At least she would be able to keep an eye on him. She wouldn't have settled for anything else.

There were no fancy preparations, nothing that the movies had led her to expect from a séance. And this *was* a séance, wasn't it? What else could you call trying to talk to a ghost? But all Ian did was stand in the living room archway with his legs splayed and his hands clenched into loose fists. He didn't even close his eyes.

Turning her attention to the window at the foot of the stairs, forcing herself to ignore the way the back of her neck kept prickling, she kept watch and waited.

It was almost like being locked in the closet when she was a child. Honor's tension grew as the last of the day's light faded away, leaving the interior of the house black, leaving the night beyond the window fathomless. She couldn't see a darn thing. How was she supposed to keep watch?

Ian hadn't moved a muscle since he'd turned his back to her. The tempo of his breathing remained steady and relaxed, and he was so silent and still that she would have thought he had fallen asleep, if he weren't standing.

Either whatever she had felt when they first returned from Pensacola had evaporated, or she had become inured to it. The house seemed empty. Echoingly empty.

It seemed, she found herself thinking with sudden uneasiness, like a huge emptiness. A vast, immense emptiness. An emptiness too big for the house.

Shivering suddenly, she turned and looked into the impenetrable darkness inside the house. Something was happening.

Suddenly Ian disturbed the absolute silence by drawing a long, deep breath. "Stay back," he whispered. "Whatever happens, stay back there."

Oh, God! She could feel it. The emptiness was growing larger, growing colder, until the air felt like ice. Beyond Ian, she could almost see something. Something darker than the dark. Something that swallowed even the last little bit of starlight that had gotten through the clouds and into the house.

A curse escaped Ian, little more than a hiss. The darkness beyond him was swirling like thick, oily smoke, growing darker but more visible, as if it were some kind of black light.

Honor's scalp crawled as fear filled her. As terror turned her blood to ice in her veins. Suddenly she was that little girl locked in the closet again, and she started to slip to the floor, to curl up into herself, to hide within her own arms from the forming horror.

But she caught herself. Gasping for air as if there were none left in the universe, with the hammering of her own heart a deafening drumbeat in her ears, she resisted the overwhelming urge to hide. Because Ian might need her. Bracing her back against the wall, she forced herself to stand straight and watch.

"Stay back," Ian whispered again.

The column of swirling smoke grew until it reached from floor to ceiling. Sudden, loud raps came from the walls and ceiling of the living room, a staccato burst that seemed somehow angry. Honor suddenly glanced upward, remembering the scratching she had heard from the attic. And now she heard it again from the floor directly above, as if...as if that thing were following her thoughts.

Shuddering with a fresh chill, she dragged her eyes down and forced herself to watch Ian. He might need her, she reminded her terrified mind and heart. He might need her. But, oh, how she wished she could run, or scream.

Ian still hadn't moved a muscle. A faint murmuring seemed to fill the air, a sense of voices that were not quite audible. The column of oily smoke began to expand, as if it meant to fill the entire room, and it seemed impossible that it made no sound save the faint murmurings and now the occasional rap on the wall. It ought to howl and roar with the fury of the storm, Honor thought. The thing she had seen as a child hadn't been like this. It hadn't carried with it this sense of...evil. Truly consuming evil.

It was moving toward Ian. Oh, God! Stiffening, she moved away from the wall and clenched her hands. Then a loud bang sounded behind her, and she whirled, expecting to see someone. But there was nothing. Not a thing.

Quickly she turned back to Ian and found him...swallowed up. Oh, dear God, that smoke had surrounded him, nearly obscuring him, winding and twisting like a million snakes that wanted to devour him. And still he never moved a muscle. He might have been carved from stone.

Oh, God. She had to *do* something! But what? If she plunged her hand into that smoke and tried to yank him out, she might infuriate that thing. It might hurt him. Or her. From what she could see now, it wasn't actually doing anything except...surrounding him.

Stay back.

There wasn't a shadow of a doubt in her that Ian had just touched her mind. It felt like him, the warmth, the concern, the distance he couldn't quite keep. The way he felt when they made love. Sobbing for air, she clung to the last shred of her control and waited. Outside, the wind picked up as it did every night, moaning forlornly around the corner of the house.

All of a sudden Ian gave a hoarse shout and threw

himself backward, out of the coiling smoke. He stumbled once, then swung around toward Honor.

"Get out of here! Now!"

"But you—"

He grabbed the knob of the deadbolt and twisted it before flinging the door wide. Outside, the night was normal—windy, warm and damp. It seemed like another world as he hustled her through the door. Behind them, something slammed violently against something else.

"Let's go," he muttered, and when she stumbled on something, he simply swept her up and carried her. He didn't walk, he trotted. His hurry worried her as much as anything he might have said.

"Ian, what happened?"

"Just wait a minute." He trotted up the steps to his back door, fumbled with the combination lock.

"Put me down and make it easy on yourself."

But he kept his hold on her. When he got the door open, he stepped swiftly inside and then locked it again before he set her down. "Stay right here. I'm going to check out the house."

"Wait." She grabbed his arm, half expecting him to throw off her touch. But he didn't. Impatient though he was, he waited, looking down at her with enigmatic eyes. "Ian, what's going on? No one could get in here past the locks."

"Maybe, maybe not. Just wait a minute while I check it out."

She stood in his kitchen, shivering with a chill that wouldn't seem to abate, and waited impatiently while he prowled through the house. Lord, he was silent, even in those big, ugly combat boots he favored. She didn't hear him, not once, not climbing the stairs or moving through the hall and bedroom above her head.

Finally he returned to the kitchen. "All clear," he said as he went for the coffeemaker and started it brewing. Then, and only then, did he turn and pull her into a warm embrace. "You're ready to burst with questions," he remarked.

She tilted back her head and pretended to glare at him, even though she was really feeling extraordinary relief that they were out of that house, that he was safe. "Wouldn't you be? It doesn't take a mind reader to know that!"

He gave a short, soft laugh. "No," he agreed. "I'm sorry I was so rough about getting you out of there, but when it realized that I'd figured out it was protecting something, it got pretty pi— You know."

"Yeah. I know." She was distracted suddenly by the stubble on his strong chin, chocolate-dark prickles that she had an instant, urgent desire to feel against her skin. She drew a sharp breath, embarrassed by the turn her thoughts had taken.

"It's okay," he said, his voice turning totally husky. "It's okay. Adrenaline makes you…hungry. It does for most people." Bending, he pressed his cheek to hers and let her feel that prickly stubble against her cheek.

Such an erotic, masculine texture, she thought. Then she sighed as she corralled her thoughts. "I was so scared," she admitted. "But I'm okay now. Tell me what you learned."

"It sounds weirder than hell," he said, straightening. "That thing—that ghost—is evidently whatever is left of Mrs. Gilhooley."

"Mrs. Gilhooley?" Honor repeated. "You mean the woman who used to live there? The one who was so mean to you?"

He nodded. Honor reached for a kitchen chair and

pulled it out from the table. Sitting, she put her elbows on her knees and wondered if she had gone stark, raving mad. And then she knew with grim certainty that she had not. Who better to be a haunt than that nasty, evil old woman?

"I almost couldn't figure it out," Ian said. "It wasn't like touching a human mind. Something is very...different. As if only *parts* of her personality are here."

"The hateful parts," Honor said, lifting her head quickly. The room immediately began swimming, and she waited a moment for the blood to reach her head again. "The vile, nasty, murdering parts of her, right?"

"Looks that way."

"Well, what the hell is she doing in my house? Why doesn't she just go away and burn in hell?" She was getting mad. Putting a name to the ghost had an incredible effect on her, banishing her fear and making her furious. "How *dare* any part of her get stuck here!"

Ian studied her for an endless moment, and then he broke into a huge, tension-breaking laugh, a laugh so unexpected that it startled her right out of her anger. It didn't last long, but while it did, it made him look years younger, erasing all the cold distance he usually kept between himself and the rest of the world.

He should laugh more often, Honor thought. And it did her heart so much good to see it that she couldn't even get mad at him.

"I'm sorry," he said a few seconds later. "I wasn't laughing at you. It was just the absurdity of the whole thing." Leaning down, he kissed her; it was a hard and quick salute that promised more later. "It sounds crazier than a loon, doesn't it? I felt stupid even saying it out loud."

He poured two cups of coffee and joined Honor at the table with them. Crossing his legs loosely, he settled back in his chair and sipped coffee.

"It was her," he said again. "Worse, it's not what I would call rational. It's more like distilled feeling with a blind purpose."

"What purpose? What is she trying to do?"

He shrugged. "Protect something. I'm not sure what, but she doesn't want something to be found. Which means, if we want to get rid of her, we're going to have to find it."

"How can you find something if you don't know what it is?"

"I have a feeling we'll know when we see it, Honor. Something tells me there'll be no mistaking it."

Sometime during the night Honor found herself standing at the window of Ian's bedroom, looking out at the windy night. The rain had stopped, and the moon sailed on a sea of stars. The trees in her yard tossed restlessly before the wind, and the moss swayed eerily in a shadowy dance.

Abomination.

She knew now where those strange, alien words came from, and she shuddered a little as she felt the touch of that thing. Mrs. Gilhooley. She shivered again.

Demon spawn.

Honor wondered if Ian had heard those epithets from that mean old woman while he was growing up. Probably. She sounded like a broken record, the same few words, over and over again. Now, dead and buried for three years, she was still up to her despicable tricks.

Personalizing the evil over there hadn't made it any less terrifying. She could feel the threat even here, with

Ian sleeping behind her. A smile almost dispelled her uneasiness as she thought about him. Evidently good sex was an antidote for insomnia. He'd been asleep for more than an hour now.

But almost as soon as it strayed, her mind returned to the threat over there. In her house. Damn! It made her mad and sad and frustrated, all at once. Why the hell hadn't she sensed the thing when she'd first seen the house? Useless question, considering there couldn't be any possible answer.

And now this. Something hidden in the house. And what was keeping her awake long past fatigue was the simple terror of knowing that it was Mrs. Gilhooley in her house, and that Mrs. Gilhooley had always hated Ian, had tried just the other night to get him killed.

What if she still wanted to kill him? What if the old woman wanted Ian's death as much as she wanted to keep her secret? What if there was no secret at all, and Ian was her real target?

"Can't sleep?" A husky voice filled her ears as strong arms closed around her waist from behind.

Honor sighed and leaned back against Ian, enjoying the warm texture of his skin and hair from her shoulders to her hips. She rested her hands over his. "You were sure sawing wood."

He blew a soft laugh right into her ear. "*La petite mort.* Such sweet death." His arms tightened just a little. "And you're over here worrying loud enough to wake the dead."

"Sorry."

"Don't be. Come back to bed and let's talk about it."

The words were like a warm wind blowing into the cold places of her heart and soul. In the six brief months of her misbegotten marriage, nothing had been discussed in bed. Bed had become a place to avoid, an instrument of torture and disappointment. Now, hearing those beautiful words out of the mouth of a man she had come to care for, she realized just how badly she had needed to have someone feel that way about her.

There was, she thought, a world of difference between a man you could go to bed with to make love with, a friend you could lie on a bed with to talk to, and a man with whom you could do both. A man who wanted to hold you while you talked.

Because the cots were so narrow, they had made a pallet on the floor with the mattresses from both their beds. They snuggled up there now, him propped against the pillows, her curled on his chest.

"When this thing materialized, did you see it?" Honor asked.

"The black smoke, you mean? Yeah."

"I was terrified when it wrapped around you. It reminded me of snakes."

"I wasn't exactly comfortable with it myself. It was like being touched by cold worms."

"Yuck!" She shuddered and tightened her hold on his waist. "I was so scared. I wanted to snatch you right away from it, but I was afraid if I did anything, it might get madder and hurt one of us."

He stroked her arm soothingly and pressed a kiss to the top of her hair.

"What made you jump back the way you did?" she asked. "What happened? You were in such a hurry to get out of there."

"She was calling somebody," he said flatly. "She was trying to get someone to come. I could feel it, and I figured it was the guy who shot me, so I wanted us both out of there fast."

"Oh, no." Her hold on him tightened even more, and unconsciously she dug her nails into him. The crease in his side was healing beautifully, but she hated to think how close it had come.

"I think," he said quietly, "that it might be wise for you to get out of here while I try to deal with this. I know it'll play hell with your sense of honor, but if something were to happen to you..."

He didn't finish, and this time she didn't really need him to. Slowly she lifted her head and looked right into his strange green eyes. Dark though the room was, they seemed to glow. "Don't you know I feel the same way? Can't you tell?"

He muttered something almost prayerful and touched her cheek with his fingers. "But you don't trust me, babe. Not yet. I can feel that, too."

Unable to deny it, she lowered her head again to rest on his chest. It was true, she thought. Partly because she had learned painfully that things were not always what they seemed, and partly because she didn't know him that well yet. And partly because of that thing in her house. It had influenced someone to shoot Ian. It had influenced her to try to kill him. How could she be sure it wasn't influencing him to do some horrible thing, possibly to her?

Because she couldn't discuss what lay between them, she turned to the problem at hand. "What are we going to do?"

He stroked her hair gently, with a tenderness that seemed odd in such a hard, harsh man.

"We're going to go over there and look for whatever it is. Short of burning down the house, there doesn't seem to be an alternative."

She huddled closer to him, wondering what the ghost

would try to do when it realized they were searching for the very thing it was trying to conceal. She had an unhappy feeling that the thing hadn't yet fully displayed its powers.

"We'll go in daylight," Ian said quietly. "It seems to gather strength in the darkness. We'll go when the sun is bright and high, and we'll search the damn place from bottom to top."

She shivered again as a cold wind touched her. "Maybe I should just give up the house. I mean, it's only money, right? I can just tell the bank I'm leaving and it's theirs. So what if my credit rating is ruined. It's only a credit rating—"

He squeezed her so tight that she gasped and covered her mouth in a devouring, demanding kiss. "No," he said when he lifted his head.

"No?" That damned word again. Frustrated and scared past bearing, she hammered her fist once against his chest. In an instant she was spread-eagled beneath him, pinned so that she couldn't move, exposed so that she couldn't defend herself.

"Nobody," he said softly, "*nobody* hits me."

Sudden fear turned her veins to ice. Looking up into those strange, glowing eyes, she looked into the eyes of a hunter. She'd done it, she realized. She'd aroused the sleeping tiger.

CHAPTER TEN

Honor had never felt so defenseless or so exposed in her life. She had been aware before of his vast strength, of his skill in using it. All along she had known he could kill her with no more effort than it would take to swat a fly. But never before had she been acutely aware that he might well do it.

Staring up into his eerie green eyes, completely helpless beneath him, she wondered if she had trusted him too much. Wondered if, once again, she had completely misjudged a man.

But she knew, too, that she should never have hit him. Gasping, trying not to struggle against his hold for fear of angering him even more, she waited, wondering what he would do. Terrified, a mouse trapped by a lion, she forced herself to go limp so as not to arouse his hunting instincts further.

For long seconds neither of them moved a muscle. Then, suddenly, with a savage oath, he levered himself off her and the bed. She heard him this time, heard him pad barefoot and naked down the stairs, heard him slam a cupboard shut. Heard him open the back door.

Oh, God, surely he wasn't going over there?

Scared in a new way, she grabbed up the first wearable piece of clothing her hand found and pulled it on. It was his olive T-shirt, big enough to make anything else unnecessary. Hurrying, she padded down the hall and stairs after him.

He had turned none of the lights on, which was why

she saw him through the screen door. The moonlight brightened the night enough that she saw him standing on the porch, hands on hips, legs splayed, head thrown back.

She thought she had been silent, but he stiffened when she reached the screen door. One way or another, he knew she was there. Uncertain whether she should do anything, she simply waited.

And in the waiting she realized that she trusted him more than she had trusted anyone since her marriage. Whatever resistance she had felt toward trusting Ian had sprung from self-doubt, not from anything he had done.

And now, even in rage, he had not hurt her, not even when she had hit him.

He turned. "I'm sorry I scared you," he said levelly.

"I'm sorry I hit you," she answered, her voice quavering just a little. "Truly sorry. I've never done that before, and I despise women who think they can hit a man, knowing he won't hit back."

"We agree on that." He turned away again, looking out into the night. "I shouldn't have scared you, though. I know my size is intimidating, and to hold you down like that…" He shook his head.

Honor pushed the screen door open and stepped out. The night was alive with cicadas and tree frogs, and she tried not to think about that huge bug she'd seen mashed on the road. She crossed the porch to stand beside him.

"I imagine," she said after a moment, "that you've suffered a lot for your size. And your unusual eyes."

He stirred a little. "I don't pay attention."

"Of course you do. You're not deaf, dumb and blind."

The wind gusted, rustling the trees in her yard and whispering sorrowfully through the darkness. It sounded as if the night were sighing. Tentatively, aware she might

well be rejected, she touched Ian's forearm with her fingertips.

He turned toward her instantly and gathered her close.
"I'm sorry," he said gruffly. "Damn it, I'm sorry. I
never wanted to scare you...."

Whether he admitted it or not, he had been hurt by the
way people reacted to him, Honor thought. Between that
and his telepathy, it was no wonder he lived behind impenetrable walls.

It felt so good to have his arms around her again, so
good to lean against his strength and feel welcome there.
She clung to him for a long while, soaking up his
warmth, and the scent that was uniquely his.

"You didn't hurt me," she said. "And that's all that
matters."

One of his big hands found her hair and tunneled into
it, combing gently. "I've never met anybody like you,"
he said roughly. "Anybody else would have run from me
ten times over."

"I guess you haven't been looking in the right places.
I'm nothing special."

Bending, he kissed the top of her head again. "That's
what *you* think. Come on, let's go inside. I don't want
anyone to see you out here with me like this."

At this hour of the morning? Honor wondered. Who
could possibly be watching? And then she remembered
the person who had shot Ian, the person the ghost had
been calling. He might be out and about. The thought
was like a chill breath on the back of her neck.

"Sorry," he said, hustling her through the door. "I'm
great at destroying a mood, too."

When they were inside and he was locking the door,
Honor turned on him. "Damn it, Ian, quit apologizing
for everything. There's not one thing you need to apol-

ogize for! I'm the one who hit you, and I deserved to be
swatted back. If I were a man, you'd probably have
nailed me to the floor.''

Satisfied with the deadbolt, he faced her. ''Maybe.''

''There's no maybe about it. All you did was scare me
a little. Quit worrying. Quit worrying about everything.''
She hated this. Hated knowing just how abnormal he felt
he was. Only years of experience could have made him
feel that everything about him was wrong, from his size
to his eyes.

Reaching out, she touched his arm. ''There's nothing
wrong with you,'' she said softly. ''Not one damn thing.
You're different, but different is *not* the same thing as
wrong.''

''There are a lot of people who wouldn't agree with
you.'' He spoke stiffly, as if for some reason he was
afraid to relax.

''Maybe so, but they're not here right now.'' And suddenly it was all very clear to her. Maybe she didn't trust
this man with her heart, maybe she still wondered if he
could be influenced by the ghost the way she had been,
but it was eminently clear now that he would never purposely hurt her.

But he expected her to be afraid of him, as so many
others had been. He never entirely relaxed, always main-
tained a rigid control, for fear he might do something to
scare her—as he had when he pinned her to the mattress.
Yes, she had been scared. Terrified, even. But the important point was that he had not hurt her.

He stood now in the kitchen, unselfconsciously naked,
a magnificent man who had been shunned all his life
because he was a telepath and because he was a deadly
fighting machine. He said he didn't care; she didn't believe it.

She took his hand gently. Raising it to her lips, she kissed the backs of his fingers and then his palm. "Everything else aside, Ian, I am *not* afraid of you."

She heard him catch his breath. Then, with the swiftness of a striking hawk, he scooped her up into his arms and headed for the stairs.

Honor knew exactly what was coming, and arousal trickled through her to her center, tingling and warm. Life had turned him into a closed-up, locked-up man, and he had only one means of expression still left to him. What he couldn't say with words, he could say with his body.

And, oh, was she ready to listen!

He was gentle at first, taking exquisite care, treating her as if she were priceless crystal. But then, at some point, he dared to let go, dared to test her declaration that she wasn't afraid of him. Dared to be himself without inhibition.

It was like catching a ride on a cyclone, Honor thought dimly and much later, when she lay trembling beneath his sweaty, exhausted body. Like riding a rocket, or driving a car without brakes. The whirlwind had swept her up and carried her to a world of sensations so intense they surpassed thought.

And there she had found a long-lost piece of herself. Smiling, she held Ian close and slipped away into a deep restful sleep.

Ian didn't sleep. He had made the ghost aware of him, and he felt the threat strengthening. Directed at him now, he thought, and not Honor at all. While she slept deeply, he went to stand at the window and watch her house through the trees. Lights flickered in the windows, in a restless movement that bounced here and there in seeming frustration. He felt it commanding him to come, but he would choose his own time.

It seemed, he found himself thinking, that he and Mrs. Gilhooley were fated to have it out. He was reluctant to think in terms of destiny and eternity, and his faith had been all but destroyed in childhood, but he stood in the dark and looked over at Mrs. Gilhooley's house and wondered why he and that nasty old woman had been locked in mortal combat since his childhood, and why the conflict seemed to have extended beyond the grave.

Given a different life, he might have been a mystic, but he wasn't a mystic, and he felt uneasy with the ideas that were rolling around in his mind now. It was, he told himself, simple happenstance. If he hadn't felt compelled to return to this house to prove to himself that the terrors of his childhood no longer had the power to hurt him, he never would have run into this mess.

He had meant his return here to be a kind of excision, a cutting-away of old scar tissue. He had told himself he was setting himself free of the last of his emotional baggage, that when he had dealt with the memories this place represented, he would be beyond the reach of anything and anyone.

Instead he found himself faced with his old nemesis and collecting fresh baggage. Wherever he went now, Honor Nightingale would haunt him. The first woman, the only woman, not to be afraid of his strange talent. The first person to become aware of his talent without thinking of him as an abomination.

This bedroom he stood in now had been his as a child. The one in which Honor had slept had belonged to his older brother, long dead. His parents' room was empty of everything, cleared out by him to remove the last traces of an abusive father and a mother who had refused to touch him ever again from the day the church had shunned him.

Nothing his father had done to him had cut him as deeply as what his mother had refused to do. He had locked those memories in the deepest, darkest vault of his mind, then had come home specifically to dig them up, face them and toss them away. It seemed amazing now, and even a little ironic, that Honor had accomplished with a few words what he hadn't managed to do in nearly a full year. She had set him free of his past.

Except for Mrs. Gilhooley, of course. There was one last raveled end to deal with, and he would deal with it first thing in the morning. The old woman had met her match. Ian McLaren was going to uncover her secret— or die trying.

"How are we going to do this?" Honor asked.

They were standing in front of her house, looking at the black, empty windows. The day had turned sunny and hot, though it was still early, and humid. She wiped her brow with the back of her arm and wished a breeze would stir.

"It seems quiet this morning," Ian said. "She was restless all night, but now...it's as if she's asleep."

Honor felt a chill despite the heat. It was disturbing to hear Ian refer to that thing as *she*.

"I guess it'll be safe if we split up," Ian said. "If she starts to get active, I should sense it. I'll start on the second floor, and you start in the front down here. I'll work my way up to the attic, while you go through everything on the ground floor." He turned and looked down at her. "I know it's a bigger task downstairs, but you're better equipped to tell what's yours and what isn't.

And I'll leave your bedroom for last, so we can do that together.''

"Fair enough."

"Unless you'd rather we do it together. We can start in the attic.''

For some reason she remembered the chill she often felt at the foot of the attic ladder and shook her head. "No, this is fine." Bad enough that she would have to go into the living room. Her mind had retained an indelible image of the swirling darkness that had surrounded Ian last night.

"If we start to come close to what we're looking for," he continued, "we may stir her up. I should sense that, too.''

"That would be a dead giveaway, if the ghost starts getting nervous.''

One corner of his mouth hitched upward. "We can always hope.''

It was really too hot for jeans, but Ian had insisted on protective clothing again. Inside the house it was cooler, from the air-conditioning, but the carrion smell had become almost asphyxiating. Gagging, Honor had to back right out the door, but Ian forged forward with a trash bag and picked up all the rotting meat.

"At least she didn't smear it all over the walls," he remarked as he passed Honor on his way out with the bag.

They opened all the doors and windows and turned on the house fan to blow the smell away, and Honor mopped the hallway with vinegar. When she had finished, the smell seemed nearly gone—or maybe her nose had just turned off, she thought sourly. Damn the old woman, anyway!

She didn't feel nearly so defiant, though, when Ian had

at last gone upstairs and she was left alone in the hallway, facing the living room. There was no longer any doubt in her mind as to why she had hesitated to paint and furnish the room. If evil had a smell, that room reeked of it.

"Miss Honor?"

Startled, she whirled around and then sighed with relief when she recognized Jeb Sidell. He was plainly agitated, shifting from one foot to the other and twisting a porkpie hat in his hands. "What's wrong?"

"Orville. He fell, and his leg busted like bad wood, and he's bleeding bad. My ma's calling for help, but—"

She ran upstairs to grab some clean pillowcases to use to make a pressure bandage. Pausing by the foot of the attic ladder, she ignored the clammy chill that clung there and called up to Ian.

"I'm going out with Jeb! Orville broke his leg and needs help!"

She didn't wait to hear if he answered. Splints. She needed something to use for splints. Forget that. It would take too long. The bleeding had to be stopped before anything else could be dealt with.

Downstairs, she hurried out the door, Jeb on her heels. "Where is he?"

"I'll drive," Jeb said, pointing at a beat-up old truck. "We'll get there faster."

She climbed up into the cab, hoping against hope that it wasn't too late for the little boy.

A surprising number of the attic floorboards were loose, as if no one had ever bothered to drive the nails back in as they worked free over time. In many places, the nails were entirely gone. And beneath each loose board was an easy hiding place between the joists that supported the flooring. A careful inspection of the lath showed that it, too, was loose in places and concealed fair-sized spaces between itself and the wood.

It would take a couple of hours, at least, to explore all the possible hiding places in the attic, Ian estimated. Mentally he blocked the entire area off in sections, intending to search section by section from one end to the other.

As he worked, he whistled softly, a habit from childhood that he'd nearly forgotten. Back then he'd whistled most of the time to avoid hearing what people were thinking. It made a kind of screen, concentrating on something like a melody. He did it now without even thinking about it. Not initially.

At some point he felt the day beginning to darken. Sitting back on his heels, he dropped a board back into place and looked toward one of the round attic windows. Beyond the filmy, dusty glass, the sky looked as blue as ever, but the sense of darkening was still there.

Glancing around, he saw that the warm-toned wood looked oddly gray, and that the light coming through the windows seemed to have lost its brightness. A glance at his watch told him it was just past noon. Too early for the light to change so drastically.

Getting to his feet, he walked over to the west window and looked down from the same place where Mrs. Gilhooley had stood when she shoved her first husband to his death. Nothing looked different out there, he thought.

Turning, he stared across the length of the attic to the other round window. There, near the middle of the attic, he thought he saw a shimmering in the air, a distortion like heat waves over pavement. The attic might almost be that hot, he thought, but something wasn't quite right.

Something about the way the air moved, the way the room beyond it was not only distorted, but subtly darkened, as well.

He smiled then, a private, rare expression of satisfaction. "We're getting close, aren't we, you old bitch?"

If he had hoped to provoke some kind of response, he was disappointed. The shimmering remained unaffected, the light staying oddly darkened. He waited a few minutes, wondering if something else would happen, or if the disturbance would disappear.

When nothing at all changed, he shrugged and reached for another board to lift. That was when it occurred to him to wonder if Honor was experiencing anything strange. If she wasn't then he would be willing to bet the item they sought was somewhere in the attic. If she was…well, they wouldn't be any worse off than they had been to start with.

He had to pass through the shimmering area to reach the ladder. The sensation was faintly unpleasant, cold and damp, like a cave, or a tomb, but after last night's encounter he hardly noticed it.

Until he reached the other side. In an instant he realized he had been duped, and fury rose hot in his blood. Turning, he looked back at the shimmering, and saw that it was a wall, ceiling to floor. And just beyond it he saw the faint gray smoke that he knew was Mrs. Gilhooley.

Sounds filled his ears now, the normal sounds of a house, of the breeze outside. Once again his mind picked up impressions, mostly vague thoughts cast adrift in the psychic either by people he would never know. All the background cacophony of life.

Sounds neither his ear nor his mind had heard for…hours? It had been so subtle that he didn't even know when it had been. He had been cut off. Deliberately.

But why?

And he thought of Honor.

He hadn't heard a sound from downstairs since the old woman had cut him off. Anything could have happened.

He dashed down the attic stairs, hoping against hope—yet he already knew. Free of the old woman's deception, he could feel Honor's absence as surely as he would have felt it if his heart had been ripped out.

The door of the linen closet in the hall stood partway open. It had been closed when he had gone up to the attic, so she had been up here since. He opened it wide, peered in and saw nothing amiss. He could feel her there, though, could sense in some subtle way that she had touched these things just recently. But why? He scanned neat stacks of towels and sheets and could see no answer.

Her room was undisturbed, as far as he could tell. There was no sign of a struggle, at any rate, and no sign of a hurried departure. He wondered if Mrs. Gilhooley had managed to scare her away again. Maybe Honor was running from him again, as she had just the other night.

Downstairs, he walked through the undisturbed rooms and found nothing. Only the front door, unlocked, told him anything at all. Outside, he found tire tracks in the driveway behind her car, which hadn't been moved since well before the last heavy rain. Someone had been here this morning.

Someone had been here, and now Honor was gone. And the only clue he had was tire tracks that headed out toward the highway. Standing beside the dirt road, he followed them with his eyes. And then he noticed that they had initially come from the other direction. From up the road, toward the Sidells' place.

Moments later he was backing out of his driveway and heading up the road to question a woman who had spoken to him only once in thirty-five years, and then to call him a murderer and wish him an eternity in hell.

She was sitting on the porch of a run-down house, looking as run-down as a woman of forty could manage. Too thin, too worn, she had plainly had a hard life. She didn't move when Ian climbed out of his Jeep, and no one came out of the house to join her. It was just the two of them and the stifling Florida day.

"Annie." He nodded, staying well back, not wanting to frighten her by approaching.

"Ian." She didn't nod, but she didn't look away or get up and leave. "Heard you were back."

A year ago, he thought. He'd come back a year ago, and she acted as if she'd just heard it. But the old bitterness was nothing beside his current worry. "Yeah. You got your wish, Annie."

She cocked her head a little. "I never got a wish in my life. What're you talking about?"

"You wished me to hell. I went."

For a long moment, she stared unwaveringly at him, her lips compressed. Then she nodded. "Me too, Ian. Me too. My boys are good, but—" She cut herself off sharply and shook her head.

Ian didn't need to hear the rest of the sentence to know Jack Sidell had the temper of an ornery rattler. At least she was talking to him. "I'm looking for my neighbor lady, Honor Nightingale."

"The nurse lady. She ain't been here, for sure."

"Well, we were at her place. I was doing something in the attic for her. When I came down, she was gone. Never said a word. Didn't leave a note or anything, but her car's there. And I saw some tire tracks in her driveway. They came from up here, pulled in the drive, then headed out to the highway. Anybody been up this way this morning?''

Annie shook her head and lifted a chapped hand to brush sweat from her brow. ''Sure been hot.''

''Mmm…''

''Jeb headed out to town 'bout an hour ago. Said he didn't know when he'd be back. Still looking for work. They don't hire him too quick, 'cause he's slow, but he's a hard worker. Ain't never been fired from a job.''

Ian nodded, restraining his impatience. ''I've heard good about the boy.''

''Nobody's got a bad word for any of my boys. I raised 'em right.''

This time he just nodded. A couple of minutes ticked by while she stared at something he couldn't see. Just as he was about to decide there was nothing to be gained here, she focused on him again and spoke.

''I'm sorry for what I said all them years ago, Ian. You didn't kill her. Maybe you knocked her up, I don't know, but you didn't kill her.''

And for the first time in all the years since, he said what no one had believed at the time. ''I never touched her, Annie. Never.''

Annie shrugged. ''Don't matter anymore. But Jeb…''

When she hesitated, Ian had to restrain himself from saying more than ''Yes?''

''Something's wrong with that boy lately,'' Annie said. ''He's not right. He's acting funny. Orville won't even go hunting with him no more. Worries me.'' She leaned forward a little bit. ''I don't know where he went. But if he's got that nurse lady, there's no good in it. No good at all. I don't know what's been driving him lately, but he kicked his coon dog last night, and I ain't never seen Jeb kick a thing in his life…''

Ian never heard the rest. He was in the car and moving.

A hundred yards down the road, though, he pulled over and set the brake. Here, where he had nothing else to concentrate on, he closed his eyes and reached out, trying to find some hint, some flicker, of Honor's mind. Or even Jeb's. Some hint of where they might have gone. Never in his life had he tried so hard to reach out with his mind. It felt like straining a long-unused muscle, and the effort left him with a blinding headache.

But he had a general idea as to which way they had gone.

Dusk was closing in, and along with it a sense of hope-lessness to add to her other miseries. Honor sat tied to the base of a tree by ropes that crisscrossed her chest and stomach. Her ankles were tightly bound, and her wrists were raw from the rope that held them together in her lap. Her face was swollen from numerous mosquito and fly bites, so swollen that her eyes opened only to slits, and the itching was driving her crazy. The only bright spot was that Ian's insistence that morning had left her wearing jeans and long sleeves, preventing further dis-comfort.

She was the prisoner of Mrs. Gilhooley, and the longer she sat here and listened to Jeb Sidell rustling in the undergrowth and talking to the ghost of his dead grand-mother, the easier Honor found it to believe.

And, worse, as night closed in, she was beginning to feel the old woman's presence herself. It was a chill in the air that trapped the brutal heat of the day in the thick vegetation, a chill that had nothing to do with tem-perature.

Suddenly Jeb appeared out of the shadows and hunkered down near her. "Water," he said, holding out a rusty tin cup.

Honor drank eagerly, having too much common sense to turn down a necessity to make a point. When he offered her pieces of a candy bar, she wolfed those down, too.

"I didn't want to do this, Miss Honor," he said as he fed her.

"Then why did you?"

"Gram said she'll hurt me if I don't do what she says."

Honor peered at him, wishing the dusk weren't concealing his expression so effectively. "Hurt you how?" Lord, was it only a couple of days ago that she'd told Ian she couldn't imagine how a ghost could hurt anyone? She was beginning to get a good idea.

"She makes things inside my head hurt."

"Oh." She accepted another bite of candy. Things inside his head. She could almost imagine it.

"She said she'd send another snake to bite Orville, too."

"Do you think she can make snakes do what she wants?" Honor shuddered, thinking of the coral snakes and water moccasins that inhabited this place. After the rain, water moccasins could be almost anywhere, too, not just in the rivers and creeks.

"Sure," said Jeb. "Easy." He gave her more candy bar.

The darkness was thickening, and with it the chilling sense of the old woman's presence. Honor looked around, wishing for light. Any light. Some source of illumination to tell her what other threats might be emerging from the dark. Mrs. Gilhooley was bad enough by herself, but the thought of snakes and bobcats and all the other things that inhabited the dark made her just as uneasy. Just as scared.

"Jeb." She looked at the young man. "What you're doing is wrong."

"I know." Even in the dark, his anguish was palpable. "I know."

"Then don't do it!"

"I have to! She'll hurt me! She'll hurt Orville!"

"Why would any grandmother want to hurt her grandchildren?"

"I don't know." It sounded as if he were crying. "I don't know. She scares me, Miss Honor. And I can't let her hurt Orville. But she's not going to hurt you. She promised she won't hurt you. I made her promise, because you saved Orville before."

For hours Honor had been dragged through the thick, junglelike growth of the forest. She'd been terrified, she'd fallen so many times that her entire body was sore and bruised, and now she was sitting in the dark with the man who had kidnapped her and dragged her for miles, and she was supposed to believe she wasn't going to get hurt because she had helped Orville. The same Orville who was being threatened by another snakebite.

Somehow she didn't feel very reassured. And she still didn't know what they were doing out here.

"Why did you drag me out here, then?" she asked Jeb. "If you're not going to hurt me, why am I tied up like this?"

"She made me." He whispered the words, as if he, too, felt the encroachment of the evil thing that was his grandmother. "She made me."

"But why? Why does she want me here in the woods like this?"

He cocked his head to one side. Though he was just a shadow in the deepening gloom, the movement was still visible. "We're gonna catch him," Jeb whispered.

Something deep inside her froze to ice. "Catch who?" she asked, her own voice dropping to a whisper. But she knew. Oh, God, she *knew*.

"Catch the demon spawn," Jeb whispered. "Catch the witch man." Then he rose and disappeared into the night.

There were more than a half-million acres of land on the air base, nearly a thousand square miles, most of it virgin forest and subtropical jungle. A man could get lost in there and never be found, and he could die from dozens of causes, everything from poisonous snakes to bobcats, from drowning to falling.

Ian knew the reservation as well as he knew the back of his hand. He'd guided troops through it for years, in daylight and pitch-darkness. He sometimes thought he could tell where he was by the smell of the vegetation and the lingering odors of explosives and jet fuel that never quite blew away.

He drove until his sixth sense warned him to stop, and there, with eyes trained by years of practice, he saw the hastily concealed signs of the recent passage of a vehicle. He didn't have to walk far into the woods to find Jeb Sidell's old truck. From there they would have walked, and anywhere a man could walk, Ian could track.

He took time, though, to check out the truck's cab. He saw two of Honor's pillowcases, crumpled on the floor boards. There was no doubt they were hers, because they smelled of her laundry soap, and faintly of her. They were dirty from muddy footprints, and spoke to him of a struggle. If Jeb had hurt her, he was going to be one sorry kid, Ian thought grimly as he slammed the cab door. One damn sorry kid.

Closing his eyes, he reached out again. Strained to feel Honor somewhere out there in the hot, muggy evening. It had taken him too long to get here, he thought. Soon it would be dark, and tracking would be harder.

And then he felt her, a whisper of her fear, of her fatigue. Just a touch, a light, almost fragile touch. Two minutes later he was on his way into the woods with night-vision goggles and his knife. He didn't need a gun. He had *never* needed a gun.

She hadn't gotten much sleep the night before, and after being dragged through the jungle and running on adrenaline for hours, Honor was exhausted. She dozed against the tree, despite the bugs, the possibility of snakes and her fears for Ian. Periodically she awoke and listened to the whispers of the breeze, but not even Jeb disturbed the nighttime silence.

Jeb was out there somewhere, waiting, his trap laid and ready to spring. Honor doubted that it could be much of a trap, given the young man's reluctance, and his slow-wittedness, but that didn't keep her from trying to "beam" a warning to Ian, wherever he was. Somehow she had never considered the possibility that he wouldn't find them. She never once worried that he might not have figured out where she had gone, never once imagined that he might not look for her.

She guessed she trusted him after all.

And that was a terrible thing to realize now, when she couldn't do anything about it and they might well both be dead before she got a chance to tell him. And if ever anybody in the world had needed to be trusted by some-one, it was Ian. He needed it the way a sturdy tree needs rain, and it was the one thing no one had ever given him. Except his army superiors, of course, but that was a different thing altogether.

Well, she trusted him, and if they lived long enough, she was damn well going to tell him.

She drifted off again, but sleep came in fits and starts, a little here, a little there, punctuated by crushing anxiety and fear.

Sometime during the endless hours of dark, Jeb finally returned. He woke her by shaking her shoulder.

"He's coming."

"Who?" She refused to let this boy know that she knew who he had meant when he referred to the "demon spawn."

"McLaren."

"Him? What do you want to hurt him for? He's never done anything wrong."

"He's a witch. He has to die."

"He is *not* a witch!" Honor was tired, hungry and fed up, and her temper was fraying. "When have you ever seen him call up a demon? Come off it, Jeb. You know damn well he's never done anything wrong!"

"Mama says the old preacher used to shun him."

"So? Have *you* seen Ian do anything wrong? With your own eyes?"

"Gram says he's evil. Evil!"

"Your gram's the evil one!"

"No! Don't you say that! She's not! She's not!"

Honor heard him hurry away, trampling vegetation as he went, trying to escape her words. If she hadn't been so scared for herself and Ian, she might even have felt pity for the young man.

And then she heard the most spine-chilling sound in the world—an abruptly cut-off shriek of terror.

"Jeb? Jeb? Jeb, answer me!"

But he never did. Apart from the whisper of the wind in the treetops, the night remained deadly silent.

CHAPTER ELEVEN

The night had been terrifying before, but now, knowing something had happened to Jeb, Honor found the dark intolerable. Tipping her head back, heedless of the way the ropes cut her as she twisted, she tried to see the stars, but the thick pine needles hid even that much from her.

Anything, anything at all, could come crawling out of that darkness now, and she couldn't even run or try to protect herself. Thoughts of foot-long bugs and giant spiders seemed a lot worse than Mrs. Gilhooley.

Who was still hovering around like a bad odor, Honor thought, shivering. Oh, God, how long till morning? How long until night would give way to dawn, until the chill would succumb to the warmth?

And Ian, even with Jeb out of commission, was walking into some kind of trap, and there was no way to warn him. Short of sending him frantic messages, which wasn't an easy thing to do when she couldn't be sure he was getting them.

Her skin prickled suddenly, as if it had been brushed by something. But nothing was there. She thought immediately of insects. Snakes. Ghosts.

And then she heard the low rumble. At first she wondered if it was a distant storm. But gradually she realized it was approaching, growing louder. Aircraft engines. Lots and lots of aircraft engines.

A bombing mission, she thought, and wondered how close it would be. It couldn't be here, of course, or there wouldn't be any trees. All the trees would long since have been knocked down or blown to smithereens.

As soon as she had the thought, the night burst with the brilliant white light of explosion. Almost before she understood what was happening, there was another...and another...and another. Coming closer. Oh, God, coming this way!

Why were they bombing the trees?

Dirt showered her, and her shoulder stung as something hit her. The shock waves kept rolling over her, leaving her breathless, and she couldn't even cover her ears with her hands. She felt as if she were caught inside the thunder.

She was going to die. There wasn't any doubt in her mind that she was going to die.

Another series of explosions began to approach from the same direction as the first. Carpet bombing. Saturation bombing. Oh, God, whatever you called it, they weren't going to leave a tree standing or an inch of ground untouched. An explosion. Another one. More dirt showered her.

Suddenly something fell on her, covering her. She opened her mouth to scream, to release the intolerable terror in the only way she could, when she realized it was a body. A body had fallen on her. Jeb?

"Honor! Honor, it's me!"

Ian! Oh, God, it was Ian! His mouth against her ear. His hands gripping her shoulders.

"We've got to get out of here," he shouted, even as he slashed at her bonds with his knife. They gave way quickly. He didn't bother with her hands. Another run of bombs was making its way toward them. He hauled her to her feet, but her legs gave way, numb from endless hours of immobility. In an instant he tossed her onto his back and held her by her wrists as he ran through the night.

She couldn't imagine how he could see anything at all. Nature had never made a night as dark as this, as dark as a cave's interior, the darkness punctuated only by the hellish explosions of the bombs. The light kept blinding her, and she couldn't see a thing. How could he?

They were both going to die, she thought as dirt struck them again, this time with enough force to sting. Ian shouted something to her, but another explosion drowned out his words.

Turning her head, she buried her face against his neck and tried to close her mind to the danger and the fear. How could he run like this with her on his back? Tirelessly, it seemed. Effortlessly.

Another bomb exploded, so close this time that her cheek stung from the heat from the blast. Then another. God, they were coming closer! She pressed her face to Ian's neck and prayed harder than she'd ever prayed in her life.

And on into the night he ran.

"Here." Slowly Ian squatted and eased her from his back to the ground.

"The bombs…"

"It's okay now," he said. "It's okay. They're heading the other way now." He reached for her wrists and began to saw away the rope.

She couldn't see a thing until another bomb exploded and the light fell across them. He was wearing some kind of goggles, she realized. That must be how he managed to see when she felt utterly blinded.

Another explosion, and she realized he was right. The

sounds were retreating now. Dirt was no longer showering them.

"Somebody's going to get hell come morning," Ian remarked, as calmly as if they were sitting on the porch sipping tea.

"Why?"

"They missed the bombing range by a quarter mile, that's why."

"They weren't supposed to blow up the trees?"

He finished cutting the rope that held her wrists, then raised his head and looked straight at her. She couldn't read his expression, because his eyes were hidden behind those strange goggles. "No," he said slowly. "They weren't supposed to blow up the trees. Or you."

Suddenly he grabbed her, and she found herself crushed to his hard, broad chest, held as if she might slip away if he didn't hold her tightly enough. And suddenly, very suddenly, she felt safer than she'd ever felt in her life. And closer to tears than at any time in her memory.

"Is it…is it okay if I get hysterical?" she asked shakily.

"Sure, baby. Sure. But…maybe you can hold off just a little longer? Until we get to the car?"

He helped her to stand again, and this time her legs were able to support her. He led the way through the thick growth at a brisk pace that kept her breathing heavily. From time to time he paused and let her catch her breath, and then they were off again. In silence. With a sense that something was following. Pursuing them.

Not until they were in Ian's Jeep did the feeling of pursuit quit. When she drew a long, sobbing breath of relief, he reached out and squeezed her thigh gently. "Just a little longer, honey. Hang on just a little longer, babe."

So she did. But it wasn't easy. As the realization of safety, however temporary, sank in, the control that had kept her going all day began to evaporate.

They were driving down the dark road at breakneck speed, and she had no idea where they were going. Some corner of her mind kept trying to tell her that she at least ought to ask, but it somehow didn't seem to matter. All that mattered was that he had found her and saved her at the risk of his own neck. After this night, there was nothing she wouldn't trust him with.

She was astonished when she realized they were on the air base proper, and even more astonished when he pulled up to what appeared to be a motel beneath towering oaks.

"What's this?" she asked.

"Base TLQ. Temporary Lodging Quarters. Be right back."

Before she could enquire further, he was out of the Jeep and headed for a brightly lit doorway. *Temporary Lodging Quarters,* she thought inanely. Count on Uncle Sam to come up with a name like that. What were they doing here?

Ian was back in just a couple of minutes. Without a word, he drove down to the end of the long, low building and then parked. "You're staying here tonight," he said.

She was? Moments later they were inside and the night was locked out. Ian stood with his back to the door like a guard and looked at her. "Now you can get hysterical."

She shook her head slowly. She didn't feel like it anymore. She felt exhausted, miserable, filthy and scared, but not hysterical. "I just want to shower. Why did you bring me here?"

"I want you someplace safe while I go take care of that old woman once and for all."

"What—?" No. She cut herself off. Not right now. Right now she was going to get in the shower. Maybe then she would be up to questioning him about his plans. But now, right now...

His arms were suddenly there; his hands were suddenly helping. Some kind of dissociative state, she thought. She was numb, and she only thought she was coping.

Gently he stripped her filthy, sweaty clothes away, then his own. Gently he helped her into the shower, and gently he washed her from head to foot, using bar soap on her hair, but that was all they had, and anyway...anyway...

She never knew when she started crying.

Afterward, she remembered Ian lifting her from the tub, wrapping her in towels, drying her as tenderly as if she were a baby, and finally tucking them both beneath the warm covers of the double bed. There he cuddled her close and let her cry her eyes out.

"I thought I was dead." Her voice was rusty, cracked, and her eyes ached from weeping.

"Me too. Oh, God, baby, me too." His voice was a husky sound in the dark. Rough. "I didn't think I'd get there in time. You kept falling asleep, and I couldn't feel you...."

"That's how you found me?"

"After dark. Before dark I tracked you. It was easy. But when it got dark...you remember that game where you're blindfolded and trying to find something, and somebody directs you by saying you're getting hotter or colder as you move? And then you'd fall asleep and there wouldn't be any 'hotter' or 'colder' to guide me."

"Something happened to Jeb. I heard him scream."

"He's dead."

There was a finality to his tone that said he was sure

of it. She didn't question him further. "It was a trap. You were supposed to get killed."

"I know. And you were the bait. I know."

"But...the planes weren't supposed to bomb there."

"Yeah." He paused and then squeezed her close. "It sure makes you think, doesn't it? If she could do something about that, affect instrument readings or whatever..." He let the words trail away.

"What do we do now? Give up?"

"Screw that," he said, steel running through his voice. "No. I'm going to put that bitch to rest for good, if I have to take that house apart board by board to do it."

He touched her damp hair and patted her shoulder with the awkwardness she found somehow endearing. "Now, try to get some sleep," he said. "I'll be right here. Nobody's going to hurt you, Honor. Ever again."

That promise warmed her deeply and eased the last of the tension from her. In a little while she was asleep, surrounded by his strength, his heat, his promise.

Pink light edged around the corners of the generic white curtains on the windows and cast a rosy glow through the room. Honor sighed, trying not to think about the problems still facing them, and turned onto her back.

And looked in cat-green eyes. Ian was propped on his elbow, watching her, and he made no secret of what he was thinking. It was plain in his eyes, in the flush on his cheekbones, on his parted lips. He wanted her.

"Like hell on fire," he said, in answer to her thoughts. "Like nothing I've ever wanted before."

She turned toward him with no thought except that the man she loved wanted her and there was no greater joy on earth. All the horror of the day before faded away beneath the brush of his hands, the heat of his mouth and, finally, the weight of his body.

"I want you to stay here while I go back and get to the bottom of this." He was lying on her, still joined to her, as the sweat on their bodies slowly dried. She was running her hands along his sides, but she stopped suddenly when he spoke.

"Why?"

"I don't want to put you at risk again. Look what happened yesterday." He lifted his head so that he could look down into her eyes. "She knows we've figured out that she's hiding something. She tried to kill you. Tried to kill us both. You don't think she's going to leave it alone now, do you?"

"So you expect me to let you go back there and face it—*her*—alone?" Her voice was calm, but she saw at once that he wasn't deceived. That was the tough part about dealing with a telepath.

Suddenly he grinned, and his incredibly boyish expression at once amazed her and warmed her to her very toes. "Don't even try," he said, his voice a deep rumble. "The better I get to know you, the easier you are to read. You're not coming with me, and that's that."

Two hours later she was beside him in his Jeep. She'd just had to be stubborn, that was all. And had to promise to stick to his side as if she were attached by glue. Not that he would have hog-tied her in the room or anything. Ian wasn't like that. He would never force her to do anything against her will.

But he could exact a lot of promises, and he had.

It wasn't that she wanted to face that ghost again. At this point she was all but ready to abandon the house and spend the rest of her life paying off the mortgage. But she couldn't let Ian face that thing alone. No way. If she had stayed behind, she would have chewed her fingers and climbed walls and finally called a cab to take her there anyway.

As they neared their neighborhood, Honor could have sworn she *felt* Mrs. Gilhooley, as if the old woman's ghost were poisoning the air with evil. And for an instant, one long instant, she allowed herself to wish she was driving away from here, never to return.

She glanced at Ian from the corner of her eye and wondered what he was thinking. Wondered if he were reading her mind. Damn it, there ought to be some kind of flag he put up, so that she would know when her privacy wasn't absolute.

But even as she had the thought, she cast it away as petty. She didn't have a thing to hide, except possibly her anxiety that he would lose interest in her the moment the ghost was gone. And to tell the truth, she honestly couldn't imagine him staying interested in her for long. Why should he? She certainly didn't have anything a billion other women didn't have.

"What are we going to do about Jeb?" she asked him as they jolted down the dirt road toward their houses.

"I already notified some people that he had been out there. They'll look for him."

"I wish I knew what happened to him. I was arguing with him, and he ran away into the woods, and then I heard him scream." And the memory of that scream was going to stay with her for a long, long time. Ian's hand settled comfortingly on her shoulder and squeezed. She gave him a grateful look.

"He probably tripped on something and broke his neck," Ian said quietly. "But all I know for sure is that he was dead before I found you. I can't explain how, but I just know when someone dies."

Honor waved her hand dismissively. "Don't even try. I probably couldn't understand in a million years what it's like for you."

If it was possible, the shadows beneath the live oaks around her house looked even darker this morning, as if the Florida sun couldn't penetrate them at all. As if they were doorways into another world.

"Listen," Ian said. "You just wait at my place while I search."

"No."

He turned his head and looked straight at her with those odd green eyes. "No?"

"You taught me how to use that word," Honor remarked as she shoved her door open. "No."

Ian filled an insulated jug with water and ice, while Honor changed into clean clothes. Then they headed next door with the jug, a couple of crowbars and two flashlights.

He really meant it, Honor thought. He was going to take the place apart board by board if necessary. And she was darn well going to help him. Enough was enough. There couldn't possibly be anything hidden in that house worth Jeb's death. Worth the attempt to kill the two of them.

The shadows sucked the heat from the day, and there was no mistaking the chill beneath the trees. It wasn't natural, Honor thought now. No way should shade be this dank and cold.

The house was worse. Never in a million years would she have bought this place if she had felt then what she felt now. Mrs. Gilhooley's presence was an evil miasma, haunting the entire house, her rage an almost palpable thing.

Honor instinctively glanced at Ian, thinking that if *she* could feel it, it must be much worse for him. His face revealed nothing, probably the best indicator that he was exercising a great deal of self-control.

"Let's start in the attic," Ian said. "Something about her antics yesterday made me think I was getting close."

"Six of one…" Honor shrugged, leaving the sentence incomplete.

At the foot of the attic stair, the chill had grown almost arctic.

"Maybe you'd better go wait at my place," Ian said as she recoiled from the cold spot. "Honor, really, all I'm going to do is wreck your attic. I can do that all by myself."

She tried to smile, but couldn't quite manage it. "I'm not leaving you alone. Quit suggesting it."

"This doesn't have anything to do with the way your dad raised you, does it?" he asked as he started climbing the stairs.

"Probably. All that stuff about not deserting your buddies got to me."

He gave a small chuckle that was probably supposed to be humorous but didn't quite make it.

Almost the instant they were both standing in the attic, the wind outside kicked up savagely. The roof creaked threateningly overhead, and branches tapped like bony fingers at the round windows.

"Probably building up to another afternoon thundershower," Ian remarked as he set down the jug and the flashlights. "Okay. I started at that end yesterday and got as far as that one raised floorboard over there. That's where we'll start. The only question I have is, do you want me to nail everything back in place as we go?''

Honor looked around and shook her head quickly. "No, damn it. Let's just get this done. I'll worry about fixing things if we managed to get rid of her."

"We might save some damage if you try to peer behind the lath with the flashlight. Chances are any place she used for hiding something would have been easy for her to get to, so it's likely to be easy for us, too."

"We wish." She jumped a little as the tree limbs tapped on the glass again and realized they had lost the sunshine. Well, so what? Picking up a flashlight and a crowbar, she started where Ian indicated.

For a long time, the only sounds were the creaking of nails being pried up, and the clatter of boards being moved, along with the protesting groans of the roof as it was battered by the growing wind. Ian stopped once to take a drink and peer out the huge round window.

"Storm's brewing," he said.

"So what's new?" She had her nose tucked into a small crack and was wishing there was some way to bend light so that she could get illumination in behind one of the thin boards.

"It's a coastal climate," Ian remarked. "We get more sun than Seattle, but we get our share of rain, too."

"There's been an awful lot lately." At last she succeeded in figuring out that there was nothing in the small crevice. "It would sure help if we knew what we were looking for. A ring could be hidden almost anywhere. A diary, on the other hand—" A loud rumble of thunder made her look up. "More of that, too, I guess."

"Yep." There was a creak as he yanked up another board and a clatter as it fell aside. Wind gusted again, and for an instant it sounded as if hail were rattling against the windowpanes.

All of a sudden, lightning flared and thunder cracked deafeningly, the strike so close that the house shook and Honor felt her hair stand on end. At just that moment the attic stairs snapped up and closed with a slam nearly as deafening as the thunder.

Honor and Ian looked at each other across a space turned gloomy by the falling light. Neither of them wanted to comment on the stairs' closing without human assistance. After a moment Ian turned his attention back to the hole he had just opened in the floor. A hollow drumbeat of thunder sounded again.

"Honor?"

She turned to look at him. "Yeah?"

"I found it."

It was a diary, the cardboard cover mildewed, many of the pages stuck together from humidity and age. Neither of them even thought of going downstairs and getting comfortable with a beer. They sat cross-legged on the floor and used both flashlights for illumination.

"I'm almost scared to see what's inside it," Honor said as Ian used the tip of a penknife to pry pages apart. "I mean, if she could murder her husband, I hate to think what else she might have done. And there must be something she really wants to hide."

A loud clap of thunder shook the house with its force as Ian lifted the flyleaf and gently folded it back.

"At least the atmosphere's right," Honor remarked, trying not to notice the way the shadows were deepening. "If we had candles, they'd blow out right about now."

He answered with a soft chuckle, but kept his attention glued to the diary. These were the answers they needed, and everything else would have to wait. "Reading this could take a while. But at least it looks as if she didn't write a whole lot on most pages."

Nor was it a very thick or large book. It was, in fact, a fifty-page marbled black composition book of the kind that Honor had used throughout elementary school. The first page was given over to the rather childish inscription My Diary, Mary Jo Schmidt.

Inside, the pages were dated, and it was soon apparent that Mrs. Gilhooley had started this diary while she was still a little girl. And it was soon equally apparent that the horrors had started early. There were tales of mutilated frogs put in other children's lunches. Later she wrote how she had drowned a little boy's new puppy. And on each page there was more.

Honor shuddered inwardly. "It looks as if she only wrote down the terrible things she did. There isn't anything else in here."

Ian nodded. "A listing of her crimes, as if they were triumphs. And look how she gloats that no one ever suspected her."

That was just as chilling as anything else, the way the child understood that her actions were wrong, hideously cruel. They weren't simply acts of petty, childish vengeance, but instead were carried out only for the pleasure they gave her.

More than once Honor looked up and met Ian's eyes, sharing their recognition that Mrs. Gilhooley had been twisted all her life.

The storm was drawing closer, growing worse. Rain rattled like machine-gun bullets at the two windows, and each gust of wind made the house groan. Neither of them noticed. As they turned the pages, one by one, they jour-

neyed deeper into the darkness of an evil mind. Whatever
had been wrong with Mary Jo Schmidt as a child had
grown into something far deadlier as an adult. The incidents became rarer, but grew worse, until at last they
found her description of killing her first husband.

I fixed it up so I could have Bill Gilhooley. Old Ted
sure did look funny when he figured out I was push-
ing that ladder over. All the way down he just
looked at me like he couldn't believe it. Man always
was such a fool. But now I can have Bill. Just have
to wait a little while so nobody wonders.
        And that devil spawn brat next door, I'll fix him,
see if I don't. I'll fix him good. He musta seen me
push that ladder. It was funny, but nobody believed
him. But I'll fix him.

Honor edged closer to Ian, instinctively wanting to offer comfort, even though the scars were a lifetime old.
He already knew all of this, and there couldn't be any
unpleasant shocks for him here, but still she wished she
could make him feel better.

He didn't seem to notice the gesture, though. He just
kept turning pages and scanning them while the storm
raged and the light faded to almost nothing.

"There," he said suddenly. "I knew there was something else to that. I wondered if the old woman ever knew
the truth of that, or if Maggie lied about me on her own."

Honor peered over his shoulder, squinting to read the
faded ink by the yellow beam of the flashlight.

Maggie says it was Bill what got her pregnant.
Swears he come to her room damn near every night.

"Bill?" Honor asked. "Her stepfather?"

Ian nodded. "Bill Gilhooley. Damn, that explains a whole lot, her knowing about that."

I ain't believing it. Gotta be someone else. Someone she's protecting. Maybe that demon next door with his witch eyes.

There was more, a lot more, about finally forcing Maggie to swear it was Ian who had gotten her pregnant. Forcing the girl to swear that Ian had "witched" her and made her do things against her will. Bill Gilhooley himself helped with the "persuasion" that forced the girl to lie. It was hardly to be wondered that she killed herself. Or that Mrs. Gilhooley, her very own mother, had given her the rat poison to do the deed.

Ian closed the composition book. "I guess there's no question what she's been trying to keep hidden."

"I guess not. It kind of makes you wonder, though, what kind of mind would do such things and then become so obsessed with hiding them, even after death."

Ian just shook his head. He'd seen plenty of the worst people could do, things that made Mrs. Gilhooley's activities seem like minor peccadilloes, but he didn't claim to understand such people.

"Well," he said, "it seems all we need to do is get this diary out of here and turn it over to the police. Then she won't have anything to hide anymore, and maybe you can live here in peace."

Instead of feeling relieved, Honor felt a piercing sense of impending loss. She could live in peace, and he could go back to his undisturbed solitude once he no longer felt honor-bound to protect her. The prospect was grim. And another thought occurred to her. "Won't she get mad now that her secret is out?"

"Probably. But only for so long as it takes us to expose it." In one smooth, easy movement, he rose to his feet and extended a hand to help her up.

"Want to celebrate?" he asked, a sudden, unexpected sparkle in his eyes.

The expression made her breath catch, and she ignored a deafening explosion of thunder. "Celebrate how?" Her mind threw up a whole series of exotic, erotic images.

"Exactly like that," he said. "Each and every one." Catching her to him, he initiated a deep, hungry kiss that promised a night filled with sensual delights. "Oh, baby," he whispered roughly, "just you wait. Now, let's get out of here so we can have fun."

Releasing her, he walked over to the attic ladder and stepped on it. The ladder, which was sprung like a fire escape, should have swung down beneath his weight. It didn't. He jumped on it a couple of times, then looked at Honor. "Has this ever gotten stuck before?"

She shook her head. "There's no way it *can* get stuck. If the springs were broken, it would just fall open. And it only locks in the open position."

He jumped again, harder, with no success. "Well, hell," he said disgustedly.

That was when Honor smelled the smoke. Ian smelled it, too, at almost the same instant. Bending, he touched the stairs with the palm of his hand. As soon as he looked up, Honor knew the worst.

They were trapped in a burning house.

Whenever it had started, the fire was seriously out of hand by the time they discovered it. A look around the shadowy attic revealed wisps of smoke that had been gathering in the air, seeping up from the floors below. Even as they looked around the attic, flames burst up between a pair of joists that Ian had left uncovered as the ceiling material below went up in smoke.

Oh my God, Honor thought numbly. Of all the ways to die, she would have picked anything else in the world. Smoke stung her eyes, and she coughed, watching with disbelief as Ian put the floorboards back over the exposed areas.

"To slow it down," he said. Reading her mind again. Then he grabbed a crowbar and went to knock out the beautiful round window at the back end of the attic. When only jagged pieces remained in the frame, he yanked off his T-shirt and used it to protect his hands as he pulled the last of the glass away.

Honor found herself standing right beside him, watching the play of his muscles as he let in the fresh, stormy wind and prepared a hope of escape for them.

"People jump," she said. "When the heat gets to be too bad, they jump rather than burn."

His strange green eyes met hers. "I know, honey. I know. If it comes to that, we'll jump together. We're only on the third floor. We'd have a shot."

Suddenly she was more scared of losing him than of dying in a fire. Much more scared.

"Ian...Ian, I never said...I never told you—oh, God, I'm so glad I met you!"

He caught her in a brief, bone-crushing embrace and muttered something in her ear that sounded like, "You're the only person on earth who's ever felt that way." Then he released her and went back to clearing the window frame of glass.

It seemed to take forever, though it probably took only a few moments. Finally he hoisted himself up and leaned over the edge, taking stock of the situation. A muffled explosion below was followed by a tinkle of glass, telling him the fire downstairs had reached flashover. It would be a raging inferno now, and the only way out would be through this window.

But the branches of the oak that had been rapping against the window were slender, bony fingers without the strength to bear even Honor's weight, and any sturdier branches were beyond their reach. Trying to jump would offer only a slim chance of success.

All of a sudden, he reached for the snap of his jeans. "Give me your jeans, too."

Confused, she didn't move immediately. She was still trying to cope with the idea that they might burn alive.

"Honor, your jeans. I'm going to make a rope."

Understanding at last, she quickly stripped them off, then watched as he slashed both pairs in half with his ever-present hunting knife. Then he tied the strips together into a rope that, while not quite long enough, would make it possible for them to get down to the first story before jumping.

"Okay, grab the other end and pull as hard as you can," he said. "See if the knots hold."

The smoke was getting thicker in the attic, and her eyes burned like fire from it. Doing as he said, she leaned back with all her might and weight to test the knots.

Suddenly the attic stairs fell open, and flames fountained straight up, almost instantly igniting the lath above it.

"That does it, babe," Ian said roughly. "Options all used up. You go out that window first. I'll hold the rope."

He was tugging her to the open window, but she resisted briefly. "How will you get down?"

"I'll nail the rope to the wall. Don't worry. I've been in tighter spots."

She didn't doubt it for an instant. But she very definitely wanted him out of this one *now*.

It was like being in gym class again, she thought wildly as she watched him wrap denim around his forearm so that it wouldn't slip. Then he was helping her over the window ledge and she was perched dizzyingly, her feet against the siding, her hands hanging on to the denim rope for dear life.

"Come on, sweetheart. You can do it. Just back down slowly. Go on."

Reaching back for skills she hadn't used in years, she inched her way down, ignoring the shrieking of her muscles, ignoring her fear, ignoring everything except the fact that the sooner she got down, the sooner Ian could come down, too.

And then she reached the end of their makeshift rope.

"Jump, Honor. Go on. It's not eight feet to the ground. The worse that'll happen..."

Is a bruise, she thought, and let go.

As soon as she hit, she knew she was going to have a football-sized bruise on her hip. But that didn't matter. Scrambling to her feet, she backed away from the burning house and looked up at Ian.

Only he wasn't there. The denim rope hung down the side of the house, but there was no Ian to be seen. And where he should have been, there was nothing but flames.

CHAPTER TWELVE

"Ian!" She shrieked his name, wondering how the fire could have gotten to him so fast. And surely, if it had, he would have jumped...

Smoke. Maybe smoke had overcome him while he'd been lowering her. But no, he'd shouted to her to jump. He hadn't sounded strangled or woozy.

"Ian! Ian, damn you, answer me!"

Smoke was pouring out the window now, great black clouds of it. She made a dozen promises to God as she shifted from one foot to the other and tried to figure out what she could do. Every window in her house was belching smoke and flame. There was no way she could go in there, no way to get to him. Even a call to the fire department would take too long. "Ian!"

And then, suddenly, filling her with a relief that nearly left her weak, she saw him. Blackened by smoke, he swung over the windowsill and climbed down the denim rope. And sticking out of the back of his black briefs was the damn diary. At any other time the sight would have been funny. Right now it just made her want to cry and scream. He'd risked his neck to bring that damn book out with him. She could have killed him.

He jumped the last ten feet, rolling with all the practiced aplomb of a paratrooper and ending up on his feet, facing her.

"What happened?" she shouted at him, furious in her relief. "Damn it, I thought—I thought—"

He knew what she had thought. He crushed her to him,

holding her so that she could barely breathe. She didn't care. She held him back every bit as hard. "The diary isn't worth this," she sobbed. "Ian, you should have left it. You could have been hurt. You could have been *hurt*."

"I had trouble getting the damn rope nailed to the wall," he said. "That's all. It wasn't the damn diary."

Her whole life was going up in flames, she thought dismally. Everything she had ever worked for was going up in that house. Even the last few mementos from her parents were burning in the vile old woman's rage. But none of that seemed to matter beside Ian's safety.

With a sudden, deafening whoosh, one of the curtains of moss burst into flame. Ian grabbed her hand and dragged her toward his house, wanting them out of there before any more moss ignited.

"Maybe we shouldn't go to your house," Honor gasped as Ian dragged her around the hedge. "What if she sets your house on fire, too?"

At the hedge, Ian halted and looked back at her house. "Do you have fire insurance?"

"Yes, of course. The bank insisted."

He nodded. "Good. Wait here a minute." Then he left her standing there while he trotted back toward her burning house. Flames were shooting out the windows now, and the front door burst open with a loud bang. Overhead, the storm raged, seeming almost paltry in comparison to the fire. A steady drizzle soaked her, chilling her.

Ten feet back from her front porch, Ian halted. He yanked the notebook out of the back of his briefs where he had tucked it; then, after only an instant's hesitation, he threw it onto the porch.

"Ian, no!" That was his proof he had done no wrong! What was he doing? She took a step forward, but it was already too late. A geyser of flame erupted through the open door and fell on the notebook, setting it on fire instantly. As if the old woman had reached out for it.

For a long time they both stood where they were, watching the book burn, watching as the house was devoured from within. An ominous groan from inside finally seemed to shake Ian as he turned and walked back to Honor, an incredible figure in nothing but soot and black briefs, his strange green eyes glowing like unearthly fire. Witch fire.

"Let's call the fire department," he said. Behind him, the roof caved in with a shower of sparks that ignited more of the moss.

Thunder rumbled in response, and the rain continued to fall.

The trees stood like ghastly black skeletons, denuded of moss and leaves. Dead. The house, too, was little more than a blackened heap of rubble, with the occasional charred finger reaching to the gray sky.

Standing on the road near her mailbox, Honor watched as the charred lump of the notebook stirred on the blackened remains of the porch and sheets of ash riffled and blew away. The last of it. The absolute last of it. Thunder rumbled, retreating.

A footstep alerted her, and she looked around to see Annie Sidell and her son Orville. Annie's eyes were red. She was weeping yet for Jeb, who had been found at the bottom of a ravine. Neither Honor nor Ian had told her the real story, leaving it to the authorities to speculate about why Jeb had been on the range, where no civilian should have been.

"I'm glad it's gone," Annie said after a moment.

"You grew up in that house." Honor hadn't expected that reaction at all.

"I lived there till I was eighteen and got out quick as I could. It's a terrible thing, Miss Honor, but I never did like my mama. She was a mean woman, mean through and through. I was…I was so scared Jeb was getting to be like her, these last few days."

Honor turned and looked at the older woman, and felt genuine compassion for her. "I'm so sorry about Jeb."

Annie merely nodded. "You'll be leaving now, I reckon."

"I…guess so." There was evidently no reason to stay. She'd slept alone on the cot in Ian's guest room last night, when he hadn't returned from the range. He had said he might be gone a few days, depending on how much the Rangers needed him to do this time. He'd told her to make herself at home, but he hadn't suggested she stay. She wondered if she should just pack her few remaining clothes and go.

The hospital had given her a week off to take care of her homeless state, and she guessed she'd better get on it. Either she had to find another place to live, or she had to think about looking for a job elsewhere. Nurses were always in demand, so she wasn't concerned about that. She could go anywhere she chose. The question was what she chose…and whether Ian wanted her to hang around.

And what she might be hanging around for. Lord, she didn't want to lose him. The very thought made her ache and brought tears to her eyes. But what could they have together if he only wanted sex from her? If he never shared himself in any other way? She knew now that a man could want her. Knowing that, she wanted so much more. If Ian couldn't give it to her…well, it would be better for them both if she moved on.

Annie headed back up the road with Orville, leaving Honor with the distinct impression that she had seen what she wanted to see, that seeing the house gone for good had satisfied her somehow. Maybe Annie, too, had felt her mother's evil presence there over the years. Maybe she, too, was feeling free at last.

Free herself, Honor went indoors and started cooking dinner for Ian and herself. He might not show up, but if he did, dinner would be ready. And maybe now he would talk to her. She had asked him twice why he'd thrown the diary into the fire, and he still hadn't answered. There were a lot of questions that needed answering before she left.

"You're not leaving."

Whirling, she saw Ian standing in the kitchen door. Dressed in camouflage and his red beret, knife and side-arm strapped to his hips, he was the archetypal soldier. Just now, for some reason, he looked bigger to her than he ever had, tall, imposing. His face was still as harsh as granite, and she didn't doubt he could kill a man with a single blow. But she also knew how infinitely gentle he could be, and the memory of his touch brought her to the edge of tears again.

"You're not leaving," he said again.

"There's no reason to stay."

"No?" He crossed the floor between them like a springing leopard and caught her right up off her feet. "Seems like we've got a few things to settle," he said, heading for the stairs.

"Dinner—"

"Can damn well burn!"

She guessed it was probably going to. "You've got to stop grabbing me like this, Ian! I don't like it! I'm not a piece of baggage for you to haul around any time you feel like it!"

"Sorry," he said unrepentantly as he set her down

beside their makeshift pallet. "We'll argue about it later. Later you can tell me how I'm supposed to treat a lady. I've never had a lady to treat right before. I've never had anyone...anyone...."

He didn't seem to be able to continue, and she no longer cared. There was something about the way he was pulling at her clothes, as if he couldn't wait another minute, yet was terrified she would shove him away, terrified he might hurt her. Such infinite gentleness and complete impatience that she nearly burst into tears on the spot. Oh, God, how she loved him.

He'd never had anyone.

He could have found no better words to reach her heart. He had someone now. He had *her,* and she wanted him to know it. She wanted him never to doubt it, and she had stopped counting the cost to herself. She was his, body, heart and soul.

He set her gently down on the mattress and stood over her, stripping away his clothes with rough, impatient hands. And when he was naked, he stood there looking down at her with such hope and longing in his eyes. Waiting. Waiting for her to invite him. Sensing, finally, that some things could not be bulldozed.

Instead of reaching for him, she rose on her knees. His jutting arousal was right before her eyes, and she heard him catch his breath as she leaned forward and pressed her face to his groin. How good he smelled, she thought as she nuzzled him. Coarse hair, satiny skin, the very essence of him. And when he trembled, she knew the first real sense of power she'd felt in her entire life.

"Tell me," she whispered. "Tell me how to please you."

She took him into her mouth and learned his textures and tastes with a hunger to reach him in ways for which there were no words. If this was the only way she could show him, tell him, let him see...

He was shaking like a leaf in a hurricane when he fell down beside her on the bed and pulled her into his arms. With his hands and mouth he painted fire over her from head to toe until she was begging him, begging him, begging him....

And then he was in her, over her, part of her, giving her the essence of himself, giving her his seed as he had given her himself. Claiming her as his very own.

She saw it in his eyes in those final moments, and she exulted fiercely.

He went downstairs and turned off the oven, the steaming rice and everything else. When he came back up, they bundled together in blankets and looked at one another in the shaft of sunlight that had somehow found its way in through the window.

"I love you," she said. But a whole bunch of doubts had risen in her. Weakening her earlier determination to stay no matter what. She couldn't force herself on him. He had to love her, too. But he hadn't said he did.

He nodded; he had read her mind after all.

"That's why I can't stay."

He shook his head. "That makes no sense."

"But it does, Ian. Don't you see? Loving you day after day when you don't love me, waiting for you to find someone else—"

He covered her mouth with his hand. He had a lot to learn about handling women. "Who said I don't love you?"

She gasped, her blue eyes widening. After a moment she yanked his hand away. "You never said you did!"

He closed his eyes briefly. "I've...never said that to

anyone. I've never had anyone to... Honor, I'm lousy at this. Ask me how to blow up a bridge, jump out of an airplane, field-strip an AK-47 blindfolded. That's stuff I know how to do. This stuff is..." He shook his head. "I don't want you to go. Ever."

She caught her breath, and a warm glow began at her center, spreading everywhere, driving away the chill left by the years. "Ever?"

He shifted uneasily. "I could understand if you don't want to stay. I know I'm unnerving to be around. Plenty of people have refused to have anything to do with me once they found out what I am."

She ached for him. Oh, how she ached for him, understanding that, however alone she had felt, he had been utterly isolated.

"I'm...unnatural," he said, his voice husky. "I know that. I understand that. And it's human instinct to avoid people who are,...mutants."

"Oh, my God." Honor barely breathed the words, as she understood fully, for the first time, the scars that this man bore.

"So I can understand why you wouldn't want to stay indefinitely."

"But you want to keep me around for...a little while?" Anger was beginning to stir in her, but not anger at him. No, it was anger against all the people who had made him feel that he wasn't good enough.

"As long as you can stand me."

Considering that he considered himself totally undesirable, that admission had taken guts. Guts of the kind she seemed to be a little short of herself. She was asking him to take a blind leap she wasn't prepared to take herself, and the understanding shamed her.

Tilting her face up, she kissed him with every ounce

of passion and love she felt for him. "Then you'd better plan on marrying me."

He went instantly still. Not stiff, not rigid, just utterly, perfectly still, as if everything in him were arrested in a moment of utter amazement. When he spoke, his voice was thick. "Marriage?"

"Kids, too, I think. We haven't exactly been behaving like responsible adults in that department, but that's okay, because I want several. Well, maybe a half dozen."

"Kids?"

He looked stunned, and she was scared half out of her mind, because there really wasn't any reason on earth why he should want her. Why he should love her. Jerry hadn't—

"Stop it," Ian said fiercely. "Stop thinking about that creep. He was wrong about you. Wrong about everything. I want you. I need you. I love you, damn it! And if you're crazy enough to love me, then I'm not crazy enough to let you get away!"

"Even if I want kids and marriage?"

"Especially if you want kids and marriage. I never hoped— Oh, God, baby, I never dared even dream it!"

For a long, long time she held him as close as she could and considered how odd it was that they had both lost their dreams and then rediscovered them because of that wicked old woman who was probably even now gracing the halls of hell.

A long time later, Honor asked the question again. "Ian, why did you burn the diary? It was proof you hadn't done anything wrong. You could have cleared your name."

He sighed and stared into the deepening twilight for a few minutes before he answered. "All that mattered," he said finally, "was that I was free. I was free of all of it, but I don't know how to explain it. It was as if reading it in that diary was a vindication for me. Nobody else mattered.''

''But Annie thinks—''

''I don't know what Annie really thinks,'' he said, interrupting her. ''Nor does it matter. She's the only person who might have been interested in the truth anymore, and I just couldn't do it to her. She's had to live with enough. She didn't need to know that her mother was a murderer, or that her stepfather raped her sister. What possible good could it do anyone now to have all that filth come out?''

''But people still think you did terrible things.''

He shrugged a shoulder. ''But *I* know I didn't. That's all that matters. I came back here with some crazy notion of laying old ghosts to rest, and that damned diary did it for me. I don't know how or why, but it did it. I'm free of my past, Honor. Finally.''

He rolled onto his side and smiled at her, really smiled, and it transformed his entire face. ''Now I have a future for the first time in my life. I want to build it with you, with our babies. I want to build it with sunshine and happiness. Away from here. Away from old ghosts and old memories. I want us both to have a fresh start, even if it's just a couple of miles up the road.

''I want us to build our own house and fill it with ghosts of our own making. Fill it with laughter and joy and all the things life should be blessed with. There's no room in tomorrow for the bitterness of yesterday.''

He sighed, his smile fading just a little bit. ''I set her free, too, Honor. She's gone. Can you feel it?''

Honor nodded and kissed his chin. ''You set us all free. I love you.''

He cupped her chin and smiled down into her misty blue eyes. ''So...will you marry me?''

"I thought that was obvious!"

He chuckled. "Honey, I may be a telepath, but I'm also a very ordinary man. I need the words as much as the next guy."

So she leaned up to his ear and whispered all the words he wanted to hear. And in her ear he whispered all the words she needed to hear.

The only thunder that night was in their hearts and minds, in their souls and bodies.

And it was just the beginning.

*   *   *   *   *

nocturne™

Save $1·⁰⁰ off

**your purchase of any
Silhouette® Nocturne™ novel.**

Receive $1.00 off

any Silhouette® Nocturne™ novel.

**Available wherever books are sold, including most
bookstores, supermarkets, drugstores and discount stores.**

Coupon expires December 1, 2006. Redeemable at participating
retail outlets in the U.S. only. Limit one coupon per customer.

RETAILER: Harlequin Enterprises Ltd. will pay the face value of this coupon plus
8¢ if submitted by the customer for this specified product only. Any other use
constitutes fraud. Coupon is nonassignable. Void if taxed, prohibited or restricted by
law. Void if copied. Consumer must pay for any government taxes. Mail to Harlequin
Enterprises Ltd., P.O. Box 880478, El Paso, TX 88588-0478, U.S.A. Cash value 1/100
cents. Limit one coupon per customer. Valid in the U.S. only.

5 65373 00076 2   (8100) 0 11265

SNCOUPUS

n o c t u r n e™

Save $1.⁰⁰ off

your purchase of any
Silhouette® Nocturne™ novel.

Receive $1.00 off

any Silhouette® Nocturne™ novel.

Available wherever books are sold, including most bookstores, supermarkets, drugstores and discount stores.

Coupon expires December 1, 2006. Redeemable at participating retail outlets in Canada only. Limit one coupon per customer.

RETAILER: Harlequin Enterprises Limited will pay the face value of this coupon plus 10.25 cents if submitted by the customer for this specified product only. Any other use constitutes fraud. Coupon is nonassignable. Void if taxed, prohibited or restricted by law. Consumer must pay any government taxes. Mail to Harlequin Enterprises Ltd., P.O. Box 3000, Saint John, New Brunswick E2L 4L3, Canada. Limit one coupon per customer. Valid in Canada only.

52607136

SNCOUPCDN

Introducing...

nocturne

a spine-tingling new line
from Silhouette Books.

These paranormal romances will
seduce you with dark, passionate tales
that stretch the boundaries of conflict,
desire, and life and death, weaving
a tapestry of sensual thrills and chills!

Don't miss the first book...

UNFORGIVEN

by *USA TODAY* bestselling author

LINDSAY McKENNA

*Launching October 2006,
wherever books are sold.*

SNIBC

If you enjoyed what you just read,
then we've got an offer you can't resist!

Take 1 bestselling
love story FREE!

Plus get a FREE surprise gift!

Clip this page and mail it to the Reader Service®

IN U.S.A.	IN CANADA
3010 Walden Ave.	P.O. Box 609
P.O. Box 1867	Fort Erie, Ontario
Buffalo, N.Y. 14240-1867	L2A 5X3

YES! Please send me one free LUNA™ novel and my free surprise gift. After receiving it, if I don't wish to receive any more, I can return the shipping statement marked cancel. If I don't cancel, I will receive one brand-new novel every month, before they're available in stores! In the U.S.A., bill me at the bargain price of $10.99 plus 50¢ shipping & handling per book and applicable sales tax, if any*. In Canada, bill me at the bargain price of $12.99 plus 50¢ shipping & handling per book and applicable taxes**. That's the complete price and a savings of 10% off the cover prices—what a great deal! I understand that accepting the free book and gift places me under no obligation ever to buy any books. I can always return a shipment and cancel at any time. Even if I never buy another book from LUNA, the free book and gift are mine to keep forever.

175 HDN D34K
375 HDN D34L

Name	(PLEASE PRINT)	
Address	Apt.#	
City	State/Prov.	Zip/Postal Code

Not valid to current LUNA™ subscribers.

Want to try another series?
Call 1-800-873-8635 or visit www.morefreebooks.com.

* Terms and prices subject to change without notice. Sales tax applicable in N.Y.
** Canadian residents will be charged applicable provincial taxes and GST.
All orders subject to approval. Offer limited to one per household.
® and ™ are registered trademarks owned and used by the trademark owner and
or its licensee.

LUNA04   ©2004 Harlequin Enterprises Limited

THE PART-TIME WIFE

by *USA TODAY* bestselling author

Maureen Child

Abby Talbot was the belle of Eastwick society;
the perfect hostess and wife. If only her
husband were more attentiive. But when
she sets out to teach him a lesson and files
for divorce, Abby quickly learns her husband's
true identity...and exposes them to scandals
and drama galore!

On sale October 2006 from Silhouette Desire!

*Available wherever books are sold,
including most bookstores, supermarkets,
discount stores and drug stores.*

Visit Silhouette Books at www.eHarlequin.com SDPTW1006

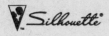

INTIMATE MOMENTS™

CAN THREE ALPHA WARRIORS WITH A BLOOD-BOND AND NO PASTS CHANGE THE SHAPE OF THE WORLD'S FUTURE?

Find out in Intimate Moments' new trilogy filled with adventure, betrayal and passion by

LORETH ANNE WHITE

THE HEART OF A MERCENARY
October 2006, #1438

A SULTAN'S RANSOM
November 2006, #1442

RULES OF REENGAGEMENT
December 2006, #1446

AVAILABLE WHEREVER YOU BUY BOOKS.

Visit Silhouette Books at www.eHarlequin.com   SIMLAW

Those sexy Irishmen are back!

Bestselling author

Kate Hoffmann

is joining the Harlequin Blaze line—and she's
brought her bestselling Temptation miniseries,
THE MIGHTY QUINNS, with her.
Because these guys are definitely Blaze-worthy....

All Quinn males, past and present, know the legend
of the first Mighty Quinn. And they've all been
warned about the family curse—that the only thing
capable of bringing down a Quinn is a woman.
Still, the last three Quinn brothers never guess
that lying low could be so sensually satisfying....

The Mighty Quinns: Marcus, on sale October 2006
The Mighty Quinns: Ian, on sale November 2006
The Mighty Quinns: Declan, on sale December 2006

Don't miss it!

Available wherever Harlequin books are sold.

www.eHarlequin.com

HBMQ1006

SAVE UP TO $30! SIGN UP TODAY!

The complete guide to your favorite
Harlequin®, Silhouette® and Love Inspired® books.

✓ Newsletter ABSOLUTELY FREE! No purchase necessary.

✓ Valuable coupons for future purchases of Harlequin,
  Silhouette and Love Inspired books in every issue!

✓ Special excerpts & previews in each issue. Learn about all
  the hottest titles before they arrive in stores.

✓ No hassle—mailed directly to your door!

✓ Comes complete with a handy shopping checklist
  so you won't miss out on any titles.

- -

SIGN ME UP TO RECEIVE INSIDE ROMANCE
ABSOLUTELY FREE
(Please print clearly)

_____
Name

_____
Address

_____
City/Town   State/Province   Zip/Postal Code

(098 KKM EJL9)   **Please mail this form to:**
            In the U.S.A.: Inside Romance, P.O. Box 9057, Buffalo, NY 14269-9057
                In Canada: Inside Romance, P.O. Box 622, Fort Erie, ON L2A 5X3
                    OR visit http://www.eHarlequin.com/insideromance

IRNBPA06R   ® and ™ are trademarks owned and used by the trademark owner and/or its licensee.